MALLORY GORMAN
WON'T BE BURIED TODAY

A Stella Kirk Mystery #5

L. P. Suzanne Atkinson

lpsabooks
http://lpsabooks.wix.com/lpsabooks#

Copyright © 2022 by L. P. Suzanne Atkinson
First Edition—March, 2023

All rights reserved

No part of this publication may be reproduced in any form, or by any means, electronic or mechanical, including photocopying, recording, or any information browsing, storage, or retrieval system without permission in writing from the publisher.

This is a work of fiction. Names, characters, and incidents either are the product of the author's imagination or are used fictitiously.

Cover Design by Majeau Designs
Editing by Tim Covell

ISBN
978-1-7776005-4-9 (Paperback)
978-1-7776005-5-6 (eBook)

1. Fiction, Mystery/Detective-Cozy/General
2. Fiction, Mystery/Detective-Amateur Sleuth
3. Fiction, Mystery/Detective-Female Sleuths

Distributed to the trade by the Ingram Book Company

Table of Contents

Recurring Characters 1
Chapter 1: Mallory Gorman Won't Be Buried Today 3
Chapter 2: I Expect You'll Be Awhile 11
Chapter 3: Why Shouldn't She Be Happy? 21
Chapter 4: Instantly Suspicious 31
Chapter 5: It's Been Almost a Hundred Years 41
Chapter 6: On My Way Downhill Fast 51
Chapter 7: Troubled and Contented 61
Chapter 8: I Refuse Further Involvement 71
Chapter 9: He Remembers 81
Chapter 10: Posh is Not the Best Descriptor 91
Chapter 11: Hard Times for Old Guys 101
Chapter 12: Don't Dead Bodies Haunt You? 111
Chapter 13: You Are Too Suspicious 121
Chapter 14: Too Many Questions 131
Chapter 15: The Tide Sneaks Its Way to High 141
Chapter 16: She Wasn't Confident 151
Chapter 17: Nervousness Proves Unfounded 159
Chapter 18: Summer is Over 169
Chapter 19: Aiden is Doomed 179
Chapter 20: Second Thoughts Niggle 189
Chapter 21: What a Mess 199
Chapter 22: Maybe She's Nearby 209
Chapter 23: Sacred Trust 219
Chapter 24: Anybody Dead? 229

Until we all start to take responsibility, until we do all we can to improve the character of our communities, we'll never break the cycle of violence and indifference.
—Carrie P. Meek

Indifference, to me, is the epitome of evil.
—Elie Wiesel

Other works by L. P. Suzanne Atkinson

~Creative Non-Fiction~
Emily's Will Be Done

~Fiction~
Ties That Bind
Station Secrets: Regarding Hayworth Book I
Hexagon Dilemma: Regarding Hayworth Book II
Segue House Connection: Regarding Hayworth Book III
Diner Revelations: Regarding Hayworth Book IV
No Visible Means: A Stella Kirk Mystery #1
Didn't Stand a Chance: A Stella Kirk Mystery #2
Sand In My Suitcase: A Stella Kirk Mystery #3
Fictional Truth: A Stella Kirk Mystery #4

For David, always

Thank you to Barb, Marguerite, Harriet, and Beverley
for their feedback, Earl for his input, and a special thanks to
my editor Tim Covell for his patience and support.

Finally, much appreciation to Barbara Frey, who won a Cozy Mystery Party
contest, and permitted her name to be assigned to a character in this book.

Recurring Characters:

Stella Kirk	Owner of Shale Cliffs RV Park; amateur sleuth
Aiden North	RCMP Detective (Sergeant Moyer)
Rosemary North	Aiden's wife (Mary Jo & Toni – her sisters)
Nick Cochran	Park Manager (Stella's love interest & soon-to-be 50% owner)
Alice & Paul Morgan	Park Employees (brother & sister)
Eve Trembly	Park Employee (Del Trembly's granddaughter)
Duke (John) Powell	Park Security (Cloris Kincaid – love interest)
Kiki	Duke's Pomeranian
Trixie Kirk	Stella's sister (Val Reguly – love interest)
Brigitte & Mia Kirk	Trixie's daughter (runs Yellow House) & granddaughter (Carter Stephens – love interest)
Norbert Kirk	Stella & Trixie's father
RV Park residents	Mildred Fox, Buddy McGarvey, Curtis Walsh & Elroy Brown, Sally & Rob Black, Ted Metcalfe
Jewel & Ken Winslow	Former fish plant workers, now caretakers at Painter Farm
Hester, Cavelle, Jacob Painter	Siblings
Lorraine Young	Murder victim May 1980
Lucy Painter	Murder victim November 1980
Paulina McAdams	Murder victim May 1981
Owen Ellis-Thomas	Murder victim September 1981

Chapter 1

Mallory Gorman Won't Be Buried Today

What am I doin' diggin' a grave when somebody's already in it?

Moments earlier, the sound of snapping branches had reached Vic Staples, perched in the open cab of the 1970 Ford 4500 backhoe Luther Greene arranged to be left for him at the graveyard. He slid off the machine and inspected the pile of dirt he'd created. Vic then extended a greasy hand and retrieved what he assumed was the splintered fragment of a tree root. He turned his puzzled face and peered into the freshly dug hole, whereupon he discovered a partially exposed, obviously human, skull.

****

"Shale Cliffs RV Park. How may I help you?"

"Hi. How are you?"

"Fine, Aiden. Getting ready for Mallory's funeral. Haven't heard from you in a while. How's Rosemary?" She sounds robotic, even to herself. Can't be helped. A month has passed since Greta Walmsley was charged with the murder of Owen Ellis-Thomas. She managed interviews alone because Aiden's wife was in the throes of a serious mental health crisis. After she wrangled a confession out of the woman, Stella's contract as a consultant with the local RCMP was abruptly cancelled.

"Mallory Gorman won't be buried today. The gravedigger found a body already in the hole."

"And you're telling me because...?" She expects her attempt at not sounding sarcastic has failed. She settles on the bed, back against the headboard.

"I need your help. The remains are skeletal. Maybe the site is old, but the police get called when bones are found in unmarked graves."

"Where's Essie?" Detective Essie Matkowski was the member who accompanied her during Greta's interviews, disapproved of civilian involvement, and made her feelings clear throughout by speaking with supervisors who agreed. Aiden notified her that Essie would be his partner going forward.

"Her mother's sick. She's on leave. Will you work the case with me?"

Stella felt used when he gave her the news a month ago, although she let him off the hook and said she was okay with the idea. Now, unable to compromise, and resistant to his old familiar spell, she chooses the hardball option. "I won't come on board without a reinstated contract."

"Covered. Can you meet me in the graveyard at one?"

"Sure," she mutters, not convinced she's made a good decision. "What should I expect?"

"I'm told the gravedigger from Royalty Funeral Services was preparing the grave for Mrs. Gorman's casket and discovered a body eight feet deep."

"Eight feet doesn't sound right."

"No. I understand the guy was the replacement for the regular employee who is off. Maybe he wasn't aware of the standard depth."

"Didn't someone say Mallory was supposed to be buried in the new and expanded part of the graveyard? I remember. Trixie told me Theodore and Mallory Gorman purchased the first plot after the expansion."

"Well, you know more than me, before we even arrive. By the way, the family and the funeral home have been contacted and told human remains were found. One o'clock?"

She forces enthusiasm. "Okay," she says, and replaces the receiver in the cradle.

"Kiki, extricate your fuzzy body from my pillows."

The little Pomeranian mutters her annoyance and snuggles deeper into the comforter, which covers the bed Stella shares with Nick—not Kiki.

She grabs Kiki, ignores the grunts of displeasure, and clumps down the stairs from the second-floor bedroom suite to the living quarters below. Still early for lunch, she doesn't expect Nick and Duke right away. After she sets the dog on the Lino, she reaches for the wall phone.

"Yellow House."

"Hi, Brigitte. Is your mother around?"

"I'll get her, Aunt Stella. She's in the kitchen with Mia and Val."

"Thanks." If Val Reguly, Trixie's latest flame, is there, Trixie will know the funeral is postponed. Val is Mallory Gorman's brother.

"Stella. I gather you've been told the funeral's off. If a dead body's involved, I trust you will be at the centre of the action." Her tone is more tease than criticism.

"I shouldn't be, but Aiden called. His new partner has an ill mother. I'm in the department's good books again."

"As long as you don't take over the interviews, eh?"

She knows her sister's remark isn't intended to hurt, but the question bites, nonetheless. "I wondered if you knew about the postponement, which you do. Gotta go—lunch followed by a graveyard trip for me, funeral or not. Tell Brigitte I'll stop in for tea if there's time. Talk later." She disconnects before Trixie argues.

A quick glance at the clock on the kitchen wall tells her waiting for Nick and Duke to wander in could be a problem. "Come for a ride, Kiki." She grabs the dog's leash before she flies out the door and jumps into her Jeep. Kiki settles on Stella's lap as she drops the shifter into drive. They're near the cliffs where she expected them to be; the old Ford farm truck parked beside a ditch. The septic trenches were completed and filled in, but the soil sank in many spots. The property is full of depressions from the construction. Both men are adding fill, preparing the areas for seed in the spring because the weather will soon turn, and the job must be finished. She hates to admit the truth, but Duke has been a huge help.

"Hi, guys." She hollers through the open window as her words are caught by the brisk winds off the bay. "Can you come to the house for lunch right away?" Kiki yelps when she sees her master. "Duke," she nods toward her passenger, "didn't want to leave her alone while I fetched you. She'll need a pee."

Duke lumbers toward the Jeep, battling the uneven ground. He's a small man who acts big. As he reaches for his dog, she swims out the window and into his arms. "Thanks for mindin' her, Stella. I'll put her in the truck cab for now. We're ready to stop for a bite, anyhow."

Nick, her lover, her partner, and the person who will soon be a fifty percent owner of the park, makes his way from the front of the Jeep, rake in hand. "What's the matter? Afraid you'll be late for the funeral?"

"No funeral today. The gravedigger found skeletal remains in the hole.

Aiden asked if I could help."

He remains silent but moves closer.

She explains. "Aiden said Essie Matkowski has a family issue. He arranged for the reinstatement of my contract. I'll tell you the story at lunch."

He leans in the window.

She smells soap, earth, and sea salt on his skin. Her breath catches in her throat. "There are lots of muffins," she whispers.

"Give us a kiss." He peers into her eyes with one of those "after-a-kiss" looks. "I can organize supper." He pats the door of the vehicle. "We'll be there in a minute."

Nick Cochran appeared on the scene a few months after she took over the park in early 1978. He needed a place, and she was desperate for help if she was to get Shale Cliffs RV Park back on its feet. He answered her ad for a handyman. How circumstances have changed. On New Year's Eve, they'll become full-fledged partners when they purchase Trixie's shares. Stella hurries back to set the table.

****

She never imagined a "love of her life," but here he is. She watches from the kitchen doorway as he strides in through the veranda entrance. Her heart flutters for the third or fourth time today as he tosses his heavy sheepskin-lined jacket on a living room chair and approaches the stairs to their suite above.

"Am I under surveillance?" His eyes are soft.

"In a way." She giggles. "Lunch—the basics," she shrugs, "is on the table. I put out juice. Do you want tea?"

"Later, when you tell me the gruesome details." He glances at his hands. "Give me a sec."

As Stella turns toward the kitchen, she hears Duke. "We're here. Kiki did her business." He hauls a stained plastic container full of kibble from his jacket pocket as he makes his way through the large front room. "Here, Sugar. Let's find a dish for your water."

He grabs a cereal bowl out of a cupboard, splashes water, and plops the fake Blue Willow china on the floor near the dog while Stella observes without comment. He meets her eyes. "Well, now she's settled, I'll wash my mitts. Lunch looks good." He eyeballs the muffins, cheeses, grapes, and mandarin oranges, while he splashes water across her counter. "I love Christmas when we can buy these little cuties." He hastily dries his hands with her tea towel, seizes an orange, and peels the loose skin.

"Take a seat, Duke." She has stopped criticizing his behaviour and hoping for improvement in his table manners.

"Don't mind if I do. Heavy work atop the cliffs with the wind whistlin'." His eyes widen and he adds, "Make no mistake. Love any chance to come out here, regardless of the weather."

"We appreciate your help. Right, Stella?" Nick fills the room with his tall and slender frame, his residue tan, and his ruddy good looks.

"By all means." Their security guard was often a pain in the arse over the last few years, but he's better now—much better. At one point, Duke was considered a suspect in a murder investigation because of his reputation as a lurker—a dirty old man who made lewd remarks and created discomfort for most young women in the vicinity. There's been a change. Throughout the past summer, Eve, and Alice, who work for her, never mentioned Duke as any cause for concern. He discovered, after Lorraine Young's death, how words matter and not everyone appreciates the advances of a near sixty-year-old loud dresser who channels John Wayne on a whim.

Duke manages security in the park throughout the summer. The job is simple enough. He opens the gate in the morning and closes it at night. He scoots around on the golf cart, checking for unattended fires or trucks parked where they block the roads. He keeps a trailer on site. Stella waives his seasonal fee in exchange for his services. She was pleased when he became involved with Cloris Kincaid. He's more settled when he has a companion. Cloris moved her fifth wheel from the Port Ephron RV Park to Shale Cliffs at the end of the season. Duke has been married and divorced three times. His new lady-friend is a handful of years older than him. Certain seasonals say she's a mirror image of the departed Loretta, Duke's mother, who died last year.

"Stella, doesn't Aiden want you at the graveyard right away? You don't seem too bothered by the time." Nick's brows furrow.

She chooses a banana muffin from the batch she made yesterday. "He said one o'clock. I expect forensics will work with those little brushes and trowels for hours. The body's probably been buried for a while."

"Why?" Duke sprays crumbs on to his place mat.

"You'd think the guy diggin' the hole would notice a new plot," Stella mumbles with her mouth full.

Duke squints. "In the expansion—where Mrs. Gorman was gonna be planted?"

"Yup." She squints. His point remains unclear.

"Well, they cut a road through and gravelled, flattened any ruts in the field, and marked out the plots. Maybe the body's fresh."

"He could be right, Stella. Your father is bound and determined his friend Willy disappeared."

"Aiden said the remains are skeletal. No predeterminations, you guys". Stella changes the subject. "How are you and Cloris getting along, Duke?"

"Not bad. Not bad. She ain't keen on my bedsitter at the motel, though." He reaches for his third orange and Stella makes a mental note to buy more when she goes into town. "I'm anglin' for an invite to stay at her place. She has a cute three-bed-bung a half mile outside Port Ephron." He bends and retrieves his Pomeranian from the floor. "Are you hot, little girl?" He removes her powder blue sweater while he continues. "Cloris don't relish the idea of a dog livin' in her house. Hell, she don't even want Kiki in her truck." He and Kiki pout in unison.

At the same moment, Nick creates a similar woebegone expression.

"Listen, you two. No dog. Duke, Kiki is yours and your responsibility. We babysit when you need us. Don't take advantage." She switches her gaze. "Nick, no."

Duke maintains his pout. "She could stay here for the winter and be with me in the summer when I'm livin' in my trailer. I'll pay her bills—and keep her in cute clothes." He bares yellowed teeth in a pleading grin.

"We'll give the notion consideration, won't we, Stella?"

She stands, clears the table, and hopes her lack of response provides an answer. She expects Cloris will invite Duke to spend the winter with her, and Kiki will be their guest. No need for acquiescence right away.

****

Shale Cliffs RV Park is situated across an isthmus from the mainland. During bad storms, when the wind blows in the right direction, the tide will cover the road and access is cut off. Besides the park and the tiny village of Shale Harbour, the spit of east coast land supports a plethora of cottages and a fish plant. She winds her way along the highway, with the view of the darkened ocean on her left. Depending on her speed, she can reach town in twenty minutes. Today, she takes her time. Aiden said one o'clock, but her enthusiasm lacks the necessary exuberance for the task. She should have refused his request and let him find another "qualified" detective to investigate with him.

Although difficult to admit, she was devastated when he explained her services as his community liaison were no longer required. She carried the writers retreat murder inquiry through to a confession from Greta Walmsley without him present—and with Essie Matkowski, assigned to fill in, undermining her at every opportunity while breathing down her neck. Now, a month later, he wants her help again. She guides the Jeep through the turn into Main Street, with the Shale Harbour Savings and Loan on her left and the playground on her right. The bank's salmon-orange paint sparkles in the midday sun.

Traffic is light for lunch hour on a Tuesday, although not unusual for the time of year. The local merchants host sales and events nearer Christmas. Hope Carlyle's weaving shop is open. She runs a steady business and keeps rooms upstairs. Her blue Victorian house stands back from the sidewalk, shrouded by maples long bereft of their leaves. The place could use a coat of paint and a tidy. A century home gobbles thousands in upkeep. Further along, she passes Cocoa and Café. The tiny bistro has done well, from what Stella can ascertain. Cars are parked out front. The restaurant stays open year-round, with shorter hours in the winter. The deck, which inches into designated parking, is empty now. The umbrellas are gone. The metal tables and chairs sit covered in a corner. Tiffany and Andrew Blair, the young owners, participate in whatever plans shopkeepers create for the lead-up to the holidays.

Stella's eyes mist as she passes Yellow House, owned and operated by her friend Paulina McAdams before her brutal assassination. Stella found the body. *Was her death a mere seven months ago?* Now Brigitte, Stella's niece, runs the business and lives upstairs with her three-and-a half-year-old, Mia. The rest of the arrangement remains in the hard-to-believe category. Trixie, Stella's sister and Brigitte's mother, dated a fellow who said he was Russ Harrison, a Human Resource Management Consultant. The title suited Harry Russell, who was subsequently revealed as a hired hit man, blackmailed by a local realtor to kill Paulina, who was embroiled in a serious liaison with the realtor's husband. Although Trixie is involved with a new love interest—a common circumstance for her younger sister—she has never fully recovered from her torrid affair with Russ / Harry. Stella wants to pop in for tea on the way home.

Parlour Antiques is across the street from Yellow House and next door to Cocoa and Café. Matt and Mercedes Savioli became friends after Paulina's murder and during the writers retreat. Their main level is piled high with Victorian treasures. They live upstairs, as many merchants in the village do. Further along, she passes the small jewellery store where the pieces are created from sea glass. A variety of souvenir shops embellish the mix before she reaches Elm Street and the Harbour Hotel on her right. She's often reminded of Somerset Maugham stories, where the location plays a pivotal role in the personality of the mysteries. Harbour Hotel is a bright turquoise three-story establishment built in the 1940s. The labyrinth of hallways and tiny dining areas on the main floor afford guests a considerable amount of privacy when they avail themselves of the restaurant. Two floors of guest rooms are housed above. The place is owned by Eugenie Charlebois, a woman Stella knows by sight alone. Pepper Ferguson, a sweet person who quit university to work for Eugenie, runs the establishment. Stella struggles with Pepper's decision, even though Pepper's choices remain none of her concern.

At the T-intersection of Main and Elm, Stella manoeuvres the Jeep left and into the parking lot of the local Groceteria, your typical village convenience—big enough for what you need, but small enough to charge exorbitant prices if you don't relish the trip across the isthmus and into Port Ephron. Stella supports the locals, most of the time. Today her task is simple—buy more clementines. She stands in line behind a mother with two unruly children and listens while the hollow sounds of "Silent Night" dribble through the PA system.

"Did you find what you needed?"

"Yes, thanks." She digs in her wallet for the required funds and leaves "Silent Night" behind her.

She checks her watch. Five to one. She'll be fashionably late to view the scene of an unknown person buried in a grave for God knows how long. They'll require the services of a forensic anthropologist from Halifax, who will ultimately determine if the remains have been in the hole for a hundred years.

Chapter 2

I Expect You'll Be Awhile

Stella guides the Jeep along narrow Graveyard Lane. Community Council's lack of originality with nomenclature crosses her mind. The land, a fine piece of real estate by any measure, sits on a bluff which overlooks the isthmus and the bay. The single property visible in the distance is Harbour Manor. *Can residents see the spot from their windows?*

Vehicles pepper the scene. Besides the backhoe, the forensics team is on site, along with Aiden's unmarked Caprice. Three other police cars and a large black station wagon frame the excavation. She turns her Jeep into a familiar sidetrack and parks some distance away, near her mother's grave. After she gives Dorothy Kirk's headstone a gentle pat, she treks into the new section, where Aiden is in conversation with an unfamiliar man. The cool sensation from granite in December lingers on her bare fingertips.

"Great, you're here." Aiden acknowledges the severe gentleman in the charcoal topcoat; the one with the comb-over he controls with limited success in the brisk breeze off the water, and adds, "Mr. King, meet Stella Kirk. She's a consultant with the department. Stella, Otto King, the new owner of Royalty Funeral Services in Port Ephron. I believe the business was called Port Ephron Funeral Home until a month or two ago?" He raises his brows at Otto, who nods.

"Charmed, Miss Kirk. I guess there's an issue." He nudges a string of hair into place.

She searches for an appropriate reaction. "Well, with the expansion, one doesn't expect burials on top of each other, right?"

His olive skin flushes. He glances at Aiden, who is focused on the view.

"Can you fill me in? I understand Mallory Gorman's interment was to be the first in the new section. Correct?" She stamps her feet in the cold.

Both men nod, but Otto contributes first. "My regular operator, Luther Greene, is away today, and he asked his friend, Vic Staples, to complete the work." He rams his fists in the pockets of his coat. "Vic didn't understand the requirements, dug far deeper than necessary, and here's the result."

"Vic has been a big help, though. Right, Aiden? Whoever is at the bottom should be identified and their story revealed. No discovery without Vic." She juts her chin toward the funeral director for emphasis.

Otto studies his leather gloves.

Aiden calls out to a forensics officer who motions for them to approach. "You stay here, Mr. King. Stella, come with me."

Despite her lack of enthusiasm, and general poor attitude she's made little attempt to hide, she follows. At the bottom of the less-than-precise excavation, which she estimates as three feet wide by eight feet long by at least eight feet deep, she can see the disturbed skeletal remains of a human being. "I expect you'll be awhile," she says to the pathologist perched on his haunches down beside the bones.

He nods. "Specialists on their way from the city."

The forensics technician nearer Aiden describes the find. He clarifies the body has been here for a considerable period.

"There's the guy over by the machine, Aiden. Shall we speak with him before we leave?" She takes a step toward Vic Staples and gives Aiden no opportunity for comment.

"Hi. My name is Stella Kirk. I help the police when needed." She waves her arm in Aiden's direction. "Detective Aiden North of the RCMP. What happened here today?"

The guy shrugs and dances from one foot to the other, as he runs a dirty hand over his spotted face. "Not much to tell. The digger was delivered out here to the new graveyard, and I dug the hole. I freaked out...not ashamed to say." He winces. "Down there could be in a horror movie. You'll find bones in the pile of dirt, too, in case nobody noticed."

"I'll remind forensics. Thanks. Are you familiar with grave work?" Aiden lifts his collar against the wind as gusts break over the bluff.

"Nope. I collect garbage for the village, but I use a digger when there's a sewer or water problem. Luther's in the Port today and he asked me to cover." He searches the group for the funeral director. "Mr. King knew I was comin'.

He marked where he wanted the hole."

"Why did you dig so deep?" Stella's curiosity directs her question.

"I weren't told how deep. Six feet. Right?"

"You dug eight feet plus, son," Aiden replies.

"Am I in trouble? Alls I did was help Luther out of a jam."

"No trouble. At six feet, the person was undetectable. Give your contact information to the officer over near the squad car with the door open. We may call you for an interview." Aiden trudges across the site once more.

Back at their vehicles, sheltered from the wind, Stella asks, "How's Rosemary? You never answered when we talked earlier."

"She's better, I guess. Toni and Mary Jo want to try another discharge—Christmas. I'm not under any illusions."

"Even if she has a pass for only a few days around the holidays, I expect the experience will be good for her."

He turns, head tilted, white hair dusting one eye. "Because Thanksgiving worked out well, right?"

"Point taken. Now—the other woman in your life—Essie Matkowski. Might she materialize and take over?"

"No way. I informed my boss I want you to work the case with me, full stop."

"Another detective could be assigned if Essie can't come back soon."

"You are the person I want." He repeats as he focuses on her eyes. "Did I misunderstand? Do you prefer I find someone else?"

"And you're sure your superiors won't fire me in the middle of the inquiry? And no covering for you, either."

He appears hurt, but she soldiers on.

"I don't care one way or the other, Aiden." She cares.

****

She snuggles the Jeep into the limited driveway behind Trixie's dilapidated VW Microbus and wonders why her sister hasn't replaced the piece of junk. If you consider the money she'll receive when the park sale goes through at the end of the month—or maybe she wants to wait for the cash, since interest rates remain in the stratosphere. The children's library and small bookstore is closed Sundays through Tuesdays, this time of year. She sidles her way past the vehicles and approaches the back entrance via the toy-strewn deck.

She opens the screen, knocks on the inside door, and hears the "come on in" which emanates from the kitchen.

Stella knows the house well. After she found Paulina, she and Aiden searched the home with a fine-toothed comb. This area is where she discovered Paulina's secret escape exit; where they later learned Farley Thompson, her lover, stayed out of view and climbed into the house at night. She executes two long strides and bypasses the converted pantry before she reaches the kitchen / family room.

"Hi, everyone. Hoped I might find a cup of tea."

Her niece, Brigitte, stands at the counter while Mia, Stella's great-niece, colours at the table.

"Hi, Aunt Stella. Mom's upstairs with Val. They shouldn't be long." She lifts her eyebrows for a second and giggles. "Not what you think. She needed help moving her furniture around. She's never satisfied."

"I hope Valentin isn't too upset with the funeral delay. What a mess." She plops her purse on the floor, hangs her jacket on the back of the chair, returns to the counter, and reaches for the kettle.

"Honest answer, he was relieved. I've heard him say often how he dreaded today."

"A random body found in Mallory's plot means a postponement, not a cancellation." Skeletal images dance in front of her eyes. Her tone sounds gruff, impatient. In her heart, she knows her agreement with Aiden was poor judgment.

"What?"

"Yes. I can tell you guys a few details once they come downstairs." She's taken a position beside Mia and watches her colour. The child offers Stella an orange crayon. "Where do you want the orange, Mia?" Her mother reports Mia is a chatterbox with Trixie and Brigitte, but quiets when anyone else is nearby.

Mia touches the outline of long hair on the little girl, who pulls a puppy in a wagon.

"Oh, she has red hair. Good choice." They colour.

The little girl offers a huge toothy grin before she focuses on the dog.

Trixie bounces into the kitchen with a less enthusiastic Valentin Reguly— he prefers Val—behind. Bounce is the operative word today. Trixie is decked out in a short skirt with lavender tights and a coordinated fluffy sweater.

Her strawberry-blond (and Stella expects dyed, but Trixie won't admit manipulation) natural curls are held back with a sequined clip. Stray tendrils frame her attractive, although aging, face.

"Hi, Stella. We'll take time for tea before we're off to Theodore's for supper. We planned on spending the day with him after the funeral. Can you tell us the issue?" She drags a chair away from the table. "Otto King said a postponement was necessary because remains were found, but he gave no other details except the police were involved." She flops onto a chair opposite Mia. The little girl hands her grandmother a purple crayon.

Valentin sits as well. Brigitte pours hot water into a giant teapot Stella remembers from when she sat at this same table with Paulina. Jane, Paulina's birth-daughter, was raised by Paulina's sister, Danielle, in New York. Jane inherited Yellow House, but Danielle and Jane requested someone else run the business.

"Stella? Are you still here? You drifted off."

"Sorry. Sorry. Thoughts of Paulina." No explanation is necessary. "Not to be blunt, but the skeletal remains of a person were found at the bottom of the grave. As for the service, I imagine forensics will remove the poor soul before the day's over and then the funeral home can reschedule."

"Did the police identify the body? I thought Mallory's plot was the first in the new expansion." Valentin doesn't meet her gaze.

"No. The bones could be a year old or a hundred. Duke mentioned earlier a fair bit of site work was completed over the last few months. If the ground was disturbed, maybe no one noticed. I'll come into town and see Aiden tomorrow. He expects a preliminary forensics report."

Trixie accepts a cup from her daughter and rests both elbows on the table. "And you are involved because? Run the rationale past me again."

"Aiden's partner is on leave because her mother is ill. He doesn't know how long she'll be gone. And he whined and snivelled to his boss that any temporary partner was unacceptable. He wanted me." She frowns as she completes the sentence. "Seriously, though, I can't scrounge much enthusiasm. After he told me last month my contract was nullified, I put investigative crap behind me."

"Who was the woman Dad yapped on about? Willy? Maybe the remains are her."

"Funny. Nick suggested the body could be a nursing home resident. Willy

Saunders moved into a guest house; we assume she wanted a cat. What reason is there to find her buried eight feet deep in an unmarked grave—an area not even a graveyard a year ago?"

She sips her tea and colours. Mia gently replaces the orange with yellow and gazes into Stella's eyes. "Glammy has streaks."

"Perfect, Mia. Happy to help." She addresses Brigitte while she remains focused on the picture, and asks, "Business has slowed now? Managing any time for yourself?"

"Yes, but we planned a special weekend for December 17 through 19—the last big push before the holidays. Every shop in town will be open from noon until eight, with promotions and specials. The newspaper will advertise, Theodore has printed flyers, and Mom, here, has promised to manage Baby Girl." She gazes with fondness at her daughter for a moment, then jumps out of her chair. "Let me find a poster so you can see."

Brigitte races to the built-in desk at the side of the large family room, grabs a flyer, and returns. She hands Stella the graphics only the artistic Theodore Gorman could produce in the village. She recalls the signage he completed for the writers retreat in the fall. "Stunning, Brigitte."

"Yes, they'll be displayed in every storefront window by Thursday. People can plan. I helped organize the promotional weekend with other members of the Shale Harbour Business Association."

****

On the trip home, the cab of her Jeep heavy with the citrus smell of oranges, Stella ponders how far Brigitte has advanced since the time when she resided in a rundown rental with her mother. She cared for Mia and didn't take advantage of any opportunities—not that there were many in Shale Harbour. She accepted the challenge of operating Yellow House because Trixie's plan was to move in with Russ / Harry. Now Brigitte's developed a solid relationship with Carter Stephens, a lawyer at the local firm. He adores Mia. She runs Paulina's Yellow House business as a bookstore and children's library and treats the place as her own. Danielle and Jane Braddon don't interfere with the status quo. As for Trixie—once New Year's Eve rolls around, she will be an independent woman with funds from the sale of her half of Shale Cliffs RV Park. Her immediate future remains a mystery.

Stella's connection with her younger sister is fragile. Trixie is the pretty one; the charismatic one. Stella, although better educated and more experienced away from Shale Harbour, feels lesser—not good-looking in the traditional sense, mousy thin hair, could never manage heeled shoes, few boyfriends, and happier in a windbreaker and jeans than a short skirt and pounds of jewellery. From the moment she and Trixie assumed responsibility for the park in 1978, Trixie arrived with clockwork regularity—hand out, constantly needing money, unhappy in her job at the fish plant, and often on the wrong side of love. Now, even before the funds transfer and share sale is official, Stella sees changes in her sister—changes which involve issues besides great hair and the right shade of lipstick. She's moved past her relationship with Russ. She has increased confidence. Stella likes her more, for reasons she struggles to describe.

Once parked, she glances at her watch. Ten after four. Contentment, paired with a measure of guilt, engulfs her. He'll be waiting. The veranda door opens as she reaches the last riser. "I stopped for tea at Yellow House. I didn't call." She wishes she had taken the necessary moment for him.

"No problem." He holds the old screen wide and reaches for her bag of oranges. "Supper's in the oven. I thought we could go for a walk. I'll show you the progress Duke and I made today before we eat."

"Wonderful." Happy she isn't expected to launch straight into a police investigation conversation, she tosses her purse on a living room chair and gallops upstairs. "Need a minute. What smells so good?"

"Duke left at three, which gave me time to get an early start on supper. I found leftover sauce in the freezer along with a loaf of French bread, so I made lasagna."

What would I do without him? She makes her way back to the main floor. *Sell and move out? Buy a condo in Halifax?* She wraps her arms around his waist and gives him a quick squeeze. "You are a fine man."

"Yes," he says, and grabs her hand. "Come on. There's another half hour before we lose the light, but I'll find a flashlight just in case." His enthusiasm bubbles.

Shale Cliffs RV Park is strategically situated at the end of a short, paved road. A gate secures the park at night and during the off-season. The old family Victorian home / office / reception centre is the first structure any visitor sees. There's parking near the front door for registrations, and the gravelled lot in the back provides easy access to their personal space via the veranda. The blacktop passes the house and proceeds straight toward the cliffs. Two roads intersect before the final stretch runs nearer the edge. The park supports one hundred lots. They changed five sites from unserviced to seasonal, for a total of fifty, and left the existing thirty-five short-stay sites, which reduced the unserviced tenting spots to fifteen. The effort to install a septic system has been gargantuan throughout the fall, but the bank cooperated with a loan and the lion's share of the work has been completed. Each serviced site will be connected next spring, beginning with those who spend the summer at Shale Cliffs.

Nick and Duke levelled many of the depressions, where the ground has sunk after the lines were run, before they quit for the day. The holding tanks are installed, and the septic field is ready. Right now, earthen veins overrun the park, inching their way from trailer sites to tanks. They will need plenty of seed to grass over the myriad of trenches in the spring.

Many of the seasonals leave their units in the park throughout the winter. With Stella and Nick in residence, vandalism is a low risk. If a bad storm moves through, they plow the roads, check each rig, and report any damage to owners—part of the service.

The first trailer they pass, after they round the corner of the house, belongs to Cloris Kincaid. She's parked in this temporary space for the winter. Cloris has avoided the awkwardness of dating her sister's beau by relocating her fifth wheel from Port Ephron RV Park to a permanent site at Shale Cliffs. Stella has assigned her a spot as far away from Duke as possible, in the event the affair doesn't work out as planned. She'll move her trailer to her seasonal site in the spring.

Stella and Nick walk arm in arm, shoulders braced, and chins tucked in against the wind off the bay. She leans into his side. He has one arm wrapped around her shoulder. They meander along the main road. Nick shouts over the gusts as they pass Mildred Fox's Cardinal on the left and Aiden and Rosemary's Holiday Rambler on the right. "See the new earth raked over the sewer lines? Duke worked his ass off today. He was a huge help, Stella."

"I'm not surprised. I said I'd pay him, but he flatly refused. I think he needs a babysitter for Kiki so he can ditch his motel room and move in with Cloris."

"More trenches to be levelled, and I imagine the same work will be needed again in April, if the next months are snowy. We've been lucky so far."

Perhaps he didn't hear her. They wander near the Blacks' rig and the big unit once owned by Louise and Bob Stone but purchased last summer by Buddy McGarvey and his bulldog, Bell. Ted Metcalfe's trailer is secure. He calls each week and checks. "You two did a great job, Nick. Not the easiest task with the wind the past few days."

He gives her shoulder a squeeze. "Kiki's no trouble."

Chapter 3

Why Shouldn't She Be Happy?

Sun streams through the office window and rests against her hunched shoulders while she examines the company books for the umpteenth time. She focuses on the warmth. Without a calendar in front of her, she could be persuaded spring was around the corner, but the truth provides more enticement. She anticipates evenings by the fire, outside work abandoned for two months or more, and kitchen aromas wrapping her in the comfort of Nick's breads and stews.

Nick is impatient to prove his commitment to Shale Cliffs and to her. He has earmarked money he inherited from his aunt to purchase most of Trixie's shares and become her equal partner in the business. In private, she had doubted his sincerity since he first appeared on the scene. She is nine years older and tortured by her failings and shortcomings. In her mind, they far outweigh any positive attributes she might possess. In the end, after their time together, she has harnessed her fears and officially joined forces with a wonderful person who claims he loves her. Why shouldn't she be happy? Who said she should remain alone? Who decided no man would ever find her attractive? She did. Her inner self needed considerable time and convincing, but she has accepted, albeit with reluctance, the idea she deserves her current life. They sign the papers midday on New Year's Eve.

"Shale Cliffs RV Park. How may I help you?"

"Lunch at the café? I'll buy." Aiden's voice trickles along the phone line.

"Good morning. Any particular reason?"

"Autopsy has completed a preliminary report. I thought we could discuss the results."

"I bet you say that to all the girls." She pauses, hoping her remark didn't sound flirtatious. "I can be at Cocoa and Café by eleven-thirty," she adds, with forced abruptness.

"Talk later." The line goes dead.

The kitchen window welcomes as much sun as her office. She retrieves boiled eggs from the fridge and putters as she makes egg salad sandwiches for Duke and Nick. She washes and prepares a handful of carrot sticks, slices cheddar, and places four butter tarts, from her freezer stash, on a side plate. Upstairs, she changes into more presentable trousers and a cardigan sweater she buttons over a camisole. Lots of time for a drive across the park to tell Nick.

When she arrives near where the men continue to shovel and tidy after yesterday's work, Nick's first question when she reveals her plan is, "What entices you more than our company?" He draws a circle in the air, which includes Duke and Kiki.

"A preliminary forensics report and autopsy results."

Nick's thoughts are no secret.

"I made you egg salad and left out other goodies. I might swing past the manor afterward, but I'll be home for tea."

"The manor? Do you need me to visit with Norbert?"

"No. Dad doesn't recognize me, but Del Trembly will, and I need to ask her some questions. The discovery of this body bothers me. See you by three."

"Dead bodies always bother you." He leans in the window and kisses her on the lips. The action holds promise.

****

Aiden is seated in the back corner of the bistro. The bells over the door tinkle for a moment as Stella makes her way to the seat across from him. The rich aroma of cheese biscuits fills the room. She drapes her coat over a spare chair as Tiffany approaches.

"Hi. Tea or coffee?"

"Coffee, please. And the special." She meets the young woman's gaze. "Whatever, as long as fresh biscuits are included."

"Lobster chowder. 'Tis the season."

"Works for me. Aiden?"

"The same, Tiffany, and more of this." He shakes his cup. "When you can."

Once Tiffany moves out of earshot, Stella asks, "What's the story? Could the body be a manor resident?"

Aiden squints. Once Tiffany's behind the counter, he begins. "Autopsy identified a man. The body was buried a year ago, or maybe longer. They need more time. Dental records will be a stretch because he has no teeth, and the fact his skull was bashed in by a blunt object of unknown origin establishes COD."

She sits straight in her chair and studies his face. "Whoever was in the grave isn't Willy Saunders, the woman my father and Del mentioned, but it could be Jasper, the old guy from the manor bridge club who's been gone for months."

Tiffany returns and places chowder and warm cheese biscuits the size of saucers in front of them. Aiden eats with relish, as if the concept of connections between a found body and two disappearances is of no interest. After several spoonsful and a bite of biscuit, he looks away from his lunch. "Describe the people at the manor you were told disappeared."

"Well, Dad's preoccupied." She doesn't minimize the circumstances or blow an innocuous event out of proportion. "He says a resident, Willy Saunders, Wilhelmina, left months ago and never came back. Del Trembly confirms. She also said a person called Jasper, who played bridge with three other old guys, flew the coop, too."

"Are they believable?"

"Dad rambles, but Del is as sane as you or me."

"Identification of the remains will be difficult. What do nursing home staff say?"

"I never discussed the man, but the day-supervisor says Willy moved into a guest house and is fine. Dad thinks she left so she could own a cat. No pets at Harbour Manor," she adds, as a means of explanation. "The curious part was they wouldn't provide me with the name of the new residence. Nick and I will take Dad and Del for a visit once I find out."

"We'll learn more about the body when the final reports are in—they say Thursday. We should interview Royalty Funeral Services afterward. You can join me." The remark represents an unasked question.

"Oh, I'll come, Aiden." Her annoyance and frustration with the previous loss of her contract slip away. "A man was probably bashed on the head and tossed in a hole that a killer thought had no chance of discovery. Council expanded the area and here we are."

"Yes." Aiden taps his mouth with his napkin. "Lots of work. I'm off to Port Ephron for a meeting with Mary Jo, Toni, and Rosemary's psychiatrist from Halifax. A big trip for a talk with a family, but apparently the good doctor comes to town once every month for consults with relatives." He presses his lips together, as if to prevent criticism from trickling out. "Lucky us."

Despite the sarcastic tone, she hears apprehension in his voice.

****

Before she alights from the Jeep, Stella takes a minute to stitch and fortify those pieces of herself most likely to crumble when she sees her father. He hasn't known her for two years. Dementia burrows through his brain in ways she finds mysterious and heart-breaking. He loves Nick and remembers who he is, although now he believes Nick has taken over Shale Cliffs RV Park and married a woman named Stella. Oftentimes he doesn't remember her name. He asks for Trixie, Brigitte, and his great-granddaughter. She swallows tattered pride and makes her way toward the entrance. She didn't call ahead.

Harbour Manor is a quality nursing home, compared to most. There are extra costs for Norbert Kirk's private room, but value for the money. The halls are wide. The lights are bright. Institutional attributes are inescapable, but both the food and the care are exceptional. Her first introduction, every visit, is the smell. The pungent, yet camouflaged, stench floats in the nostrils as an aroma caught between disinfectant and stale urine. The odour never retreats; never improves. The reception desk is vacant. She increases her speed on her way to her father, but the day-supervisor, Maura Martin, materializes out of nowhere.

"Ah, Stella Kirk. You didn't call. Are you here to see your father?" Her lips are pulled away from her teeth, but the smile is forced.

"Yes. I was in the village and thought I'd run over for a few minutes to chat with Dad and Del Trembly." She refuses to ask if her behaviour is permissible.

"Norbert might be napping after lunch. Del is in the lounge. Her TV is on the blink. I think her soaps are on television and she won't appreciate the interruption."

Stella matches the polite, albeit hollow, simper of the nurse. "I'll only be a few minutes, Ms. Martin." Before a response is composed, Stella resumes her sprint along the hall.

He's stretched out on his hospital issue bed, dressed in corduroy pants and a flannel shirt. The sweater she and Nick gave him for Christmas last year is wrapped around his shoulders. She pushes the wide door further ajar and steps inside.

"Hi, Miss. What can I do ya for?" A familiar question when campers arrived at the office.

"Norbert, I'm Stella. You remember. Nick's wife?" A wave of abject sadness washes over her.

Grunting with the effort, he sits and throws his legs over the side of the bed. Bleary eyes search the room. "Is Nick here? Where's Nick? Is he comin'?"

"No. You're stuck with me today. Can we talk?"

"I guess." His posture curves. Disappointment rests on his shoulders.

"The body of a man was found at the bottom of a grave when they were digging Mallory Gorman's yesterday."

"Well, weren't me." His loud and cackling guffaw is unexpected.

"Funny guy, Norbert."

"Not Willy?"

"No, they're sure the remains are a man. Is Jasper your friend?"

"He left a long time ago. The boys don't play bridge no more. They keep waitin' for him to come back. He was polite—a real gentleman." Norbert stops and peers at Stella. "He was a ladies' man."

"Good idea for me to meet with the female residents, I guess, eh?"

"When's Nick comin' by? Can't remember when I seen him last."

"Nick's been hard at work on the new septic system at the park. Wait 'til you see the construction we've done."

Norbert stretches out on his bed once more. The visit is over. "Bye."

She pulls the door closed and soon reaches the common area, equipped with card tables, lounge chairs, a big television, and a patio used when the weather is warmer. Del isn't difficult to find, flaked out in the biggest chair, fixated on the television screen. Stella waits until the ads appear before she approaches.

Del Trembly is the grandmother of Eve, one of Stella's summer staff, and an aunt to the Painters—Cavelle, Hester, and Jacob. She has been helpful during past investigations, with her abiding knowledge of the community and keen observations of human nature. Del is a resident of Harbour Manor because of her weight and poor mobility. She can't take care of her personal needs and requires assistance to complete most tasks. She's perceptive and curious—in Stella's eyes, two admirable qualities.

"Hi, Del. Gotta minute?"

The senior swivels her broad shoulders and meets the originator of the voice with a wide and genuine smile. "Sure do. Did I miss a message?"

"No message. I suppose you heard we found a body over in the new part of the graveyard."

She reaches out and pats the chair beside her. "No one's around. Turn off the squawk box for me and sit."

"Nurse Martin suggested you might be too busy with your soaps."

"Oh, never mind her. I could miss a week of shows and still figure out what's goin' on. Sit. Sit." She leans across the arm as far as her hefty frame will allow. "Did the cops identify Willy?"

"They've determined the body's male, Del."

"Must be Jasper." She throws her body into the back of the lounger, disgust clouding her face.

"Describe Jasper for me. I stopped in to see Dad. He said the guy was a gentleman and the ladies around here liked his company. The other three in the bridge club refuse to play since he left, apparently. Do you remember when? And what's his last name?"

"Jasper Nunn, he is. Well, he wasn't here for Christmas and we're almost there again. I assumed he moved. He walks real good and has kept his marbles. I figured he found a place with more freedom."

Stella leaves her chair and surveys the land around the nursing home through the garden doors, which lead to the patio. The graveyard extension is visible above the wall outside. When she turns, she asks, "Did you ever hear machinery over by the new part?"

"Yesterday, people said they heard noises. The TV's loud in here. I'm not a good judge. Norbert's room's on this side, and he's mentioned there was diggin', but nobody took him serious. They hadn't started the expansion when he was complainin'. Jasper is tall, lotsa hair, and great teeth. No wonder the ladies fell over him. Do you think he was in the hole?"

"Between you and me, forensics says the man has no teeth."

Del pats Stella's hand. "You'll solve the puzzle, dear. You always do. I hope the body's not Jasper, but maybe his beautiful choppers were store-bought, and he lost 'em."

On her way out, Maura Martin stops Stella in the corridor. She has feline qualities and appears when least expected.

"How was your father? Did he call you by name?"

"No. Dad's advanced, Maura." She replies with exaggerated patience, as if speaking with a young child. "You understand his condition better than most."

The supervisor winces.

The result satisfies Stella's urge to knock the nurse off her game. Maura Martin misses no opportunity to remark how Norbert remembers others in the family, but not Stella. "Besides, his recognition of me has no relevance today."

"Another murder inquiry? You should visit Regina and find a red serge jacket."

Stella bends nearer the much shorter woman. "No RCMP uniform necessary for the completion of an investigation, Maura." Extra emphasis. "I'm off. Trixie and Brigitte will be over soon. I'll make sure they contact you first."

"Your sister isn't required to call."

****

She slams her rump into the driver's seat of the Jeep. Did she hold her breath on the return trip to her vehicle? *Why does Maura Martin crawl under my skin? Is she taunting me because my father can't remember who I am?* The endless trails and blind corners of Norbert's dementia, and how his condition has weighed on her, are well understood by any person who works with the elderly every day. The nurse's attitude disturbs her.

Once she returns home and climbs the veranda steps, the first object she sees is a bag of dog food propped near the back door. Duke obviously made plans with Cloris. "Anybody around?"

Nails skid across the hardwood as Kiki rounds the corner and propels her fluffy body into Stella's calf. "Well, here you are, little cutie."

The Pomeranian wiggles and squirms in her powder blue and sparkling turtleneck sweater. Stella drops her handbag on the sofa nearest the door before she scoops the dog off the floor. "Nick? Are you here?"

With quiet and measured caution, Nick appears at the kitchen entry. "Duke left her with us after we finished for the day."

"Is she our house guest for the duration?"

He saunters across the expanse of the living room and wraps both Stella and Kiki in his arms.

Duke's petite canine closes her eyes in what Stella interprets as pure bliss. "I think she's answered my question," Stella adds, with a giggle.

"You're not cross?"

"No. What's the point? Cloris isn't a dog-person. Kiki can stay with us for the winter." She expects this visit will become permanent, but she plays along for the time being.

"Tea is ready. We missed you. Let's go in the kitchen. Tell me what you learned at your lunch meeting."

"And on my Harbour Manor trip."

He lifts his eyebrows but remains silent.

Kiki, curled in her basket nearby, keeps watch on the couple.

Stella, elbows on the table and both hands wrapped around her mug of rooibos tea, lets her shoulders drop. Over the next half hour, she tells Nick the information Aiden relayed at lunch and more details related to Jasper Nunn. These discussions with Nick are her release. Aiden is aware they review each case. Nick's trustworthiness and confidence are invaluable to her.

"I guess I'm hooked, Nick. A man was whacked and buried deep enough to remain hidden if the council hadn't expanded the graveyard…and if Vic Staples knew how to dig a proper hole. The status, or even the safety, of two previous residents of Harbour Manor remains questionable…and I don't like Maura Martin, the day-supervisor."

"How does your opinion of her relate to a body found at the bottom of Mallory Gorman's grave?"

"No idea."

Sleep doesn't come easy. Kiki stays in her bedroom basket, under a white fluffy blanket decorated with paw prints. She snores and snorts. Nick rumbles. Stella's thoughts drift. Old people in this world with no one representing them or interfering on their behalf, when necessary, are vulnerable. A man is buried for God knows how long and never missed. The questions of identity and cause of death hold too much mystery to ignore.

What if she had remained in the city, struggling to create a career as a journalist, in the same circumstances—no family close by, nobody who knew her, or cared where she was or what she did? She might have become another old lady, alone in a nursing home with no advocate to speak on her behalf. The fate of Mildred Fox flits through her mind as she begins to drift.

She turns into Nick's shoulder and closes her eyes. Her move to Shale

Cliffs was the right decision: taking over the park, supporting her father, and rekindling relationships with her sister and niece. This man beside her is a welcome bonus for what she perceived as her sacrifices. As she falls asleep, she senses a slight movement at the edge of the bed. The solid warmth of Kiki snuggles into the small of her back.

Chapter 4

Instantly Suspicious

Two cups of hazelnut coffee create a balancing challenge as Stella picks her way along the narrow driveway toward the machine shop. Ruts, plus a ribbon of grass asking to be mowed one last time although December is upon them, make the five-minute trek precarious.

Aiden called earlier. He asked if she could meet him at the Port Ephron RCMP detachment. The final autopsy was completed, and the visiting pathologist finished a last scour of the hole. She agreed to accompany him to Royalty Funeral Services for informal interviews with the owner. Luther Greene, the fellow who was supposed to dig the grave, will be available, too. Vic Staples has been summoned to the office in Shale Harbour for later in the afternoon. Since she plans to leave Nick on his own yet again, a cup of coffee and the promise of a tasty lunch are her means of compensation.

She discovers him part way under the truck. His khaki-covered legs protrude as he grunts with the effort of jacking up one side. She approaches and stands near the back fender until he notices. The frame groans as the wheel leaves the gravel and becomes suspended in the air.

A muffled "Hi, you," emits from the undercarriage before he scrunches his way into the open.

"Hi. I brought you coffee."

"I see. Are you here to help?"

His indulgent guise suggests he expects no such behaviour. She sets the mugs on the lowered, and tilted, tailgate. "Aiden asked if I could drive to the Port later and discuss the autopsy, then meet with the funeral home director."

Nick peers at her over the rim of his cup, an action she recognizes as his pause in case she says more. "I'll be back for supper. You're quiet." His silence unnerves her.

"Are you sure about your involvement in another inquiry, Stella?"

"I'm okay. I appreciate your concern," she smiles her gratitude, "but I've made my peace with the contract issue. My return will be one-time only. Essie Matkowski will finish her family duties and return to her partnering job with Aiden on the next file. He asked me to be part of this case until we find a resolution, and his bosses agreed." She sips and frowns. "I realize I'm probably jumping to conclusions, but I think this unsanctioned burial must be nursing home related, though I can't figure out how, yet." She continues to argue with herself out loud. "And there's not even any reason to believe the man they found is elderly. Has anyone else left Harbour Manor besides Jasper Nunn and Willy Saunders?" She doesn't expect Nick to answer. "I never realized how vulnerable seniors are when they have no support. Who knows? There might be other old people missing."

He places his empty cup on the grass near the vehicle. "Don't let Aiden take advantage" He holds both palms in the air. "'Nuff said. Help me lift the wheel off, okay?"

She bends beside him and steadies the tire as he removes the nuts and wiggles it off the bolts. When the unit falls away, the weight catches her by surprise. "Yikes. I could never manage a flat on my own."

His laugh is soft. "If you're alone, place a block of wood, if you can find one, below the tire to make a step." He turns and pulls a piece of wood out of the back, grinning as he waves it in front of her. "There's one in the Jeep, too. Lots of people pull and drop, though. Will you stick around while I do the other side?"

"Soup's ready to be heated for lunch. There's crackers and cheese." She checks her watch. It was her mother's. *If my eyesight gets much worse, I'll need one with bigger numbers.* "I can stay." In a sudden fit of realization, she asks, "Where's Kiki?"

Nick lifts his brows.

Without words needed, Stella sneaks a quick peek inside the cab. She sees Kiki, curled on Nick's jacket, sound asleep.

"Glad the morning hasn't turned colder while I'm outside. Makin' do with my sweater." His glance toward the front seat is indulgent.

They work in companionable silence while they install both winter tires on the back of the old Ford pickup. "When are you due in the Port?"

"Not until one-thirty. I told Aiden I wanted lunch with you and plan on leaving the park at one—my attempt at assertiveness."

"Good. If you take Kiki up to the house, I'll be along once I put my tools away. I won't forget the mugs."

She opens the cab and retrieves Kiki and her leash. No surprise she was snuggled into Nick's jacket. She is without attire and the fluff of her fur, as she walks, resembles a huge dust mote floating in the air. "You need a sweater, little one." The dog leads the way, with surprising enthusiasm, along the trail.

****

Stella has never felt comfortable in the Port Ephron police detachment, regardless of the status of her contract. She isn't acquainted with the staff and hasn't spent enough time in the area to cope with the constant change in reception personnel. When she informs the young person manning the phones that she's arrived for an appointment with Detective North, the disinterested response is familiar. She waits in the front lobby. Ten minutes pass before Aiden is called. When he pushes open the glass entry door into the foyer from the main part of the building, the first words out of her mouth, in sufficient volume to be overheard, are, "I was punctual, Aiden."

"The front desk didn't call because my phone extension was lit. I spoke with Otto King and made sure he'll see us today."

"Good. I drove over here specifically for a meeting with him." Her tone is churlish.

Aiden frowns.

Aware of her annoyed response, she doesn't care. Maybe she hasn't reconciled the past after all.

In his office, they review the limited autopsy results and discover little more than they knew before. The victim is male, older than middle-aged, has no teeth, medium height, and has been in the ground for one to three years. The team discovered remnants of a blue flannel shirt and overalls with metal buckles at the bib. Besides a huge dent in his skull, they found no other broken bones, or signs of disease. Identification will be a matter of elimination. "We can speak with manor residents and determine if anyone remembers him."

"I've assigned a detective to search missing persons reports, but feel free to talk with the old folks. We'll discover more with that avenue of inquiry, I'm sure. We'd best be on our way."

From the moment she meets the man on his own turf, Stella isn't impressed with Otto King. He acts guilty, with his clammy handshake, his black suit, and his shiny shoes. Imagine trading on his last name to call the funeral home *"Royalty"* Funeral Services.

Their discussion begins in the parlour, where people gather to celebrate the life of a loved one. Lucy Painter was buried from here. Dorothy Kirk, too. Stella knows the establishment well. The business occupies a renovated century home, which smells musty and tired.

"Mr. and Mrs. Gorman chose the particular plot in the expansion for Mrs. Gorman?" Aiden starts with the obvious.

"Not a clue—no idea." He launches into what feels like a rehearsed explanation for the uninformed. "The Village Council owns the land, sells the plots, and manages the graveyard. Any funeral service can conduct a burial. The Gorman couple chose us. I gave the local man, who took Luther's place, the lot for the grave. Royalty Funeral Services has no connection to the discovered body."

Stella watches as King grows increasingly haughty and defensive. She revels in his uneasiness. "Do you know Vic Staples?"

"No. Luther told me he was reliable and competent. He dug the hole eight feet deep, for heaven's sake!" He twists his hands.

"And good job he did. Repeating what I said at the site, Mr. King, the victim was discovered because of Vic Staple's inexperience."

"I guess," he acquiesces. "Shall we sit for a moment in my office? Once I've finished with your questions, Luther is here, and you may talk with him as well."

He shows them into a mahogany-panelled room Stella expects is Otto King's sanctum. The desk is constructed of the same shiny, red-highlighted wood as the walls. The leather chair behind the unit is of the richest brown she's ever seen. The oak floor is protected by an Aubusson carpet Stella is sure came directly from France. None of the décor existed when the business was called Port Ephron Funeral Home. She remembers planning her mother's funeral in a room full of file cabinets and casket samples.

Wrestling her sarcasm, she remarks, "Nice office, Mr. King."

With his chest puffed, he gazes around the space and acknowledges her hollow compliment. "The renovations took weeks and were expensive, but I felt the ordeal was necessary for the comfort of clients in a stressful time."

Otto will be the comfortable one. "Is Mallory's funeral rescheduled?"

"We are striving for Saturday afternoon at two. I hope you'll attend," he simpers.

Her skin crawls at the sound of his voice.

"Police clearance is required." Aiden is blunt.

King frowns but doesn't reply.

"You never sell plots, Mr. King?" Aiden refocuses the conversation.

"Mercy, no." He lifts a manicured hand and covers his mouth. "At the risk of repetition, Village Council allotted the expansion and sells the lots. I manage the service and dig a grave in the space owned by the deceased or their family." He waves for them to be seated and rounds the wide desk to access his chair. He's now framed, with mathematical perfection, by a pair of mahogany bookcases. "I'm surprised you aren't aware of the process, Detective."

Admonished, Aiden remains silent, and Stella interjects. "Why did Vic Staples dig Mallory's grave? Where was Luther Greene?"

"He said he had a family matter requiring his attention here in town, Ms. Kirk. He advised me he couldn't complete the task at the time required and suggested I hire Mr. Staples. He has experience." Sarcasm bleeds into his tone when he adds, "I thought."

Stella can't wait to meet Luther Greene.

"Luther is out in the back. The hearse needed a wash. Let's go find him." Aiden stands.

Stella presumes he's impatient to vacate the hot mahogany humidor in which they've been sequestered for the last half hour.

Otto King's assistant could be described as a heartthrob if one used Rosemary North's vernacular when she takes on the persona of a prom queen from the 1950s. His chiselled features are highlighted by tanned skin and deep blue eyes, the colour of the ocean in the summer. He's outfitted in tight denim jeans and a plaid cotton shirt open at the neck. The temperature in the shelter of the garages is above the norm, and his jacket rests on the lawn.

"Luther. Please meet Stella Kirk and Detective Aiden North from the RCMP. They wish to discuss the issue with Mallory Gorman's grave on Tuesday."

"Charmed." He holds out a soapy hand as evidence before he adds, "I'd shake your hands, but…."

A sheepish and fake grin accompanies his remark—an overt attempt at friendliness, and Stella is instantly suspicious.

Aiden begins with a statement of fact. "You suggested your boss hire Vic Staples to cover your shift at the graveyard in Shale Harbour on Tuesday."

"Right on, Detective. I wasn't anywhere near the dead body."

"Why Vic?"

"What?"

"Why were you not at work and why did you suggest Vic Staples take your place?"

With exaggerated slowness, Luther squeezes the saturated sponge in the bucket, reaches for a towel, dries his hands, and meets Aiden's gaze. "I was busy. Since I went to school with Vic, I thought he might appreciate the extra cash. He took his saved time off from the village and worked for Mr. King."

"Are you folks finished out here?" The funeral director has reappeared at the back door. "The car must be available by three."

"We're done. Thank you for your cooperation." Aiden nods toward each of them in turn.

"Detective," Luther interjects before they leave, "Shale Harbour employees cleared the land, plotted the sites, and built a road—with the help of a local engineer. One of them coulda noticed a recent disturbance in the dirt." Luther's eyes become round, as if in sudden surprise at his own idea. "One of them coulda even disposed of a body while the ground was torn apart." He squares his shoulders. "Here at Royalty Funeral Services, we bury people whose family wants them buried." He glances toward his boss.

As far as Stella is concerned, both Otto and Luther have given her and Aiden a show, and she's determined to uncover the reason.

****

"I shouldn't be here. Knocked off work early. You already talked to me." Vic Staples sits slumped in a chair in the interview room at the Shale Harbour RCMP station. Sergeant Moyer was at the front desk when they arrived from Port Ephron and reported the guy had been waiting for thirty minutes.

"There are additional questions, Vic, and we appreciate your help."

He squirms, as if he has a rash on his butt.

"Were you on the crew when the graveyard expansion work was completed?" Aiden wastes no time.

"Not me. Two heavy machinery operators and the engineer who works for the village and Port Ephron were on the site. I filled in for one day, but the job was almost done. I spread gravel on the new road goin' through."

"Who supervised?"

"The town manager, Philip Lewis, I suppose. I saw him talkin' with the engineer when I was workin'."

"Do you know how many men were involved in the project?" Vic isn't a reliable source because he wasn't around much, but she wants an idea.

"I told you—two machine operators, and I filled in once, the Shale Harbour manager, and the engineer. His name is Evan somebody," he shrugs.

Aiden turns to Stella. "Evan Fleguel is based in Port Ephron. He works over here, too."

Vic adds little more.

After he's escorted out, they regroup in Aiden's office.

"We should have a conversation with Lewis and Fleguel, and the two equipment operators. There's a chance one of them buried a body during construction."

Aiden parrots Luther Greene but Stella's not convinced. "They started work on the expansion last spring. Didn't the autopsy say the guy was in the hole for at least a year?" She nibbles a thumb nail. "Why don't we interview staff and residents at Harbour Manor? The property overlooks the graveyard, albeit not next door. Many folks are alert—Del Trembly, for instance."

"I'm not sure. Missing Persons, along with the detective I assigned, will run checks on disappeared men over the last three years. Their work might find us a lead." He frowns. "You follow the manor angle, if you want, while I interview village employees. Mary Jo and Toni need my help with preparations for Rosemary's arrival, so I'll be taking two or three days off right away."

She understands the pressure Aiden's under with a wife who often experiences acute mental health challenges and has been institutionalized for months, but she's reluctant to accept responsibility for any part of this investigation. He doesn't believe the nursing home is involved, so she'll make an exception. "When can we get together and go through what we've discovered?" He's not treated their inquiry with any urgency, which is of concern, and she wants clear direction.

"Let's meet next week—Thursday or Friday—and compare notes."

****

Back in the park, Nick greets her at the door, wine in hand. "I guessed you put in a long afternoon."

Kiki nuzzles her ankles, and she accepts the drink with a flourish. "I learned one valuable piece of information. We do not want Otto King of Royalty Funeral Services conducting our funerals. I'd rather Trixie manage the event, no matter how many boas and sequins are involved."

He throws his head back and guffaws—a deep and wonderful sound she often tries hard to elicit. "I bet you've a story to tell me."

"Correct, but I need to make a phone call first." She races into her office and contacts the manor before Maura Martin, the supervisor, is gone for the day.

"Harbour Manor. May I help you?"

"Maura Martin, please. Stella Kirk."

She listens to classical piano while on hold. "Good afternoon, Miss Kirk. I'm on my way out the door and yes, you may come visit your father."

"Great." She attempts an upbeat tone, although she could reach through the phone line and choke the woman. She's suddenly aware she has felt impatience with many people over the last month. A quiet Christmas with Nick, and now Kiki, will be a welcome reprieve. "I wondered if I could bring my dog, Kiki, when I visit. The residents might enjoy her company tomorrow."

"Dog. I didn't know you owned a dog, Stella."

"Kiki is a Pomeranian who is our house guest for the winter. She's an old friend, well-behaved, and loves people."

Supervisor Martin hesitates for a moment before she replies with a wary, "Okay. There are rules, though."

"Understood. And Nick and I can both be there and provide adequate supervision."

"I assume, Kiki is her name? I assume Kiki is house-trained and clean?"

Stella softens her tone. "Kiki is a sweet little dog who will create lots of joy for your residents. We can come over in the afternoons, tomorrow and Saturday. What do you think?"

"Okay. I'll be here tomorrow. We'll see from there. Several residents become maudlin near the holidays and a dog visit might be the exact medicine needed. Thank you, Stella."

After the call, Stella sips her wine and pets Kiki, now perched in her lap. "You are my ticket to resident interviews, little one."

Chapter 5

It's Been Almost a Hundred Years

"Grab her purple sweater with the sparkles, Nick. Are we ready?" Stella thunders down the stairs, rounds the corner, and slides into the kitchen, breathless.

"Are we behind or are you excited at the thought of a manor visit?" He ruffles Kiki's ears while he wrangles her into her attire.

"We'll have fun with the dog and the residents." She pauses long enough to see he's caught the glint in her eye. "I'll manage a few questions regarding our mysterious dead man at the same time." Aiden disagrees with her theory that people at Harbour Manor vanished, but she will persevere.

"You're determined there's a problem."

He states the obvious, and she knows he expects an explanation. "The manor is run by the Board of Directors. They receive their funding from the village and the province. There must be records kept of former residents and their current whereabouts. If I'm forced to write letters, I will."

"Consider Willy Saunders and the man named Jasper Nunn might have left of their own volition. Nothing ominous about a move to a better situation."

"I need to understand, Nick. Why isn't information about them available? All I'm asking for is a forwarding address, for God's sake." She slams her feet into loafers. Thank God there's no snow yet. She reaches for a leash from many hung on a hook by the veranda entrance. "Changing the subject, I hope Duke doesn't mind sharing Kiki with residents of the nursing home."

Nick scoops the dog off the floor and wedges her under his arm. "He left her with us. You're mine, now, Princess." He ruffles what fur is exposed around the neck of her sweater and they make their way toward the Jeep.

****

"Hi, Norbert. Take a gander at who I brought for a visit." Nick has pushed open the door and approached Stella's father, who snoozes in his chair facing the window. Stella lags in the doorway.

"What? Hey. Whatcha holdin?" He extends his arms. "Hi, Kiki. Hi, Nick. Where's Duke?" Kiki does her job and snuggles with the old man.

He hasn't acknowledged Stella. She approaches with trepidation. "Hey, Norbert. We're Kiki's babysitters for a while and figured folks here at the manor might appreciate a visit."

Norbert pats the dog. His hands are heavy and veined. Kiki squints her eyes each time his palm falls on her fuzzy skull, too polite to refuse his weighted attention. "And you're Stella, right? Nick's wife."

She lifts her lips into a forced smile. "Brigitte and Trixie will be over to see you soon."

"Good. Hope they bring the little one." He pauses and furrows his brow. "Mia, right?"

"Right." Her heart breaks. "Can we talk about the body buried in the hole over in the field?" She points out the window.

"What?"

He doesn't recall the incident. The logic of his memory loss escapes her. None exists. "They dug Mallory Gorman's grave and found a guy. He'd been dead for over a year. You told me you heard machinery noises. Do you remember when?"

Her father focuses on Kiki. "I'm no different from your pup here. What I call to mind could be a few minutes ago, yesterday, or last year. I got a blender for a brain."

"Okay. No problem, Norbert. Let me describe the man, and you can tell me if he sounds familiar."

Kiki accepts the heavy-handed pats and shut her eyes.

"Forensics says he wasn't tall, had no teeth, and was wearing a plaid flannel shirt and bib overalls."

He shakes his head. "No friend a mine. Nick, you gonna stay?"

Nick glances at Stella. "Sure, I'll sit with you. Stella wants to take Kiki to Del's room for a few minutes, though."

Reaching over, she retrieves the dog and makes her goodbyes, happy to escape the man who once was her father. As she travels along the wide and bright corridor, then around the corner in Del's direction, various residents out for exercise with their walkers stop and touch Kiki for a moment. She promises visits later.

Stella steps into her friend's room. "Hi, Del. I brought a friend to say hello."

The old woman's squeals confirm her delight. "Sit her in my lap. Sit her in my lap."

She rushes over and places Kiki on Del's ample thighs as if she were a sacrificial lamb.

"Oh, I miss my little dogs. I owned three over the years. They were fluff balls, too. Not Kiki's breed, mind you. Mine were Shih tzus—a pain in the arse to comb, but good doggies." She ruffles Kiki's fur. "I don't imagine a dog visit is the main reason you came round. Any chance the body be Jasper?"

"No, Del." She describes forensics' report once more.

Del ponders. "Never met a short man wearin' overalls, that I remember. Could be anybody, I suppose. I told folks you were investigatin'. Whatcha gonna do now?"

"Talk with residents and see if someone recalls a guy who resembles the person we found." She frowns. "My theory is that only certain men wear overalls all the time. They're a style statement more than work attire once you reach a certain age. Maybe we can narrow the search. The man, for sure, had no teeth and the consensus is Jasper sported a full set."

"If they weren't false, but Jasper was dapper, never be caught dead in overalls." Her cackle at her own joke borders on hysterical. Kiki flattens her ears. "I'm glad you didn't find him."

"Thanks for your help, Del. I must meet with Supervisor Martin for a minute. Nick is with Dad. Dad remembered Kiki, but he doesn't remember me."

"Poor dear," she remarks, as Stella leaves.

Did Del mean her or Norbert?

****

She finds Maura Martin at the nurses' station and plasters an open expression on her face. She expects resistance. "Good afternoon. I thought I'd stop by and check in before I start my visits."

Maura jumps from her chair and reaches for Kiki over the top of the reception desk. "What a sweet little dog. What's her name, again?"

"Meet Kiki. Her owner is one of our seasonal employees. He's spending the winter in a spot where he can't keep her. Now she's our house guest for the foreseeable future."

"Aren't you cute in your purple sweater?" She meets Stella's gaze. "I love dogs. I must advise you, Del Trembly has told anyone who will listen how 'her friend' is working to identify the body found the other day."

"I'll provide a description and ask, if you don't mind." Stella can't believe her good fortune. Maura Martin is unusually agreeable.

"Residents are excited, especially about Kiki. I said you were visiting today and tomorrow with a dog. The bridge club is in the common room for a game of crib and their tea. Is the body Jasper Nunn?"

"Still unidentified, Maura." She tells the nurse what she knows. Like Del, the description proves unfamiliar. Permission to visit again tomorrow has been given, albeit with subtlety.

"Come on. I'll carry Kiki and we'll go meet the boys, right little one?" She hugs the Pomeranian against her generous bosom. Kiki's ears flatten again.

****

Stella tags behind while Maura breezes into the common room with Kiki tucked into the pit of her arm. "Good afternoon, gentlemen. Your tea and biscuits should be along any minute. This is Kiki. She's a Pomeranian and a friend of Stella Kirk's."

"Del Trembly told us about you," the man with a ragged ponytail accuses. He makes eye contact with his companions, but points at Stella. "Her father is Norbert, but he don't know her from Adam." He peers in Stella's direction again. "Am I right?"

"Let me introduce the men, Stella." She hands Kiki back. "Meet Guy Boucher, retired military." She indicates the gentleman wearing shorts in December. "Did you do your fitness workout today, Guy?" She explains, "Guy keeps a set of weights in his room. He's been with us for two years."

"A fella needs ta stay in shape for the ladies." He squares his shoulders and touches his sparse blond hair.

"And Elmer Richards. The contraption parked by the table is his."

Stella eyes the walker, wrapped in duct tape at various joints.

"Pleased to meetcha." Elmer's face is fleshy and puffed. His lower lip protrudes, so his speech is garbled. Significant saliva escapes along his chin. He mops the offensive liquid with a soiled blue handkerchief, which he stuffs into the pocket of pants with the waistband around his chest.

"Elmer moved in at the same time as your father, Stella, after his sweet wife died of a sudden heart attack."

"I'm sorry," she mumbles.

"My missus took care of me. This arthritis put me in a tangle." He holds out gnarled and crooked fingers. "Can't peel too many taters anymore."

"And last but not least, please meet Caleb Hall, our resident know-it-all."

Caleb stands and throws his long ponytail over his shoulder. "Never mind old Maura, here. She and me, well, we don't see eye-to-eye most of the time." He straightens his plaid cotton shirt and khaki pants, which appear a size too small for a man of his girth. His white socks, paired with heavy leather sandals, are exposed below his cuffs.

"Caleb's lived in many places before Harbour Manor, but moved in here with Guy. I'll leave you, now. If you need my help, give a shout." She bustles out into the hall, and Stella hears the rhythmic squish of her soft-soled shoes as she moves further away.

"Can I hold her?"

"Sure." She puts Kiki on Elmer's lap. He uses his wrists to keep her secure, although Kiki settles without a problem.

"Del says you work with the police and you're findin' out who the funeral home found in the hole." Caleb leans forward.

"Correct, Mr. Hall. If I give you a description, will you guys think of anyone who fits?"

"Fire away," spouts Guy, with an enthusiasm Stella finds unsettling.

She takes her time and mentions each characteristic related to the uncovered body. The men nod while they listen. Elmer cuddles with Kiki. He drools.

After a moment of silence, Guy and Caleb exchange glances and Caleb responds. "Don't sound familiar. Covered over for a year or more, you say? And call me Caleb. Everybody does."

"Yes. Forensics claims the body's been buried for more than a year—timelines aren't an exact science."

Tea arrives. Staff added a cup for Stella. She pours milk and waits while the men doctor theirs. "Shall I take Kiki while you enjoy your wafers, Elmer? She's a mooch."

"Can I give her a treat?"

"Tiny pieces. She's put on weight over the last few months."

Elmer mumbles to Kiki. "You're not overweight, my dear. Take a gander at Caleb. He eats too much, and you see the result. At least your sweater fits you."

"Keep your trap shut, old man." Caleb raises his voice.

"You can't hurt me. I'm a cripple and you can't hurt a crip." Elmer's bottom lip protrudes more than normal when he leans toward his friend.

"Cut it out, you two. Stella, here, is gonna think we got no manners." Guy takes a quick sip of his tea. "You're barkin' up the wrong tree, my dear. We'll ponder the problem, though. You should go talk with Addie and Eula. They've been here for a hundred years and know everybody."

"The corpse ain't Jasper?"

"Not likely, Elmer. The body has no teeth. Del says Jasper was dapper, with beautiful teeth." She reaches for Kiki. "Do Addie and Eula enjoy dogs? We can visit with them before the afternoon's over."

"We all miss Jasper." Guy sighs.

"A dog's no problem. Let me escort you." Caleb grunts as he rises. "I'll be back, fellas." As they wander along the wide corridor, he enlightens Stella on the fascinating subjects of Eula Cameron and Addie LaPointe.

****

On the short trek to a room shared by the two ladies, Caleb filled Stella in on what he considered was their unique history. She clutched Kiki and deciphered little of his disjointed ramblings about farms and husbands.

"Hi, girls. Can we come in?"

Stella hears a giggle. "Certainly, Caleb. We're pleased to see you, aren't we, Addie?" Without pausing for a response, she adds, "You haven't cut your mop. What's the matter with you? Bald in the front and a horse's tail in the back. You look like an idiot."

She elicits a grunt from Caleb.

"Who's here?" Eula scrutinizes Stella at the doorway, before she focuses milky eyes on Kiki.

"Meet Stella Kirk and her dog, Kiki. Stella's the daughter Norbert Kirk can't remember."

"Oh."

Stella studies Eula's face, awash in sympathy. Meanwhile, Addie watches her with a steady gaze.

"Pleased to meet you both. I came for a visit with Dad and to let everyone cuddle with Kiki."

"The real reason she's here is because of the dead guy they found in the graveyard—the one what was a surprise."

Addie and Eula sit in twin glider rockers, side by side, in a room around the same size as Norbert's. "Del Trembly said you're lookin' for sweet Jasper." Eula glances at Addie, who nods but now keeps her eyes on her heavily veined and twisted fingers.

"Well, the man in the grave is probably not Jasper, but we still must determine who he is. I hoped you might help. Caleb tells me you've lived here at Harbour Manor the longest."

"Can Addie hold the dog? I understand what she's thinkin', and she wants to hold the dog."

"No problem." As Stella places Kiki on Addie's knee, Caleb waves his goodbyes and saunters back along the hall for his tea and crib game. "Guy said you two have been friends for a hundred years now," she teases, "but you girls are far too young."

The sharp bark emitted by Addie reminds Stella of her friend Hester.

"Addie doesn't talk anymore, but she understands. The stroke, I'm afraid."

"Sorry." Stella is lost for words, as she apologizes again for the consequences of age.

"Let me see. Addie and I were born two years apart on farms along the same road. I'm older. I'm ninety-six and she's ninety-four. I met her right after she was born. Caleb is wrong. We've been friends for ninety-four years." The women titter in unison.

Eula explains. "Addie and I grew up as best friends. After high school, we married brothers from the next county. We lived on farms side by side. We birthed our kids at the same time. She raised two boys, and me—a boy and a girl. We gave the farms to our sons at the same time and moved into old folks' apartments in Port Ephron. The place didn't suit us, did it, Addie?"

The older woman slides her face back and forth with unnecessary vigour.

"Our men died a year apart. After Addie took her stroke, she needed me for help. We signed in here in 1965. Harbour Manor was new. We're the first in this room, and yes, it's been almost a hundred years." A ripple of sadness creases her brow.

Lightening the mood before she asks questions focused on disappeared people and discovered corpses, Stella states, "You could write a book and tell the story of your lives, Eula."

"No. A tale of two girls who stayed beside one another and never changed isn't real interestin', but a full life, nonetheless."

Addie nods and runs a flaccid hand over Kiki's back. The little dog has closed her eyes and curled into the woman's lap.

Without a spare chair in the room, Stella perches on the foot of a twin bed. "Let me describe what we found." She launches into a commentary on the body and clothes in the grave. Neither woman recognizes any of her descriptors.

"Only men we've known who wore overalls were our husbands, and your guy ain't one of them." She pats Addie's knee. Both women giggle again.

"The poor fella ain't Jasper either, 'cause the man has the nicest teeth an old feller could ever want—and thick white hair." She pauses. "Nope. Wherever Jasper is, he's not in the hole."

"Thank you for your help today." Stella stands and reaches for Kiki.

"Our pleasure, eh, Addie?"

Addie nods but doesn't lift her face.

On her return trip toward her father's room, she meets a gentleman walking with exaggerated briskness along the corridor. He tips an imaginary hat as he races past. "Please discuss your investigation with me," he whispers, as he whizzes by. "I'm two doors away from Norbert. My hearing is excellent," he pants.

"We're back tomorrow, Mr. ah…."

"Dewey Laird, Miss Kirk, but call me Dewey, and I hope we can talk."

He flies along before she answers. His hips swing in a competitive walker's gait as he disappears around the corner.

A quick stop at the desk results in confirmation of permission for her to visit again the next afternoon. The all-seeing Maura adds a piece of advice and a request. "Pay no attention to Dewey," she hisses in Stella's ear. "He's heard voices all his life." In a more normal tone, she adds, "While you're here tomorrow, make time for Miriam Sylvester. Her son, William, never visits…

oh, and Connie Gee. She has ALS, but her mind is fine." She absently pats Kiki. "Connie's a sweet person with a heavy burden."

"I'm sure you'll tire of me, Maura, but may I talk with staff and volunteers the first of the week?" She ignores Maura's comment about Dewey.

"Will you bring police personnel with you?"

"No, but if you prefer that I not meet with employees alone, I can arrange for RCMP presence." She thinks of Sergeant Moyer, who will help if asked.

"You've misunderstood, Stella. Staff may be unnerved if interviewed by authorities. You're welcome to talk with them yourself if your investigation remains informal."

Nick is waiting for her when she reaches the entry. After a pause on the frozen grass for Kiki, the couple returns to the Jeep and heads for home. "A gentleman named Dewey Laird asked to see me tomorrow. I'm curious. He says he has great hearing. I expect he'll report machinery sounds, although Maura suggested what he often hears are voices in his head. She gave me permission to interview staff and volunteers next week, which was a pleasant surprise. She likes Kiki and I'm in her good books now. Nice visit with Dad?"

"Yeah. I described the septic system. He isn't interested in the park anymore."

Chapter 6

On My Way Downhill Fast

Stella leaves Nick and Kiki with her father. As promised on yesterday's visit, she trots toward Dewey Laird's location but discovers his room empty. He rounds the corner at top speed and rushes past her in a blur of waving arms. "Come with me," he puffs.

She follows him, albeit at a slower pace, back the way she came. Dewey's personal space is organized chaos. She identifies a stereo system and a television, a bookcase stuffed with titles, and a small desk, more suitable for a child, covered in reams of loose-leaf paper.

After he flops into his rocker, his gaze bounces around the clutter. "I'm writing a book," he proclaims, by means of explanation. He takes a swig of water from a finger-print-smeared glass, then stretches out his arms in a sweep. "As you can tell, I prefer my own company. People describe me as quirky, and I don't deny the affliction. I imagine Maura suggested you show skepticism when listening to me." He taps his skull with red knuckles. "She says my ramblings originate in my noggin and not from outside."

"May I sit?"

He jumps to remove papers from his desk chair and spins it around to face the room. "Be my guest."

"What's your book called, Dewey?"

"Living with Schizophrenia. Catchy, eh?"

She's not sure if he's serious. "I've heard worse titles, and yours makes a point. Tell me more." She likes Dewey. As with her friend Hester, he has social dysfunction—a forwardness—which could well put many off, but she appreciates his forthrightness.

"My parents thought I was weird from the time I was a teenager. The voices started when I was six, but I never told anyone until I was seventeen."

"Why did they think you were weird?"

"I mumbled to myself. I played alone. I loved our cat and often bragged she talked to me. As a teen, other kids taunted me. A doctor diagnosed my condition after I confessed to Mom."

"Life can be a challenge when you're different." The simplest response is often the best.

"You understand." The muscles of his face relax. "Anyway, Maura no doubt suggested I fabricate issues, but I don't. I'm much better now. The more I age, the less medication I need because the voices have retired, too." His laugh is soft. "They still come around once in a while, though. I miss them."

"How long have you lived here, Dewey?"

"Seven years. I worked as a labourer in construction my whole life. At sixty-five, I collected my pension and moved in here. They take your cheques, but give you a few dollars back for incidentals, and I'm content. Three hots and a cot—a work buddy, who was in jail, used to say, as I remember." His voice adopts a wistful tone. "Three hots and a cot," he repeats.

"Any family?"

"No. Never took on a woman. I had a sister, but she died a long time ago—cancer. She never had kids either. Me, myself, and I." He sits straighter in his chair. "And I didn't even include the voices." His self-deprecation comes out in a low rumbling chuckle.

"You told me, yesterday, about your excellent hearing, Dewey."

"Correct. Tell me when the body was buried, and I'll double-check my diary."

Stella rattles off the basic information she shared with other residents and Maura Martin. She keeps the details succinct and consistent. She is unable to provide a date.

Dewey lifts his thin frame out of his rocker and takes two steps toward his desk.

"I marked the time I heard the machinery noise in my daybook, as I do with most events each day. I wasn't lookin' for attention." He passes her an agenda with the page opened at December 15, 1979. "The weather was snowy and windy—twenty-five degrees Fahrenheit." He runs a finger over his notes. "I document the details. I report the weather and temperature." He winces. "Never got the hang of Celsius."

"Either is fine, Dewey. Will you tell me what happened on December 15, 1979?"

After he crosses his legs and settles, he says, "There were mechanical sounds I assumed were a digger, but I couldn't see much."

"Why not? Was it snowing heavily?"

"What did I write in the diary?"

Stella squints at the small cursive script. "You say this occurred while you readied for bed at nine-thirty?" She confirms the details by waiting for his nod. "You looked out the window and thought the noise came from the direction of where the paper said the graveyard expansion might go, but you couldn't tell?"

"Right. In the end, the village didn't do the work until this spring. The noises never made sense until you found a spare body. Do you suppose the man in the grave was buried on December 15, 1979?"

"No idea yet, Dewey, but you've provided evidence helpful in our investigation."

"You can keep my diary from 1979." He points out a similar day planner open on his desk to December 5, 1981. "I'll document our conversation and establish a record. Shall I expect an interview with the real police?"

Stella acknowledges the inference. "I work with Detective Aiden North. He'll no doubt confirm the information. Perhaps we can photocopy the page of your diary for now. You keep your day planner in a safe place, and I'll take the copy, okay?"

"Sounds fine. We can walk back to the office together."

"Not if you travel at your regular pace, Dewey." She grins at her new friend.

They pass her father's room, where she steps inside and tells Nick she'll return soon. They move toward the office, situated behind reception. When they approach the side door, Dewey knocks with polite firmness.

"Come in."

"Why, Olive, what are you doin' tucked away here?"

"Came in before my shift so I could finish paperwork. Good workspace since we don't employ a secretary. Who's this person, Dewey?"

"Oh, me and my manners," he self-admonishes. "Meet Stella Kirk—Norbert's girl. She's here with her dog Kiki, but we need a page in my diary photocopied. Can you help?"

"Sure. No problem," she replies, with a puzzled frown.

Stella extends her hand. "Hi. Pleased to meet you."

The nurse accepts. "I'm Olive Urback, the night supervisor. Dog?"

"Kiki's with my dad and my partner, Nick. I visited with Dewey and now I'm off for a chat with Miriam Sylvester."

"Do you know dear Miriam?"

Dewey interrupts with a gush. "Stella helps the police and they're figurin' out who they found in the hole?"

Stella meets Olive's eyes while the nurse stands in front of the copier. "We thought the body was Jasper Nunn." She provides Olive with the standard information. She's never known a man who wears bib overalls either. "As for Miriam, we crossed paths when I helped the police on another case. Such a dear soul."

"Did I do the right page?" Olive holds out the copy for inspection.

"Perfect," says Dewey, and crooks his thumb at Stella. "The paper's for her."

"Thanks, Olive. Perhaps we'll chat again before the investigation's over."

****

After she pops into her father's room and grabs a bewildered Kiki, she races to find Miriam Sylvester.

"You've been given a make-over, Mrs. Sylvester," Stella exclaims. The change, from the time Stella first met her after Lucy Painter's death in 1979, is remarkable. The woman was the mother of one of the murder suspects. Her son, William, her primary care giver, was eliminated from the investigation. He was a rudderless young man who proved neglectful in his responsibilities. Stella and Aiden found Miriam on the floor with her wheelchair landed on top of her. She was admitted into hospital and placed at Harbour Manor in January 1980.

Miriam sits in her wheelchair. A contraption designed for holding a book is fitted on one arm of the chair. The woman lifts a hand, supported by a limp wrist, and turns a page. Stella can't imagine her engaging in this behaviour a year ago. Speaking was an extreme exertion at the time, and she couldn't move without help.

"Wonderful seeing you and your little friend, Stella. Please call me Miriam." Her head hangs on her neck, lacking necessary support, but her eyes meet Stella's in a direct and open stare. "May I hold the dog?"

"Kiki will enjoy a visit with you."

"Don't worry. She'll be safe. The doctor put me on a new medication designed for people with cancer, but the pills give me extra strength."

The little dog does her job and settles into Miriam's lap. Stella relaxes.

"They say you're looking for Jasper Nunn. Nice fella'. Thought the world of Connie."

"Did someone tell you we found a mysterious man in the grave dug for Mallory Gorman?"

"A person is privy to lots of gossip at mealtime. The dining room vibrates with stories." She titters quietly.

"Let me give you the description." Stella describes the body and his clothes.

"My old handyman fits the bill. The yard work became too hard for me back in '75. For two years, I pestered William, but he did all the chores in the house and balked at more." She stops and inhales slow breaths. "You remember his attitude." She flushes at the recollection. "I hired a man for odd jobs, after William wouldn't even cut the lawn. He came every few weeks, and he wore overalls." She pauses again. "He said he needed extra money because his pension didn't cover his bills. I couldn't pay much, but I assumed he worked for others besides me."

Stella stays calm. "Do you remember his name, Miriam?"

"Ira. I never knew his last name, and I paid him cash. He came around and asked what I wanted done, but after a while he never returned."

"How did you meet him in the first place?"

"He probably knocked on doors." Her eyes widen. "He no doubt approached houses with messy yards. How ingenious. I often wish William had shown more initiative."

Although she might be on the brink of an identification, Stella takes a moment and asks, "And how is William? Does he still work for the car dealership in Port Ephron?"

"Oh no. William moved out to Alberta. He works for a trucking firm in what they call the oil patch. He says he makes lots of money. I can't worry. Once I was placed here, the sale of the house was earmarked for my care. No reason for him to stay around." She pats Kiki by rubbing the side of her hand against the dog while she focuses on regulating her breathing. "I don't blame him. Life was hard after his father left and I got sick. You learn to let go." She glances out the window.

"William's made his own way, Miriam. You're happy here?"

"If I take my condition into consideration, I am. They use a lift to manage me in and out of bed and put me in the big tub. The medication helps." Her smile doesn't quite reach her eyes. "Meals are good, the doctor visits once a month, and he checks on me if they call him. I know the staff are sad because I have no visitors, but I talk with Connie, Addie, and Eula every day. We eat at the same table." She snorts. "Those of us ladies in here who still possess our faculties stick together. I enjoy the days when entertainers come, too. I never miss."

"Did Ira mention where he lived?"

"I don't think he ever said, Stella. A place in the village, though, because he didn't use a car."

Stella approaches Miriam and retrieves Kiki. "I can't tell you how helpful you've been. I'm pleased you're settled in and your MS is managed. I'll stop and say hello any time I come to the manor." A visit with Miriam will be more satisfying than one with her father, any day.

"Great, Stella." She lifts her limp wrist. Her hand dangles at the end as she waves goodbye. "Go find Connie. The whereabouts of Willy and Jasper weigh on her mind. They were friends."

"She's next on my list."

****

Connie Gee has a private room two doors away from Miriam. As Stella approaches, she spies the thin, middle-aged woman in a wheelchair. Her head is tied with a red bandanna, secured around the built-in upright headrest, and her eyes are closed. Stella taps on the door frame.

"Connie?" Stella whispers.

"Come in, Ms. Kirk. Maura Martin said you might visit," she gulps. "We should speak."

With encouragement, Stella enters Connie's room with Kiki. "Afraid I can't hold the dog. An indignity of ALS. One of many." Her breath comes in forced gasps. "The nurses tie my head now. At least I can see more than my lap. I'll appreciate her presence. What a cutie."

"Kiki's a social butterfly. She's fine on her leash. Miriam tells me you miss Willy and Jasper."

"I do. I do. Listen." Her chest heaves. "Please roll me to the courtyard. I need a cigarette. The volunteer hasn't shown her face yet. One of them often makes time."

"Can't you smoke here?"

"Not in rooms. Only the lounge, and the bridge club objects. I prefer the outdoors."

"The air is cool, Connie." Stella isn't sure what her purpose will be. The woman is held upright by a belted affair around her chest and the red sash headband. Her hands are fixed on the arms of the wheelchair, and she demonstrates no ability to lift them.

"Only chance for a trek outside." Her eyes glance left. "You grab my cigs. and lighter from the dresser, and the blanket from the foot of my bed. Cover my legs and wheel me." She spits her directions in short puffs. "I'll give you instructions. Smoking is my only enjoyment, although my sister would debate the point."

Stella does as she's told and pushes Connie into the dining room. They enter the courtyard from garden doors at the side. The yard is closed off by a brick wall—no escape.

"Okay. Do you indulge in the curse of tobacco?"

"No. Tried a few times. Never got hooked."

"I won't ask you to light one for me," she snickers. "Put a smoke in my mouth."

Again, Stella does as she's told.

"Now, the lighter," she mumbles. Connie inhales a long drag. She whispers, "Take," before a fit of coughing overwhelms her.

Stella pulls the cigarette from Connie's lips and holds the unpleasant item like a pencil.

Connie exhales a plume of bluish-grey haze. "Man, I needed a puff." She studies Stella's face. "Don't worry. I won't let you share," she teases. "Now, shall we discuss Willy or Jasper?"

"Whatever you can tell me."

She blinks as her forehead presses against the red cotton. Stella fits the cigarette between Connie's lips.

"The person in the grave isn't Jasper, but male. Right?" More smoke drifts past Stella.

"Correct." She repeats her description and what Miriam shared.

Connie peers at Stella in a manner she interprets as the need for another puff. She doesn't ask but rather indicates, as if she's saving her air for more important words.

"Research the boarding homes in the vicinity." Her voice is breathier and more forced. "I investigated them before I moved here two years ago." She gulps again. "But I was too far gone. I talked with four. One for men and one for women weren't licensed by the government." She pauses. "Made me nervous. The two owned by the town are expensive. In the end, I came straight here."

"A good decision?"

"I'm on my way downhill fast. Certain people deteriorate in a short time." Her chest heaves behind the strap. "Others don't. Can't decide if I'm one of the lucky ones."

They sit in companionable silence for a few moments while Stella holds Connie's cigarette. Kiki has retreated under Stella's chair, not a fan of the tobacco. "You were friends with Willy?"

"She was a sweet woman. I liked her a lot. She hated Harbour Manor. Walked everywhere in her dead husband's topcoat, carrying her godforsaken string bag." Another pause. Connie's strength wanes. "Never saw her without. I often reminded her, 'Willy, you're exposing your wallet', but she didn't care." Her sigh is more of a shudder. "I was shocked she never said goodbye, but many folks prefer to fade away."

Her eyes reflect a longing that breaks Stella's heart.

"I hope she found a place where she could adopt a cat."

"My father thought the same."

She accepts another puff.

"And Jasper?"

"Handsome fella. He often disappeared for long walks. He's been gone since before last Christmas. I missed him at the concert." Her head drifts forward, but remains upright, cradled by the bandanna. "He told me he'd sit beside me and help keep my face lifted—before I progressed to the point where I needed this," she adds by way of explanation, while rolling her eyes skyward.

"Jasper and Willy leave without a word—reasonable behaviour?"

"I wish the answer was a firm 'no'." Another pause. Stella waits.

"People get funny when they're institutionalized. You turn your life over to others. You hope they do right by you." Her tone develops a rattle. "I guess, if the supervisor said they found a better place for me, I'd accept." She stops, wheezes, and meets Stella's gaze. "I'm accountable to no one but myself, even in this condition." Her expression hardens. "Folks arrive and later they leave, often under a sheet on a gurney, or maybe home with family. Some go into hospital and never come back—final stages for the old and disabled." Although breathless, she watches the cigarette.

After her last drag, Stella snubs out the offensive butt. "I appreciate the information you've shared with me today. May I visit again?"

"Anytime, if you'll hold a girl's fag for her." A fit of coughing stops her from saying more.

As Stella manoeuvres the wheelchair, and Kiki, along the hallway, Miriam calls out from her room. "Come on in and say hi, Connie. Your sister's here."

Stella points Connie into Miriam's space. A tiny woman is perched on the side of Miriam's bed.

"Meet my sister, Tess." Connie fruitlessly attempts to turn her neck. "Stella Kirk, Tess. She rolled me into the courtyard for a smoke."

"Hello, Stella." Tess turns her attention toward her sister. "As if you needed a cigarette," she admonishes. "The tobacco will kill you long before the ALS."

"Here's hoping," Connie hisses.

"I came over to fetch your laundry and stay for lunch, if you girls want my company."

Stella retrieves Kiki and makes her goodbyes, struck by how Miriam and Connie take overwhelming daily challenges and consciously make the best of their circumstances. She lifts a finger, scratches her nose, suddenly aware of such a simple task, and concludes she'll need a shower when she returns home. Tobacco clings to her cuffs. "Thank you," she sings in Olive's direction on her way past reception. Maura was correct. Connie and Miriam provided her with a few more puzzle pieces. She anticipates a debrief with Aiden soon. Who knows? Maybe he uncovered a lead or two from the town employees yesterday. A house-to-house in Miriam's old neighbourhood might be wise. Perhaps Ira, the handyman, worked for others.

Chapter 7

Troubled and Contented

Yesterday was quiet. She spent the better part of her morning compiling a report for Aiden. He didn't call. Rosemary's discharge from the provincial psychiatric hospital in Halifax, into Toni's home, is a big decision. Last fall, in anticipation of Rosemary's discharge to Toni's, Mary Jo rented her house. She and Toni lasted until Thanksgiving when Rosemary, unpredictably, became violent. While Aiden reassembled the pieces of his family relationships, Stella managed the writers retreat investigation. Now, Aiden and his sisters-in-law are preparing for Rosemary's return before the holidays. Stella has no idea if Rosemary will live at Toni's again, or whether Aiden will take on the added burden of managing his wife's mental health on his own while he works.

She staples the pages of her observations and conclusions together after a last read and reaches for the phone. Kiki remains curled on her lap. With Christmas approaching, and Brigitte now the manager of a bookstore, Stella mobilized her resources and searched out an alternate gift for her great-niece, Mia. "Hi, Hope. I thought you might be around on a Monday morning, and I'd check on Mia's dress."

"I finished yesterday, Stella, and planned to call today. The red velveteen you chose is perfect and sewed easily. I added lace along the hem and edged the collar, too."

Few people are aware that Hope Carlyle is an excellent seamstress as well as an accomplished weaver. Stella has never given any present besides a book to Mia, because Trixie spoils her with toys. The child now lives in a house full of books, so this year her gift must be different. She felt Hope was the perfect person for the task.

"You can add whatever you want. You're the expert. I'll stop by later today on my way to the manor. What's the total price?"

"Still fifty dollars. No problem."

"But you added lace, Hope."

"The trim was in the house. Fifty dollars, as we agreed."

"Appreciated."

She no sooner drops the receiver into the cradle than the contraption jangles. "Shale Cliffs...."

"Brigitte asked me to call and invite you for a holiday lunch on Thursday. We plan to decorate, and she thought you'd enjoy a visit." Trixie isn't fond of familiar salutations like hello.

"Is she sorry for me because Nick and I still prefer our quiet day?" Without waiting for a reply, she adds, "I'll take the book I ordered from her for Nick—and we expect Christmas Eve at Yellow House will be spectacular," she teases. "No pressure, Trixie." Their tradition, since she returned to Shale Harbour and took over the park, has been that Trixie and Brigitte host a Christmas Eve dinner. Nick and Stella treasure their solitude on Christmas Day, and Norbert prefers dinner and festivities with friends at Harbour Manor. Their holiday option works for everyone.

Her sister huffs and ignores her. "The book you ordered weighs a ton. Will you come? Brigitte is excited to start a new custom—girls' lunch before Christmas."

"Thanks for the invite. How can I contribute?"

"Be on time—Thursday, noon."

The phone goes dead before she says goodbye—another old Trixie trick.

Stella drives into town, purchases Mia's Christmas dress, and arrives at the manor near two o'clock. Her plan is to interview staff while they go on their break and catch Olive Urback at four o'clock shift change. Maura Martin meets her at the door.

"Hi, Stella. Everyone is arranged to speak with you. Lulu, my second in command, and Stevie, one of our volunteers, will see you right away. Tomorrow, you can touch base with Clara, my other practical nurse, and Arlene. We call her a volunteer, but she feeds her husband his supper and no more. He doesn't even recognize her."

Stella gulps her sympathy. "Sounds great, Maura. I want a word with Del, too, and I'll wait until Olive comes on shift, to talk with her."

Maura frowns. "Fine. I'll telephone Olive. If you're here tomorrow afternoon, you'll meet Todd and Hattie, who cover nights when Olive isn't here."

"Good. And I have a few more questions for Connie."

"How can Connie help you? And what about your father?"

"I'll go visit Del for a second now." Stella ignores the question, turns her back on Maura, and races to the common room. The bridge club is in a corner, hunched over the crib board. They wave. They haven't played bridge since Jasper disappeared and might need a new name. Stella cruises toward Del and taps her arm. "Hi, my friend. Are you snoozing, or watching your story?"

"Came in here for the company, but she was snoozin'," yells Caleb.

Del glares as she twists in her chair, summarily ignoring the remark. "Hi. You're back."

"Two more days. I'm interviewing staff and volunteers, which will take me through tomorrow. I'll meet as many as possible from both shifts."

"Remember Jack Lawson? You won't find her here."

"I recall Jack. She asked Dad and you both if you needed a money manager. She isn't here anymore?"

"I heard she stays home and helps her mother, who was havin' strokes, poor dear."

"When did she stop her volunteer work?"

"Almost a year ago, now. Time plays tricks on ya at my age."

Lavender wraps around her as she hugs Del goodbye.

"They're on lunch break in the staff room," Maura sings out as Stella approaches reception. She points at another space behind what she thought was the secretary's office, although there is no secretary.

For a moment, Stella observes the two women, sitting at a circular Arborite-covered table near the centre of the empty room. "Hi. I'm Stella Kirk."

Both wave, albeit with reluctance. "I'm Lulu." She extends her hand. Energy vibrates through her. "I don't often take breaks—too busy," she says, as she pats her pale blue top.

"Well, you do excellent work with my father. The care here is marvellous." The other woman, a scrawny and frail person of indeterminate age, is missing teeth and fidgets in her chair. Her knuckles are chafed and red. "And you must be Stevie."

Stevie nods, but keeps her hands clasped in her lap.

"Did Maura tell you why I'm here?"

"Yes." They answer in unison.

She tells them the story of the body discovered in the graveyard expansion, the words falling from her mouth as if she's reciting a familiar poem from childhood. No one can think who the person might be, and they provide no clues. As for Willy and Jasper—old people go away or die, the bed is filled with a new admission, but the work never changes. Stella shifts in her chair, unsettled by their collective observations.

The two women depart for the floor. As Stella lags, Olive approaches. "Maura called me and said you were here. I came in before my shift, and it's no bother, Stella, but I told you I don't recall anyone who wore bib overalls."

"Hi, Olive. I would've waited for you, but I'm happy you're here. My visit is to determine what people remember about Willy and Jasper." Reminded of her brief conversation with Del, she adds, "And the volunteer, Jack Lawson."

"Jack? She hasn't been around for ages."

"Did she help with people's money?"

Olive's face clouds. "I didn't interact with her much. She worked days and went home before I start my shift."

"They say she takes care of her mother."

"Perhaps."

****

The next day, and after one more gulp of her tea, Stella grabs her coat and races out the door. Nick and Duke are somewhere in the park, and they took Kiki with them. Stella's goal is arrival at Harbour Manor before staff change at three-thirty. There are four more staff slotted for interviews and maybe Connie Gee remembers the names of the care homes she researched.

She found no listings for boarding homes of any sort when she scoured the phone book earlier. She called the local social services office. They gave her the regulations and policies but wouldn't discuss each location with her—privacy rules coupled with their guidelines against the recommendation of unlicensed facilities. The legislation states a residential boarding home is one where no more than three guests, not family members of the owner(s), may dwell and obtain basic room and board. Help might include medication management and minimal assistance with personal hygiene. The resident must be safe on stairs if necessary and evacuate the premises under their own power in the event of an emergency. Only people diagnosed with mild memory issues by a physician will be accepted. No advanced dementia cases are permitted. A staff person is required on site twenty-four hours per day. Both private and public care homes in the province are inspected annually. They said a municipal board of directors manages Easy Living Boarding Home and Cliffs Guest Residence. Addresses and phone numbers were provided.

As Stella approaches reception, Maura Martin hands responsibilities over to a young man. He waves his boss off as one would a temporary annoyance, sits in the chair, and surveys his domain. Stella flutters her fingers in his direction. He crosses his arms and frowns.

"I told Todd you're here to discuss Jasper, Willy, and whoever was found in the graveyard, with a few more of the staff. Good luck." Her tone, laced with sarcasm, matches her dismissive wave.

Todd shrugs, but nods.

"Hi. I'm Stella Kirk and I support the police by conducting interviews. Maura tells me your name is Todd."

"At your service. You won't learn much from folks in here. Most of 'em are loony-tunes."

"Discussions with the evening staff are important. Will you give me a minute?"

Todd reaches under the desk and retrieves two small hand weights. "I keep in shape, even if I'm stuck here," he explains.

Stella describes her mission and the unidentified body. Todd is of little help. He confirms Jasper departed the manor a year ago, in November, and says Willy has been gone for more than three months. Her bed was filled with a new admission who has advanced Alzheimer's. "She makes your father seem good. At least he knows your sister."

Whether malice was behind the remark or not is a challenge of interpretation. "I'll stop in and speak with Connie Gee for a moment, before I meet staff."

"No problem. Connie ain't goin' nowhere fast. Clara can stick around after her shift. Arlene stays for supper, and Hattie, my nighttime volunteer," he holds his weight with a twisted wrist and glances at his watch, "should be here in ten minutes." He continues his bicep curls.

****

"Hi, Connie. May I come in?"

"Yes, yes. Stella, you're back. Where's Kiki?"

"Oh, Kiki's home with the guys today. I'm interviewing three or four staff, but you are at the top of my list. There's an issue."

"Sit and we'll talk."

"Do you remember the names of the care homes you researched before you chose the manor?"

She furrows her brow as she thinks. "I recall one licensed place called Cliffs Guest Residence. I guess the name reference reminds me of your Shale Cliffs RV Park. Anyway, the file folder is in my closet. All the information is inside."

Relieved, and after a search and retrieval mission, Stella finds the notes. Connie has listed each boarding home with their pros and cons. "How did you locate their numbers?"

"Blind luck with the unlicensed ones. Nobody advertises. Friend of a friend." She encourages Stella. "Make use of my paperwork if the stuff helps."

"If Willy moved into one of the places you researched, Connie, I'll drive her back for a visit—promise."

Connie tee-hees. "If she's happy, she won't let you, I'm sure."

When she approaches the now-stretching Todd, behind the desk, he volunteers, "Supper is soon, and Arlene will be in a dither, but she and Clara are waiting for you in the staff room."

"Thanks."

Clara, round and wholesome in a sunny yellow uniform, is flaked out on a sofa in the corner, munching on a banana. With her mouth full, she waves her response. An elderly lady with swollen ankles and sprigs of white hair taps the tabletop. "I must help my husband. Supper will be ready soon. I can't leave him for long."

"Arlene. Relax. Your hubby is fine." Clara turns her attention toward Stella. "Todd says you'll take five minutes. Is he right?"

"Correct." She introduces herself and rattles off the story. Neither woman adds more. Clara wants to go home, and Arlene has one foot out the door—no help whatsoever.

Hattie, the night volunteer, arrives as the two women leave. She oozes efficiency and kindness. She speaks of Willy as if she were a relative, loves her community work at the manor, and never misses a shift. Stella's description of the man in the grave is unfamiliar. She never met Jasper because she started after Christmas last year.

Discouraged, Stella departs for the park. She glances into her father's room on the way past, but he must be off for his meal. She nods goodbye to various faces and takes a gulp of cool, fresh air when she reaches the outside. Weather forecasters are predicting a storm for tomorrow—a good excuse to stay home, maybe make buns, and discuss the business. She needs down time with Nick.

****

"Aiden should call today," she muses, both hands wrapped around a pottery coffee mug. The north wind rattles the old kitchen windowpanes. Snow blusters in circles. "Can a person be troubled and contented at once?"

Nick reaches for more jam. "I guess the obvious answer is 'yes' if I take your expression into consideration. What's on your mind?"

"Long term care culture has me in a hole as deep as the one where they found the body. At first, Dad was my only concern when I thought about placement for the elderly. Now I've discovered a variety of boarding homes, licence issues, even costs, which might be unreasonable. Connie Gee gave me information about the four places she contacted before her final decision to move into the manor. Willy Saunders, the woman whom Dad misses, must be in one of them. I'll call each residence and find out where she is—Jasper, too. Once I determine their whereabouts, I'll take Dad and Del for visits, or drive both to the manor."

"And the guy in the hole?"

"I've uncovered a lead for Aiden and will follow up with the boarding homes when I connect." She explains her interview with Miriam Sylvester. "Who hit him or put him in the ground remains a mystery, but I've discovered the date he was buried, and a potential first name. A door-to-door canvas in Miriam's old neighbourhood is necessary."

"Police work, Stella."

"Right. I know. I won't be knocking on doors in Shale Harbour. I'll suggest my idea if Aiden ever makes contact."

"When was the last time you spoke with him?"

"Thursday, when we visited Royalty Funeral Services. He said he needed a week, but since the weather's nasty today, I hope he calls."

"Will you help me?"

Stella imagines standing in the wind-swept dooryard with a wrench clutched in her frozen fist. "How?"

"Kiki and me—we're gonna make buns and put on a pot of chili for supper." He cuddles the sleepy dog and nuzzles her into his neck.

"Sure. Let me finish my notes first, okay?"

Nick snorts. "On our own, little one." He returns his attention to Stella. "I'll mix the dough. Let's talk about the share transfer, too. Christmas is on the doorstep, and we'll be celebrating New Year's Eve in no time." He tilts his head and stares into her eyes. "You're still comfortable with the idea? No second thoughts?"

"Don't worry, Nick. A review is good." He will give her the option to renege until the last moment, because he wants her to be certain. "Let me re-read my report. If Aiden calls, I want to be ready." A chill runs across her shoulders. "The wind blows straight through the house."

"We need new windows. A project for the future. I'll tend the fire and turn on the oven; you'll be toasty in no time."

****

After an hour at her desk, where she reached for the phone more than once, but lost her nerve, she wraps her ugly Christmas cardigan around her torso and enters the kitchen. The green sweater could not flatter her less, but everyone understands the difficult task of looking sexy when you're freezing cold. She shrugs and shivers simultaneously.

Nick has the coffee pot plugged in, and dough for his buns in her mother's English pottery mixing bowl, covered with a gingham tea towel. The scent of yeast fills the space, and he's busy opening cans of red kidney beans when she enters. "Start the perk, my love. Break-time while the dough rises. Did you finish?"

"Yup. I'm at a dead end until Aiden surfaces. By the way, we don't perk coffee anymore."

"Right, but it will always be a percolator to me." He snickers. "Talked with Duke a few minutes ago. I know you'll be at Brigitte's for lunch tomorrow. I thought we should clean and store the last of the tools and machinery. With

Duke's help, I can finish." He glances out the kitchen window. The inclement weather is barely visible through the frost.

"He'll tear himself away from cuddling Cloris long enough for another day out here—in the cold?"

Ignoring her facetious question, he remarks, "Speaking of couples, while we wait for coffee, tell me about any persistent concerns or issues you have regarding our partnership agreement for the end of the month."

On December 31, she and Nick will become fifty-fifty partners in Shale Cliffs RV Park. Last year, she and her sister each gave Nick five of their shares, in exchange for his financial contribution toward the water and electrical system upgrades. Now, he will purchase forty of Trixie's shares while Stella will buy the final five. She stressed for weeks but found the money in her shareholder's loan. The sewer work is half completed. The bank loaned them the funds because the stipend Stella has paid Trixie each month since the two of them took over ownership from their father in 1978, is now earmarked as payment toward the loan. Trixie will become financially independent. A New Year's Eve dinner at the Purple Tulip in Port Ephron is planned after the purchase agreement is signed.

The arrangement has created uneasiness she can't define. She and Nick love one another and she's confident they are compatible, although their age difference has been a source of insecurity, when her demons of inadequacy bubble. She blinks negative thoughts away. There comes a point in one's life when chances should be taken, and December 31, 1981, is Stella Kirk taking a chance.

"The paperwork is well in hand, Nick. Andrea Picard is a great lawyer."

Chapter 8

I Refuse Further Involvement

"Olive Urback, please."

"Speaking."

"Hi, Olive. Sorry I've bothered you at home. Stella Kirk here."

"How did you find me?"

Despite the reason for her call, she makes her voice sound light and airy. "You're the one Urback in the Shale Harbour phone directory."

Earlier in the evening, while the fire crackled and with supper completed, Stella and Nick cuddled on the sofa, both with a book. Kiki snuggled between them. The wind rattled the windows, and the snow swirled. Her thoughts wandered away from her book and fixated on the night nurse at Harbour Manor. Olive was affable enough, but her answers were vague and tenuous. Stella expected Olive was at home tonight because Todd was on shift. She patted Nick's foot and Kiki's head while she explained she needed to make a call.

Now in her office, with the woman on the other end of the line, she wonders if her plan was well-founded. "I was puzzled by a remark you made yesterday."

"And what did I say?" Olive's response sounds forced.

"When I said Jack Lawson left because of her mother, you replied, 'perhaps'."

"I've no direct knowledge."

"But ideas."

"I won't repeat rumour and innuendo. A person can create lots of trouble if they spread untruths."

"Fair enough." She will not push. She wants Olive to become her ally. "Do you share any local boarding home information with prospective residents?"

"They're around. The unlicensed ones are in the shadows. The municipality doesn't want one facility recommending another. Doctors might, or people in town. I'm aware of four nearby, some licensed by the government and some not."

"Connie gave me her list. If I read them to you, will you tell me of any others that might be in the area?" The line is quiet long enough for Stella to suspect the wind disrupted the connection.

"You don't back down, do you?"

"My goal is the location of Willy and Jasper. And there's an unidentified man in a grave." Without a pause, she lists off the names before Olive changes her mind. "Connie researched Easy Living Boarding Home, Cliffs Guest Residence, Jane's Retirement Home for Ladies, and Merlon's Place for Gentlemen. Any one of them sound familiar?"

Silence.

"Olive, are you still there?"

"Yes. Don't drag me into the middle of your investigation, Stella. I need my job." Another pause.

Patience is a virtue. Her mother's words ring in her ears.

"Jane's and Merlon's are mentioned now and then. I think Maura talks about them, although policy states otherwise. I've heard of the other two, as well. They're municipal and expensive. We leave recommendations in the hands of physicians and families," she re-emphasizes.

"And Jack Lawson?"

"She might volunteer for one of them. I can't be sure, but she discussed her mother's potential move into Jane's—the reason I said, 'perhaps'."

"Thanks. I'll contact each of the guest homes after I report to Detective North." *If he ever calls.* "This is a huge help."

"Don't ask again, Stella. Whatever the problem, I refuse further involvement."

Without acknowledging her response, Stella wishes her well and ends the call.

Back in the living room, Nick has wheeled the television stand out of the corner, and she sees Perry Mason's persona grace the screen. "I thought we could watch a detective show. You're already in the mood." A sly smirk crosses his face.

She gives him a shove when she sits, letting him know she acknowledges the innuendo. Kiki doesn't open her eyes. Stella waits for the ads. "Nick, why do you suppose a person says they can't help out at Harbour Manor because they care for their sick mother at home, but then they volunteer at a guest house?"

He shrugs. "Because they put their mom in the place and spend time there instead. Simple."

Makes sense. Jack's mother didn't need enough assistance for the manor, but the burden was too difficult for Jack to manage at home. She moved her into Jane's and now volunteers, so she's nearby. "I might have exaggerated Jack Lawson's interest in the financial status of residents. I sometimes see a problem where none exists."

"Certainly not the first time." Nick's mumble is accompanied by a light-hearted jab.

****

Storms and sex. Perry Mason didn't kill the mood, and neither did thoughts of Jack Lawson and Olive Urback, which now rattle around in her brain again. Lulled by Nick's and Kiki's contented rumbles, she snuggles under the comforter. The wind sounds more menacing on the second floor.

Olive Urback has opinions, despite her lack of forthrightness. The exact circumstances of Willy Saunders' or Jasper Nunn's departures are elusive, and the details of local boarding homes may be vague, but she has ideas. Stella is determined to build trust with Olive, who's uncomfortable sharing information—right now. No doubt Aiden will consider her assumptions speculation. Even if he doesn't call, and he must call, she'll contact each guest house and ask if Willy or Jasper are residents. No detecting skills required to telephone a residence and search for an old lady or gentleman so her demented father can relax because his friends are okay.

The wind howls. The windowpanes rattle. Nick will need to plow the driveway before she's able to make her way to Yellow House, and Duke can arrive to help him. Trixie said noon but Duke will be early. Her thoughts tumble. Willy and Jasper may not be connected to the poor man she now identifies as Ira buried in the grave. She tucks the cotton sheet under her chin as she drifts off, wrapped in the lingering scent of their lovemaking.

L. P. Suzanne Atkinson

****

There are occasions when she wishes she possessed an artistic bone or two in her body. Alas, such is not the case. As Stella motors along Main Street toward Yellow House, the images of heavy snow on the trees, roofs covered in white frosting, people dressed in layers as they shovel driveways inspire a desire to capture the images—a photograph, a film, a watercolour—preservation of the moment in one's art, if one could make art, tease her sensibilities. Her goal was investigative journalism, but the death of her mother and her father's steady decline led to her current circumstances. She's not sorry, anymore. The newspaper business was misogynistic, and any rise above obituaries and lost dogs would have no doubt been remote. Regrets flit past—mosquitoes buzzing her ear before they're gone.

She nudges the Jeep into a cleared spot in the driveway behind Trixie's van. Val nods and carries on shovelling the front walkway and steps. She climbs out and checks her watch before she approaches. Eleven-thirty. Tension in her shoulders releases.

"Good morning, Val. I see Trixie gave you chores." She teases the man who provides caretaker services for both the Shale Harbour Community Hall and Playhouse—the former Presbyterian Church—and the new Presbyterian Church.

"Keepin' busy, Stella. Not here for lunch. Brigitte and Trixie are puttin' on a spread. Smells great." His grin brightens his dark complexion, and a shock of greasy hair falls over one eye. "Any news on when we can bury my sister?" He tosses a shovelful of snow across the lawn. "If the hole weren't already dug, she'd be waitin' in the cemetery vault until spring, for sure."

"No update yet. I've made progress, though, and expect a talk with Detective North tomorrow. Honestly, I'm surprised the event hasn't been rescheduled. Did you speak with Mr. King?"

"Theo did. We hope for Saturday at two, but the funeral home needs clearance from North and he's among the missin'."

Stella's eyes narrow as she maintains a neutral guise. "The wait shouldn't be much longer. The police will call."

When the front door opens, Brigitte materializes. Almost-four-year-old Mia peeks from behind her mother's leg. Stella's heart swells. Although Trixie's challenges were many over the years—raising a daughter on her own and helping to raise a granddaughter as well—every sacrifice has been worth the rewards. Brigitte, now twenty-one, has blossomed into an efficient and creative young woman. She's taken on the business of Yellow House with a passion. Mia is a sweet child. She has a mind of her own and can be ornery at times, a reflection of her grandmother more than her mother.

"Good morning, you two. Happy Christmas lunch."

"Present?" Mia fixates on Stella.

"Not today, little one. We must wait until Christmas Eve."

"Hi, Aunt Stella. She thinks anyone who arrives will bring a gift for her." Mia runs inside as Trixie shouts for her help.

"Don't put party clothes on her before our Christmas Eve supper, Brigitte," Stella whispers. "I asked Hope Carlyle to make her a red velvet dress for the occasion."

"No book?" Brigitte giggles.

Stella sweeps her arm around the children's library. "I think I've been trumped by these surroundings and wanted a special gift this year."

The warmth of Brigitte's hug washes over her. Her niece more than compensates for those momentary perceived losses she sometimes experiences.

As they wander into the kitchen in a companionable embrace, Stella's first view is of Trixie's hind end, in tight jeans, bent over the open oven. With a relish only her sister can portray, she lifts the pan of biscuits out, swirls, and shouts "ta-da!" Dressed in one of her signature angora short sweaters, a bright red version, and tight jeans, she hobbles on platform heels toward the counter and sets the tin on a cooling rack. "You're here on time," she observes, while her back remains turned.

She ignores her sister's slur in favour of a compliment. "Trixie, you make the best biscuits. They smell good."

"Lobster salad and cheese biscuits are on the menu today, Aunt Stella. I made mincemeat tarts for dessert."

"Sounds like competition for Cocoa and Café. Lots of fuss for a decorating afternoon," Stella swoons.

"We craved a girls' day. Carter's at his office. Val's back to the church when he finishes our walkways, because the church ladies are adding more decorations and he wants to supervise." She casts her eyes toward the ceiling. "I assume Nick still has piles of snow to move at the park. The party is for us.

We can decorate without interference."

Brigitte and Carter Stephens appear serious. He is good to Mia, which pleases Stella.

Trixie and Valentin Reguly are a good match, too. He's a kind man who treats her with respect, a missing commodity in most of her previous affairs. She's changed, too. With monetary independence around the corner, Trixie's new-found confidence and serenity are on full display. The transformation is palpable.

"Nick and Duke are plowing and winterizing machinery today—not feeling even a twinge of guilt."

After lunch, where conversation centred on how lights and garland would be woven into the business areas of the house, they start work by unpacking boxes. The tree, which stood naked in the family room near the back window, soon becomes the object of a string of multi-coloured lights and a carton of mismatched ornaments, some new and many Stella remembers from their childhood.

"I imagine Val asked, but any news on a funeral? Poor Mallory shouldn't be buried on Christmas Eve."

Stella shuts her eyes for a moment. The wait has been long, and unfair of Aiden, who has not released the scene for Royalty Funeral Services. "I expect Aiden back tomorrow. I told Val. Rosemary will be discharged soon. Her sisters want her home for good. Aiden took time off and met with her psychiatrist. Everyone wants to prevent a re-occurrence of Thanksgiving."

"We understand." Trixie drapes garland over a picture on the wall of the front room. "The waiting is hard on Theo and Val, though."

"The minute I hear from him, I'll express your concerns. He'll make the calls. Luther Greene will fix the grave and the service can proceed." *Hopefully.*

"Luther is a nice man. He has a four-year-old boy he brings to children's reading hour." Brigitte sorts the lights. "Whenever he can't leave work, that nurse from the manor comes instead. What's her name? Maura?"

"Maura Martin? Why is she involved?" Stella frowns.

"She's Luther's aunt. At least, he calls her Aunt Maura."

"Aunt Maura and Otto King aren't married, by any chance?" Her mind races.

"Oh, Aunt Stella. Why would you think that? Maura's husband is Hector."

****

"Hello, stranger." Stella is not magnanimous when she hears Aiden's voice the next morning.

"Don't be sarcastic. Once you understand what we've been through, you'll forgive my absence."

He wants her to ask, and she will, but not now. "I've drafted a report for you."

"Been busy, I gather. Lunch at the café? You can tell me what you discovered."

"How did your conversations go with the town? Did anyone talk with the guys who created the new graveyard?"

"Moyer spoke to Philip Lewis, the village manager. I talked with Evan Fleguel, the engineer for Port Ephron and Shale Harbour. He was on site for the construction operation and observed no indications of a disruption. No one noticed any disturbances. We've released the site."

"Because the 'disturbance', as you describe, took place December 15—two years ago." Control of her churlish tone proves difficult.

"December 15? 1979? How in hell did you come across that date?"

"I'll see you at noon. You can read the report. I'm plowing through a stack of my own work this morning. Bye." She pulls Trixie's trick and disconnects. Nick stands in the office doorway.

"If you don't mind my opinion, you should quit the investigation or build a bridge and find a way over your anger, Stella."

"Not easy." She gulps cold coffee. "I'll present my report at lunch and see how the information is received. Aiden is focused on other issues besides an unidentified body in a hole and two old people my demented father misses." She gazes into his face, forgetting Aiden and the investigation for a moment. "You can manage by yourself?" She knows the answer.

"I'm fine. Give me a call if you go anywhere afterward. There's more snow that needs moving around the yard and I thought I'd run the plow along the main road through the park again before this mess freezes. Warm weather is expected, but we might be stuck with the white stuff for good."

Stella's furrowed brows prompt another response. "I'll keep Kiki with me. She loves the truck."

"How was Duke with her yesterday?"

"He adores Kiki, but I'm not convinced he misses the responsibility. We'll see what happens in the spring when he moves back."

****

By eleven, she's cleared her desk, so scurries upstairs to change for lunch. Soft navy slacks and a white cotton sweater paired with a cranberry scarf and earrings complete the picture. Stella finds scarves a challenge. If their purpose is not keeping your neck warm under a coat, why wear extra fabric for decoration? The result is a hot neck. Trixie insists she adorn herself, not simply dress in a T-shirt and blue jeans, with hoops in her ears. She tries her best but is rarely satisfied and never meets Trixie's high standards despite her efforts.

After she parks the Jeep in the back lot of the local RCMP detachment, she tiptoes around to the front. The sidewalk is icy. Inside, Sergeant Moyer greets her and points toward Aiden's office. She's expected.

He glances at her from his desk, covered in manila folders. She has never seen this space in such disarray. "Hi. A week off and I'm swamped. Ready for lunch?"

"Sure. We can talk and eat."

"Are you okay?" He rearranges files and doesn't meet her eyes.

For a moment, the weight of her suppressed anger makes the composition of a response difficult. She remembers Nick's words and stands taller. "Fine. In my digging, I've discovered answers, but more questions, too. We're good, Aiden." She turns toward the door.

At the café, coffees in hand, they wait for tomato soup and grilled cheese sandwiches. She opens her folder. "I interviewed most of the residents of the manor who can converse and are without memory problems. Miriam Sylvester, you recall Miriam, told me she hired a man who wore overalls. He did yard work for her. She paid him cash, his first name was Ira, and he lived nearby because he walked everywhere. I think a door-to-door is needed in her old neighbourhood. Another homeowner might remember him and know his surname and address."

"Okay. And your reason?"

"He stopped appearing at Miriam's in the late fall of 1979. He's the only man anyone remembers who wore overalls."

"Okay," Aiden repeats. "And the date?"

"Re-interview Dewey Laird at Harbour Manor, who keeps a diary of each day, the weather, and any occurrences of interest. Dewey said he heard machinery at nine-thirty on the evening of December 15, 1979. He showed me his documentation, and the photocopied page is with my report—a fussy and unusual man."

"Why is he at Harbour Manor?"

"He has a history of schizophrenia."

"Stella, he can't be a witness." Aiden leans back and crosses his arms over his chest. "The sounds could be in his imagination."

Confident in Dewey and undeterred, she continues. "Connie Gee, another resident, described four local boarding homes—two private and two run by the village. I'd never heard of them. Had no idea they existed. She researched the option before her ALS progressed to the point where she required extensive care. I think Ira lived at one of those guest houses."

"I'm surprised at your lack of knowledge. I thought you were aware of everybody in town," he taunts.

"Thanks for the vote of confidence, but when Trixie and I placed Dad, there was no choice but Harbour Manor because of his memory challenges. The boarding homes are found by word of mouth. The unlicensed ones keep quiet. N. S. Social Services won't make referrals or discuss them for confidentiality reasons." She bites her lower lip. "Since Connie provided numbers, I want to call each of them over the weekend, determine if a man named Ira lived at any of them, and check whether Jasper Nunn or Willy Saunders are in residence."

Aiden sips his soup. "Busy lady."

She's secretly vindicated. "Your people can interview the staff at the manor and obtain statements from them and the lucid residents. My visits were informal." Focused on the matters at hand, she adds, "Here are two more items of information. Jack Lawson, a woman who volunteered at Harbour Manor, left because she started caring for her ailing mother at home, but now volunteers at one of the guest houses."

"I bet she moved her mother into the place."

"Nick agrees. I'll find out. And Luther Greene, who works at the funeral home?"

"Yes."

"His aunt is Maura Martin, and her husband's name is Hector."

"Relevancy?" He wipes his lips with a paper napkin.

"Not sure. Brigitte told me Maura often takes Luther's son to her children's reading group, if Luther is needed at work. I wonder why neither of them mentioned the other."

"We'll visit Royalty Funeral Services before you leave for home. Let's call from the station and tell them we're on our way."

"Theodore Gorman needs to bury his wife, Aiden."

"The scene will be released today, and they can confirm the funeral parlour's schedule." He reaches for both bills. "Let me."

She doesn't argue. "Thanks. I'll telephone Nick, too."

Chapter 9

He Remembers

Otto King stands ramrod-stiff at the front door. His foot, encased in a polished black shoe, taps. He moves sideways when Aiden and Stella struggle inside the vestibule. They follow him into the larger reception room. Despite the lack of any services in the immediate past, the space smells of grief and loss. She ignores the cling of former ceremonies and relishes the warmth.

"You want to meet with Luther again? He's outside."

Stella glances toward Aiden. "I understand you've been at the helm for fewer than six months, Mr. King, but are records kept of the machinery and when it's used?"

"Certainly, Miss Kirk." He exaggerates the formalities. "Tell me, how may I assist?"

A quick nod from Aiden spurs her on. "May we see documentation of the digger's jobs over the past couple of years?"

"We keep track of hours of use for maintenance scheduling. The unit isn't housed on the property. Arrangements are required for pickup and delivery to specific locations."

"Could you explain in more detail?"

"Certainly. When a grave is needed, we contact the storage yard and request transport to a specific site. Our operator, Luther, supervises the move. When he's finished, they're called to retrieve the machine. My business owns the backhoe, but not the truck and trailer. We are billed quarterly." He runs a hand over thin hair. "When I purchased the funeral home, the arrangement proved convenient. I can show you the records."

"We're interested in December 15, 1979."

His voice rises an octave. "Pop into my office for a few moments while I review the files."

They enter his inner sanctum for the second time. He bustles toward a cabinet, struggles locating a folder, then turns with an uncharacteristic "a ha" response on his face.

"Sit." He indicates the two chairs in front of his massive desk and waves a limp wrist. "December 15, 1979. Luther borrowed the digger. Not sure why."

Aiden finds his voice. "Does the business loan the backhoe often, Mr. King?"

"Permission is granted on an as needed basis." Otto's jaw sets. "He pays for use. I'm not aware of a problem. I have merely carried on a tradition of the previous owner."

Stella checks Aiden's face before she continues. "A few minutes with Luther will help with clarification if you don't mind. There are outstanding questions."

With a brisk nod, Otto leads them toward the rear of the building. They find Luther in a room filled with coffins. Stella swallows while she watches him polish hinges.

"Luther, Detective North and Miss Kirk wish to speak with you. I'll be in my office." The director spins on his heel and leaves.

The young man nods and places his rag on a small table in the corner—the kind of furniture easily moved out of the way when a family arrives to choose a coffin. The bereaved need not be troubled by day-to-day maintenance.

"Good afternoon, Luther. Stella and I are interested in a day two years ago when you borrowed the business' backhoe."

Luther's eyes narrow. "I take the digger out every now and again, dig a trench for a friend, or post holes for a fence. Otto's fair and lets me do the same as when the other owners were here."

Stella jumps in. Her impatience bests her. "What did you do with the backhoe on December 15, 1979?"

One could argue the response never happened, but Stella saw his jaw clench and his eyes widen. "No clue. If the records say I took the stupid digger, I did."

"On a Saturday, Luther. You spent a Saturday two years ago using the machine. You must remember."

"A cousin needed a sewer line dug; an aunt wanted a garden plot." He shrugs.

"In the middle of December, no one wanted a garden plot." Aiden's annoyance is palpable in his tone. "Did you loan the funeral home property to a friend? Vic Staples, for example? Come on, Luther."

"Nothin' rings a bell." He grabs his polishing cloth. "Are you two done? I got work." He flutters the stained rag in their direction.

"Okay. Thanks for your time."

Once inside the police issue vehicle, on the return trip to Shale Harbour, Stella states the obvious. "He remembers what happened with the digger on December 15, 1979."

Aiden's eyes remain focused on the road although his impatience ripples against Stella. "A resident at the manor, with mental health issues, claims he heard a noise on the night in question…and the night in question is determined because he keeps a journal. The date is weak. Not much in the way of hard evidence," he mutters.

"Agreed, but I want another conversation with Maura, in any event—find out exactly how she and Luther are related."

"Irrelevant, Stella, but suit yourself. I'll organize a house-to-house in Miriam Sylvester's old neighbourhood. We can meet at the manor on Monday. Satisfy your curiosity with Nurse Martin and we'll double-check what Dewy Laird reported. I bet, by Monday, he has a different date."

She refuses the bait. She expected a man found in a grave, buried for two years, coupled with two missing nursing home residents, might garner more attention from Aiden. "I understand your stress with Rosemary's circumstances, Aiden. I'll call the four guest homes tomorrow, check for Jasper and Willy, and determine if someone named Ira ever resided in any of them."

"I can assign staff in the office to make any calls related to the body, Stella."

"No problem. I'm the one with the father and friend who brought up Jasper and Willy. Let me know what time I should be at Harbour Manor on Monday."

****

While Nick inspects the property, Stella plants herself behind her desk. She's waited until after ten on Saturday morning to allow for post-breakfast cleaning and hopes residents will be occupied in one way or another. Her first call is to Easy Living Boarding Home.

"Easy Living. How may I help you?"

"Good morning. My name is Stella Kirk and I'm inquiring after a resident. I'd like to speak with the person in charge?"

The voice on the other end of the line chuckles. "We're at capacity, Miss Kirk."

"No. You've misunderstood. I've called to determine if Willy, Wilhelmina Saunders and / or Jasper Nunn are among your residents."

"None of our three guests are Willy or Jasper—if they were, we can't reveal their identities because of confidentiality."

"And a man named Ira? Maybe he wore overalls. Did he ever call Easy Living home?"

"He doesn't sound familiar."

"I see. And who owns Easy Living Boarding Home?"

"We are owned by the village and operations are supervised by a council committee. If you want further information, please contact them."

"Thank you, and you are…?"

"My name is Fannie. I live here and manage the day-to-day work—meals, laundry, and cleaning. We've got a day nurse Monday through Friday and a night nurse as well."

"Thank you, Fannie. I appreciate your time."

Stella replaces the receiver in the cradle and frowns. Boarding homes can welcome a maximum of three residents. They must complete their own personal care and be sufficiently mobile to evacuate the residence in case of an emergency. The business is owned by Shale Harbour and is no doubt in full compliance with government legislation. Aiden's badge may be required to gain access and talk with staff and guests, though.

She wanders into the kitchen and replenishes her now cooled coffee with fresh. Kiki is with Nick and the old house is quiet, which gives her ample ruminating time. Connecting the dots and sorting through the clutter of information remains a struggle. She pads back into her office on slippered feet and places a second call.

Her conversation with the live-in staff person at Cliffs Guest Residence, a young-sounding woman called Kelly, mirrored her interaction with Fannie from Easy Living. Kelly did not reveal the names of current residents but admitted none were Willy or Jasper, and she didn't recall a man named Ira. She reiterated the same personnel arrangement as Easy Living, where professional care comes on duty for both day and night shifts five days a week. Kelly mentioned they rotated emergency call on the weekend. She described her charges as capable, and any emergencies are most often medical in nature.

After she takes a few moments and jot names and notes describing each location, Stella reaches for the phone again and calls Jane's Retirement Home for Ladies.

"Jane's. May speakin'."

"Hi. My name is Stella Kirk and I'm calling each boarding home near Shale Harbour in search of two friends of mine. Can you help?"

"Whatever."

"Okay." Stella attempts an upbeat tone. Her impression is the woman on the other end sounds bored. "A lady named Willy Saunders. Does she live at Jane's or did she in the past?"

"Nope."

"Okay," Stella repeats. "Are you the owner, or is the owner nearby?"

A gruff cackle trickles into Stella's ear. "I work here seven until four, every day. A casual is called if I need a day off. They give me my breakfast, lunch, and a pay cheque."

"And night staff?"

The cackle rumbles again. "Nobody on nights. I go home to my old man. Told them I'd work seven days a week but not live here."

"Who's your boss?"

"My cheque says JanlonNS."

Since May answers her questions, Stella continues. "What does the signature say?"

"I've never ciphered the name, but the last part is EENE."

"Who interviewed you for the job?"

"Some guy on the phone." Silence. "Who are you, again?"

"An old friend of a lady named Willy Saunders and I hope she lives with you."

"Nope," she emphasizes. "Roxy, stay in your chair. Gotta go." The dropped receiver bangs in Stella's ear.

Based on May's last remark, Jane's Retirement Home for Ladies houses a person who needs more supervision than boarding home regulations dictate. If Roxy isn't a pet, JanlonNS might be required to explain why a guest requires twenty-four-hour attention and no one lives on the premises or works the night shift. Aiden's presence will certainly be necessary when she visits. As she lifts and peers under the secretive rock of private boarding homes, the yield proves unexpected.

"Merlon's."

"Good morning. I'm Stella Kirk and I hope you can help me. Who is this?"

"Elsie, the live-in. What do ya want?"

"Does a man called Jasper Nunn board at Merlon's Place for Gentlemen?"

"Can't tell ya who lives here. Against the rules."

"Did a fellow named Ira have a room there? He wore overalls."

"Nobody here named Ira. Can't help. I'm busy makin' lunch for everybody right now."

"Must be a job making three meals a day for three people, eh? You work hard."

"Try four."

"Elsie, who owns Merlon's?"

"We're owned by JanlonNS. If one of the men is a problem—and Helga, who works nights, does the same—we call the cops. Sorry I couldn't help. Bye."

Stella swivels in her chair and gazes out the office window. Clouds are heavy in the sky and more snow is promised. As Aiden's name crosses her mind, the phone jangles.

"Hi. I organized a trip to Harbour Manor for us on Monday morning. Are you still in?"

"Yes. I've been on the blower calling the four boarding homes we discussed. I discovered distinct differences between the two owned by Shale Harbour Village and the two independents. The latter are owned by JanlonNS, but I don't know who the actual owners are yet. They require visits, Aiden. The municipal places said no one named Willy or Jasper lived there and the name Ira is unfamiliar, but the other two troubled me. One doesn't employ overnight staff and the other houses at least four guests."

"Another rabbit hole, Stella? The police don't inspect boarding homes. You're way off track."

"I want conversations with their residents, and I need you to pull rank." She frowns into the receiver. "Will you help or not?"

"Are you annoyed with me? You sound put out."

"In truth, I'm alarmed. Ira may have lived near Miriam Sylvester's neighbourhood. Jasper and Willy moved to parts unknown. With no family, too many pieces of the puzzle are still missing. One item of interest is in the form of the person who is the lone employee of Jane's Retirement Home for Ladies. She told me her pay cheque comes from this company, JanlonNS." She checks her notes. "Although she couldn't read the signature, the last letters of the last name are EENE. Luther's last name is Greene."

****

While she tears along the hall at the manor, intent on a visit with Del before her scheduled informal interview with Maura Martin, Stella hears her father's voice as he talks with a care giver. "I wonder why Nick's wife didn't stop on her way by."

With her focus disturbed, she examines her reaction. She sailed past without stopping at her father's room. He sees her as Nick's wife and doesn't realize she's his daughter, but today she never gave him a second thought. The question becomes: Does she no longer care he's forgotten her? Where are those gut-wrenching claws of jealousy tearing through her when he remembers Trixie and Brigitte, but not her? Where is the deep disappointment which has most often accompanied her visits? Has she let go? She checks her watch. No time for pondering her inner consciousness right now. She has a five-minute slot for Del before Aiden arrives.

"Hi, Del. Morning snooze?" The old lady is stretched out in her lounger, eyes closed against the winter sunshine which blasts through the thin curtains.

"Hi, Stella. What a surprise. Visiting Norbert?"

"No. Official business."

"Nice you stopped here. You sound busy."

"I wanted to report information from the four boarding homes I discovered. None of them say Willy or Jasper live there."

Del's face muscles sag. "Too bad. I expected you'd find 'em."

"Me, too, but I've not lost hope. I'll interview the residents because no one would provide names. Good idea?"

She nods.

Stella senses Del's nap was, in fact, interrupted, as the woman's eyelids sag. "I'll keep you posted. I'm off to see if Aiden is on the premises yet."

She races back and finds him in her father's doorway. She listens. "Well, hi there, good detective. Am I a witness or a criminal today?"

"Neither, Mr. Kirk. Stopped for a quick hello on my way into an interview. How are you?"

"Fit as a fiddle, if you don't count the grey matter." He roars at his joke.

Frozen in place across the hall and one door back, she has not let go.

Once Aiden steps out, she meets his gaze. "You're here. I saw Del. Shall we speak with Maura before Dewey?"

Aiden's unspoken and personal question written on a face of obvious concern is easily read, but she ignores any discussion of her father.

"Fine. Maura first."

They sit side by side in Maura's tiny office. Stella recalls an experience as a schoolgirl awaiting disciplinary action.

"As I mentioned," she begins, "the identification of the body found in Mallory Gorman's grave is so far undetermined. We will assume his name was Ira, for now. You said you never met anyone by that name, correct?"

Maura, elbows on her desk and hands clasped in front of her, nods.

"And Luther Greene, who works for Royalty Funeral Services, is your nephew."

"Statement or question?"

"Statement. You often take his young son to Yellow House."

The nurse's shoulders relax. "Yes. Your niece runs the little bookstore. I see the connection."

"You refer people to Jane's Retirement Home for Ladies or Merlon's Place for Gentlemen."

She sits straight in her chair. "Harbour Manor policy frowns on boarding home referrals."

"Was I misinformed?"

"Families ask. A person wants to help. I'm a helper. I might advise. Advice isn't against the law." She glances at Aiden.

"What does your husband do for work, Maura?"

"I don't see how my husband's employment is any of your business. How does Hector's job relate to the identification of a body?"

"Luther is your sister's son. Nephew with a different last name, or Hector's sister's son."

"Hector's brother's son, in fact." Eagerly correcting an assumption, Maura falls into the trap of providing information when none was requested.

"And what does your husband, Hector Greene, do for a living?"

"My husband's retired. He takes care of me so I can work. He injured his back years ago and receives a disability pension."

Stella turns to Aiden. "Any other questions, Detective?"

"What? Oh, no. Thanks for your time, Nurse Martin. We are on our way to visit Dewey Laird."

On their walk along the corridor, Stella nibbles her lip, preventing her annoyance from spilling out. Aiden was adrift throughout her interview with Maura, but no matter. She's sure she knows who's behind JanlonNS.

Aiden marginally engaged with Dewey, who was twitchy and excited to speak to the real police officer with the documentation Stella copied earlier. Aiden murmured politely. He didn't dismiss Dewey's records out of hand but asked if the man was certain the noise occurred outside the building.

"You wonder if the noises were in my head, don't you, Detective?" The question was rhetorical. After a quick glance in Stella's direction, he continued. "I document my life in journals. I can distinguish the real from the fabricated, Sir. The voices come only rarely now because the medication works, and staff administers each dose. They give me no choice. I am a sound and reliable witness. Stella is convinced, right?"

She nodded.

Aiden shrugged.

Out in the parking lot, she studies her friend's face for clues. "Aiden, whatever has you bothered should be sorted. Your mind sure as hell isn't on the identification of our dead body, let alone the location of Willy or Jasper."

"First off, finding two old people who don't live here anymore is not police business. Neither person is reported missing, Stella. You can stick your nose into their affairs if you feel the need, but those cases aren't related."

Her torso retracts as if she's been slapped. She focuses on her core and calms herself. "Aiden, Maura Martin's husband's last name is Greene. A pay cheque at one of the guest homes is signed by a person whose last name ends in EENE."

"It is neither a crime nor misdemeanour to own a boarding home."

She ignores his churlish response and verifies her plans. "I want to meet and interview the residents of each of the four guest houses tomorrow. Will you come with me?" Her expectations are low. "I'll even throw in dinner at the park as an enticement."

He nods without enthusiasm, eyes closed for a moment. "We can find out who the managers are, for contact purposes, and explore clearer identification of Ira. I accept both your offers." His tone continues to resemble that of a surly teenager.

Chapter 10

Posh is Not the Best Descriptor

Easy Living Boarding Home is a sprawling bungalow with a glass sunroom addition. Situated on a side street behind the Harbour Hotel, the dwelling presents as a large single-family house. Stella pushes the bell while Aiden admires the cove view in the distance.

Because they called from Aiden's office, they're expected. A middle-aged, fit, and white-haired woman answers the door and ushers them in. "I'm Kay, the day nurse. Welcome to our little oasis here in Shale Harbour. Residents are assembled in the solarium. May I fetch you tea or coffee?"

"Good morning, Kay." *Take a breath, lady.* "I'm Stella Kirk and this is RCMP Detective Aiden North."

Aiden peers around the entry hall. "Picturesque spot. Much turnover in guests?"

"Moves are rare," Kay replies. "As I told you on the phone, and as Fannie mentioned to Miss Kirk, we don't know anyone named Ira. Follow me. I'll introduce you to the group."

Stella suspects Aiden's thoughts were more personal when he queried their turnover. He may be in search of a spot for Rosemary.

"Come in. Hi everyone. Fannie is on the way with your coffee and muffins. Bobby, she has a treat for you, too." She turns to Aiden and Stella while she points toward a bent elderly man with white hair tumbled over one eye, much the same as Aiden. "Meet Bobby. He's been with us five years now and knows all the residents both coming and going."

They nod in his direction.

"And this is Duncan." She pats a younger man on the arm. He dozes in his chair. "Say hello, Duncan. These folks want to ask some questions."

"Hello." He blinks.

Stoic, and at the back of the room, stands an elderly woman. "You took your time getting around to me. I'm Barbara Frey. Please call me Barbara. I'm from Texas and we never shorten our names. No Babs or Barb for me. Barbara, plain and simple." She toddles forward and shakes their hands. "Stella, Detective. Nice to meet you. How can I be of assistance?"

Kay titters. "Barbara acts as our spokesperson. You might have guessed." Her smile is sly. "We're on the lookout for Nelson, our night nurse. He promised he would come by, too. He's replacing an element in the stove for Fannie. He's our handyman as well," she adds, as a means of explanation.

Aiden and Stella make themselves comfortable in coordinated wingback chairs while Kay rushes out in search of Fannie. In five minutes, everyone is settled with coffee or tea and a muffin—except for Bobby, who munches on a digestive cookie. Stella suspects he's diabetic.

When she asks if any of them ever heard of a man named Ira, and describes his affinity for overalls, there is little response.

"My late husband wore overalls," Barbara Frey adds, in an obvious attempt to contribute to a stalled conversation. "He fished, and I emigrated from Texas and married him in 1925. I hated those damnable pants. They could hang on the line for two days and still not be dry in the humidity around here. The air is dryer in Texas."

Duncan, preoccupied with his snack, volunteers little. As a result, Stella stares wide-eyed when he barks, "No one here wears overalls because pants don't hang on the line for two days."

"Correct, Duncan." Kay nods toward Stella. "Duncan helps Fannie with the laundry. He likes acting as her assistant."

"We peel vegetables," Bobby spouts.

"Everyone pitches in." Kay surveys her charges.

"Detective North and I are in search of a woman named Willy Saunders and a man called Jasper Nunn. Any thoughts?"

Heads move back and forth in unison.

Aiden's glance toward Stella is deadpan.

"While we wait for Nelson, tell me why you chose Easy Living Boarding Home. My father lives at Harbour Manor."

"Easy Living is expensive, Stella." Barbara Frey sits on a hard chair and clasps bent arthritic fingers in her lap. "I live here because I pay them every month but keep my finances between me and my adviser. Other places take control of your money and give you an allowance. My husband left me comfortable." She squints at each of them in turn. "I refuse to relinquish my nest egg to strangers, even if I can't cook anymore." She glances at her twisted hands.

After a quick nod toward Kay, Stella stands. "I've enjoyed meeting each of you and hope we can visit again."

"I pray your friends are okay." Duncan studies his muffin as he talks.

Before departure, they speak with Nelson, busy in the kitchen. No further information reveals itself.

****

Cliffs Guest Residence is near Shale Cliffs RV Park, and Stella assumed the big house accommodated one family, until now. The two-story mansard roof design imposes on the skyline. They are greeted by Edna, the day staff person who provides housekeeping as part of her duties. She shows them around before she invites them into the double parlours where residents spend their time together on winter days. The original heavy oak woodwork and the wallpaper are authentic for the period, which, in this case, is the late 1800s. A small cast-iron wood stove is installed where a coal burning unit once sat.

They meet Everett, an active man who helps around the place. He has a daughter nearby and comes and goes with her routinely.

Grace, vacant of emotion, sits in her rocker. She has mild dementia. Edna emphasizes how Grace meets the guidelines for residency in a boarding home because she has a large family, and her relatives visit—to the point of annoyance.

Lizzie, a younger woman of no more than forty, lives with Parkinson's disease. Her illness, and how her relations make their homes far away, clutter her mutterings. She clutches her bouquet of depression in front of her—so her condition can be seen and appreciated.

Each resident has a private room downstairs. Staff occupy rooms on the second floor. Charlotte covers nights, delivers the evening snack, and spends most of her time with the residents since she lives here, too. She approaches Stella as they leave, none the wiser for their questions.

"May I talk with you alone?"

Stella's eyes dart around for an out-of-the-way corner.

"Come upstairs."

They climb the long staircase and enter the second space on the right. A single bed, dresser, desk, and a bookcase which holds a small television, furnish the room. An antique braided rug decorates the pine floor while rose wallpaper gives the impression one is sitting in a flower basket.

"I love my room, Stella. I love living here and I don't want any trouble. I assume you and the detective will visit Jane's Retirement Home for Ladies?"

Stella nods.

"I worked at Jane's and the place scares me."

"Tell me why, Charlotte. May I sit?" She eyes the chair in front of the desk.

"Yes, yes. Sit. Everyone hates Jane's. The ladies are often heavy care and more than the three allowed—even five at times. They once let a woman live in the workshop out back. I took her food but didn't ever know her name. I couldn't stay at Jane's anymore. I was upset all the time. When May arrived one morning, I left and walked here with my suitcase, because Kelly told me their night person already delivered her baby and they needed someone right away. Jane's never hired a replacement for nights."

"Who owns Jane's?"

Charlotte shrugs. "I didn't write them a proper letter because I didn't know where to send one. I left a note with May and my address here." She focuses on the writing paper on the desk. "I have no family nearby, but I keep in touch with my cousins. The council gave me a desk. Generous, right?"

"Nice, Charlotte." She shakes the girl's hand. "I appreciate your help."

****

"The invitation was supper, not lunch," Nick teases as he opens the veranda door and welcomes them both.

"Stella insisted, since we're in the neighbourhood, we should stop here instead of going into town. Hope this isn't inconvenient for you."

"Not in the least, Aiden. Grilled cheese?"

Her appreciation translates into a kiss on his cheek and a soft rub of his back. "Thanks, big guy. Sorry I couldn't call. We'll visit the other two guest houses this afternoon, Nick—the unlicensed ones. Supper is still on, though."

"Good. I've planned a ginger chicken stir fry, and I bought egg rolls from the hotel."

With wide eyes, she asks, "The hotel makes egg rolls?"

As Aiden turns from side to side and watches them interact, Nick chuckles and serves their sandwiches. "I called Pepper and discovered what they might offer and ran into town earlier. I'm not above some investigation, myself." He chuckles again. "I collected them, along with the veggies. I'm set."

"And what else did Pepper 'find' for you?" Stella raises her eyebrows.

"A pecan pie."

A sudden guffaw reminds her there's another person at their table, watching their banter.

"You two crack me up," Aiden says, as he finishes his grilled cheese. "You have supper well under control, Nick. Now, if we can figure out why a man who might be named Ira, was buried in December 1979, we'll be all set."

"I'll help you clear before we leave for Jane's Retirement Home for Ladies."

"Sounds posh," Nick remarks as he gathers silverware and turns toward the sink.

"If what the day staff person, May, said on the phone, and what Charlotte, the night staff at Cliffs Guest Residence confided, are any indication, posh is not the best descriptor."

Aiden waits at the veranda door when she whispers in Nick's ear, "Thanks. I'll make your efforts worthwhile later tonight."

****

Jane's is a dilapidated Victorian house in desperate need of paint and landscaping attention. The bleak windows make Stella think of ghosts. When they knock, a dishevelled and fretful May answers. "I remembered you were comin', but I ain't cleaned yet. Roxy's been havin' one of her days. Come on in."

They enter a wide foyer with hooks for coats and trays for boots. Steep and worn stairs rise from the lower hall to two additional levels. They remove their footwear but keep their coats.

Stella begins. "May, as I mentioned when we spoke on the phone, we want to meet each of your residents for a moment, if possible. We won't disrupt your routine for long."

May turns and runs toward the kitchen at the back. She hollers over her shoulder, "Roxy's out here with me. She needs watchin'. Flora and Ethel are upstairs. Start with them. Ethel can't tell you much, but Flora will talk your ear off."

Aiden's puzzled expression does not go unnoticed by Stella. As they trudge up the staircase, each tread worn from many trips, they hear Roxy bellow from the back of the house. "Don't touch me! You're hurting me. Stop!"

"I'll check out the noise, Stella."

She examines her surroundings. Three bedrooms and a bathroom are on the upper level. One door has a deadbolt, another appears closed tight, and the third stands ajar. Stella chooses the last one and taps on the casing.

"Come in. We're here."

Two women sit beside one another in rickety recliners. A tiny lady is bent in half, focused on her shoes. She plucks at the laces and doesn't acknowledge the presence of anyone in the room.

"I'm Flora and this here is Ethel." She points at the person beside her, whose chin rests on her breasts. Sprigs of black hair try in vain to cover Ethel's skull. "What's your name?"

"Hi, Flora. I'm Stella. We are meeting the people who live here, so we can learn about previous residents, as well as you."

"Can't tell ya nuthin'. May says I should shut my pie hole. I watch Ethel. She don't talk."

With no seating space except for one of the single beds, Stella remains standing. "Flora, do you know a lady named Willy Saunders? She likes cats and wears a man's overcoat."

Flora squints and pushes her chin forward. "Nope. Told ya, I can't tell ya nuthin'."

"All right. Why do you live at Jane's?"

"I took a big fall five years ago." She pats her head. "I can be hard to handle. The doctor said I should stay here and let folks care for me. Insurance sends extra money 'cause it wasn't my fault I fell at the liquor store."

"Has the choice worked out okay for you?"

Flora stares at Stella before she answers. "They take my pension and my insurance cheque. They feed me. Can't ask for much more. Ethel was in rough shape when the police brought her here a year ago. She don't talk," Flora repeats. "Never had no kids. She watches her feet all day. What a life." She consoles Ethel with a pat.

"What's wrong with Roxy?"

Aiden enters the room, his face pale.

"She's what they called paranoid." Flora patiently informs the uninformed. "She imagines people will hit her, or rape her, or kill her. She screams rape if a man gets close."

"Learned the hard way," Aiden grumbles.

"Roxy needs a lot of care." Stella states the obvious. "Where does she sleep?"

"Next door. Minnie was there, too, but she's gone—probably died."

"Why do you think she died?"

"Because May put Roxy in with us for a night." She lifts her hands like a magician who just made a rabbit disappear, "and in the morning, no Minnie."

"Where does Roxy sleep now?"

"In the other room, but she most often comes in here and curls in a ball on the floor. Monica Lawson died, too. She weren't here long. Her daughter visited and helped May. They took Monica's body in the middle of the night. That was almost six months ago. Jack still volunteers on Thursdays."

"And the third bedroom with the lock?"

"Reserved for a night person, but the room's empty since Charlotte left. I liked Charlotte."

"Thank you, ladies. We might come back for another visit if that's okay with you." Stella focuses her attention on the crusty Flora.

Flora nods. "Ethel. Time for a pee." She grabs the other woman by the armpit and hoists her away from the fixation on her shoes.

Aiden and Stella make their way downstairs. At the landing, Stella turns toward the kitchen. "Give me a second. I want a word with May."

She approaches the sunny space and sees Roxy tied to a wooden armchair. She's asleep. "May, are you around?"

"Out back. Gimme a minute." The frazzled woman returns with a load of sheets out of the dryer.

"One quick question before we leave. What happened to Minnie, who lived upstairs and shared a room with Roxy?"

May hesitates for a fraction of a second.

"Moved."

"I see. Good. Flora assumed she died. What's her last name?"

May swallows. Her eyes are empty of any emotion.

"Gardiner. Flora talks too much."

Back in the car, Stella frowns. "May lied. She said a former resident, Minnie Gardiner, moved. Flora said she died."

"Stella, if a woman died upstairs at Jane's, two people would be required to carry the body down. Minnie moved, I'm sure. Jane's is a hell hole."

"If you're right, then what about Monica Lawson? Flora said they took her body away in the middle of the night."

****

Merlon's Place for Gentlemen is a regular, although large, mid-twentieth-century structure, with two stories and three windows across the top. The lower floor boasts a centre double-entry and picture windows on either side. A large, aproned woman greets them at the door. "Good morning. I am Helga and work at night, but I live here and help Elsie sometimes."

"Thanks for your help today." Aiden takes the lead. "We are in search of information on two gentlemen and wonder if they are residents or if they lived here in the past."

"Come inside. I will fetch tea." She lumbers off in the general direction of the back of the house.

The front living room resembles a funeral parlour with individual chairs in a semi-circle and a large coffee table in the middle; arranged for a meeting or a vigil.

Helga returns with a tray. "Elsie must take in the laundry. The dryer is still not working. She will be here in a moment." She drops her offerings on the solid surface, then turns.

"We want to interview the residents, if we can, but first, Helga, have you ever met a man called Jasper Nunn, or known a fellow named Ira who wore overalls most of the time and did yard work for people in town?"

"I'm not good with names. Elsie will be finished soon."

Alone again, Aiden and Stella stare at one another. "This place gives me the creeps, Aiden."

"If Elsie isn't here in a minute, I'll go upstairs."

Elsie, a petite woman of indeterminate age, blusters in. She wipes sweat off her brow with the back of her hand. "You are Stella Kirk and Detective North, right? I see Helga has made herself useful. Most of our residents are in their rooms for rest time. I'll lead the way." She trundles toward the stairs.

"Meet Horace and Cecil. As you can tell, Horace isn't mobile and uses a walker. Say hello to the police, Horace." Without waiting for a reply, she points to the second man in the room. "Meet Cecil. Poor old boy can't remember the day of the week, but he's a good guy, right Cecil? We've roomed them together because Horace has the brains and Cecil has the brawn. They help one another, right fellas?"

Horace nods.

Their questions about Ira and Jasper go unanswered, although Stella sees a spark of recognition in Horace's eyes when she describes Jasper Nunn.

Elsie hustles them along. In the second room, she gushes, "Meet poor old Fred. His wife died a year ago. Married sixty years and never learned to take care of himself. Couldn't boil water, could ya, Fred? Now he sits around day in and day out, missin' his lady."

They ask their questions. Fred attempts a remark, but Elsie interrupts.

"We board three men here—our limit. Are we done? Time for me to start supper."

On their way back to the car, Stella mumbles, "I bet the old boys know Jasper. Elsie railroaded us through the place." A tall, athletic-looking gentleman with piles of white hair pops out from behind the thicket which borders the driveway. "You might want me."

Aiden eyes him with suspicion. "And you are?"

"Jasper Nunn. I lived at Harbour Manor, but I moved out over a year ago, now. Elsie said I should keep outta sight because they're over the limit, havin' four men in the house."

Stella, momentarily at a loss for words, extends her hand. "I'm Stella Kirk. The bridge club and my father are worried, Jasper."

"Can we talk in your car? Elsie will be out lookin' for me any minute."

Once seated inside, Aiden drives a block away, and Jasper explains. "Sorry about folks bein' concerned." He stares at his lap. "People my age avoid goodbyes. You figure it might be the last one. If you drift off, no one's the wiser."

"Why did you move into Merlon's?"

"My savings was runnin' out. I needed a cheaper place. My health is fair, so I don't qualify for government help. I signed over my pension cheque and I can come and go as I please. I walk the back roads outside town. Elsie and Helga said I could share a room with Fred, but I need to keep quiet and stay out of the way."

"May I tell your friends at the manor?"

He gives a worried nod. "I hope Merlon's don't toss me out."

Aiden drops Jasper around the corner from Merlon's Place for Gentlemen and they return to the park.

Over their Chinese supper created by Nick and the hotel, they begin a discussion focused on the homes. She has questions for the unlicensed facilities. "We should report our concerns to social services. Surely, they conduct regular inspections for compliance with the regulations. And call the fire department, too. Jane's is a fire trap, and those women could never evacuate on their own in an emergency." She pauses for breath. "And Horace and Cecil are too far gone. They don't meet the boarding home criteria."

"Yes. Assessments are necessary, for sure." Aiden takes a final swallow of his beer. "I'll instruct staff to call the homes and obtain contacts for each of the residents. The extra information might help sort out their details. Maybe I should be a social worker," he adds. "We'll talk tomorrow. Great supper, Nick."

"Before you go, will Rosemary still be home for Christmas?"

He nods but with obvious hesitation. "That's the plan—December 20, Sunday. I don't know if she'll stay." A quick wave and he's out the door.

Chapter 11

Hard Times for Old Guys

Aiden's call happens during lunch preparations. Nick is busy in the machine shop. Kiki is with him, content in the truck. Stella imagines he'll be cold when he returns, so she tended the fire. She opened a tin of soup and dug in the pantry for crackers. The wall phone in the kitchen is an easy reach as she sets the table.

"Stella, here's the information uncovered by the crew when they visited each boarding home earlier today and asked for background on residents. Not much of value, I'm afraid."

"Background? And confidentiality?"

"Out the window when the police knock. People don't understand they can refuse information." He huffs. "Anyway, Easy Living and Cliffs Guest Residence cooperated, no problem. Barbara Frey has a daughter nearby. Duncan has two nephews who visit and take him for car rides. Bobby gardens, and his son owns the plant nursery in Port Ephron."

"And Cliffs?"

"Let me see."

She hears papers shuffle.

"Everett's daughter volunteers. Grace has a different family member come in every day. Lizzie's relations don't live close, but she has a friend who visits and takes her for tea and to the shops."

"Did they determine how the finances work?"

"Yes. Both homes are run by Village Council and each resident has a designated Power of Attorney, billed each month, if they're unable to manage their own money. Monthly charges are expensive—half again as much as an Old Age Pension cheque."

"Barbara Frey commented on the cost. And the other two? The private ones?"

"At Jane's, they said Roxy and Ethel have no contacts, and Flora has a sister in Florida." He stops.

"What's the matter?"

"I wonder what our circumstances will be when we reach the age where we need care. Neither one of us has kids."

Aiden's morose tone has tainted his speech for weeks. "I'll share Brigitte and Mia with you." Her light-hardheartedness goes unrewarded.

"Merlon's is no different, Stella. Horace and Cecil are without family. Fred has a daughter who Elsie, the day person, says won't come near him. She lives in the north somewhere. Jasper is alone in the world, too. He waited outside again and spoke with my staff."

"Does the money work the same as the licensed places?"

"Not even close. When you move into Jane's or Merlon's, they take Power of Attorney over your finances."

"Exactly what Jasper said. Is the process legal?"

"If an individual is in their right mind, they can give POA to whomever they want. Most people possess limited resources when they choose a private home—their Old Age Pension, maybe a scrap of savings. Jane's or Merlon's becomes the best option in the circumstances. Jasper said he left Harbour Manor because he couldn't pay their bill anymore." He sighs. "This isn't police business, Stella. I got the information as a favour, but we must focus on the old fella in the hole."

"Okay." She has no intention of letting the matter go. Finding Willy Saunders is important, too. "I plan to run over to the manor after lunch with Jasper, if he wants to go."

"Sounds fine. Did you hear that Mrs. Gorman's funeral is tomorrow? Will you attend?"

"Yes. Nick and I are going. You?"

"No, but keep an eye on people—Otto King and Luther Greene in particular. I'm convinced they're involved in our clandestine burial." When she doesn't respond, he continues. "We need to focus on the body we found, Stella, not on a couple of folks where one is no longer even missing."

****

Nick rolls into the kitchen as she replaces the receiver on the wall. Kiki wiggles around between her feet, waiting for pats and treats. "How about a drive later?"

"Sure." He leans in and kisses her cheek. "Let me wash my hands and you can tell me what plot has thickened now."

"A trip to Merlon's Place for Gentlemen, plus a Harbour Manor visit. Are you in?" She hollers at his retreating form.

"I'm in."

She gives Kiki a biscuit and pats her dog bed, positioned behind the table. She ladles hot soup into bowls and places them in their spots. She surveys lunch, which never tastes as good as when Nick takes charge.

"Smells great," he spouts, when he returns. "Your plan is a visit for Jasper at the manor? You'll shock the old folks."

"I'll call Maura first. She'll tell them we're on our way. I wish Willy Saunders could be found safe and sound, too, but I'm afraid life hasn't ended well for Willy."

Nick dips crackers in his soup and eyes the bowl of fruit in the centre of the table. "Why are you worried, Stella?"

"Aiden made a serious point when he called with contact information on the boarding home residents. Without children or close relatives, the elderly are vulnerable. With limited funds, they're forced into unlicensed facilities where owners take their POA and their money. They turn over control."

"I guess we're lucky with Brigitte and Mia."

"Correct. I told Aiden he could share, despite the fact he insisted on no more boarding home investigations by the police. Sad, eh?"

She makes a quick call, ignores Elsie's protestations, and insists Jasper be alerted. She then contacts the manor. Maura Martin's abruptness, when she suggests a visit from Jasper, sets an unwelcoming tone.

****

Jasper stands erect on the front steps of Merlon's. He stamps his feet for warmth. His jacket is worn and tattered at the cuffs. Stella jumps out of the Jeep and opens the back door while Nick holds Kiki, snuggled into her fisherman's cable-knit sweater.

"Climb in, my friend. I called Nurse Martin and advised her we were on our way."

The old gentleman, with added care on arthritic knees, folds himself into the seat. "She won't be none too happy."

"Why, Jasper? She reported you'd moved, but she didn't know the address."

"Merlon's was Maura's idea. She told me if I couldn't pay my bills and my savin's was runnin' out, I should move in. The home takes your money, but you're set."

As they drive, Stella frowns and glances at Nick. "How exactly do they take your money, Jasper?"

"I signed papers at the boarding house and at the bank. Gave them my little savin's account. Not much—a few hundred. Now my Old Age Pension is mailed direct. I don't even sign the back. Simple."

"Standard for everyone?"

"Seems so. We're each given an allowance."

"An allowance?"

"Yup. Fifteen dollars a month. They keep the money, mind you, but I can ask for a couple of bucks to buy myself shavin' cream and soap. If I need new pants or underwear, they take the charges outta my stipend, too."

"Are your happy with the arrangement?"

"Askin' for my allowance and tellin' somebody I need new underwear is humblin', but I'm okay. I keep track of what I spend and make sure I don't git gypped. Cute dog." He reaches over the seat and tweaks Kiki's ears.

Why did Maura Martin act as if Jasper Nunn's location was unknown? Because she recommended Merlon's, and referrals are against Harbour Manor policy?

"I admit I miss this place," Jasper mutters, as Nick pulls the Jeep into the lot at the manor.

"I'm not surprised," Stella replies as she jumps out. "You made good friends here."

"At my age, a feller don't want good friends. Leavin' 'em hurts and sayin' goodbye hurts, too." He meets Stella's gaze. "Don't get me wrong. The chance for a visit, since folks were worried, is good."

Stella can't help but recall Eula and Addie, who live here, and share a room because they've been neighbours and friends all their lives. The thought of the death of one of them proves beyond her imagination.

"We've assembled everyone in the lounge. I see you brought your dog—without prior approval." She glances in Jasper's general direction. "Hello,

Jasper. You're doing well?"

"Keepin' busy, Maura. Out for my walks every day. Excited I can pop in and say hi."

Residents pack the common room. Her father and Del Trembly sit side by side in matching recliners. The bridge club stands in unison when Jasper Nunn ambles into view. Dewey Laird perches on a straight-backed chair beside a sofa where Eula Cameron and Addie LaPointe are settled. Dewey can't stop wriggling. For a second, Stella wonders if they'll clap.

While Jasper makes his rounds in one direction, Stella, Nick, and Kiki visit with Del and Norbert.

"Where's Willy?" Norbert pats Kiki and doesn't make eye contact with Stella or Nick.

Nick glances at Stella before he replies. "Willy isn't located yet, but we're still on the lookout, Norbert."

"Willy moved away. She has a cat now. Right, Del?"

"Possible, eh Stella?" The cast in her eyes says otherwise when she touches Stella's hand.

After a chat with Del and Norbert, Jasper tells Stella, "I'm gonna wander along the hall and visit with Connie and Miriam before we go, since nobody wheeled the girls in here."

Stella makes her way across the room toward the bridge club, Kiki under her arm. "Hi, guys. Nice to see Jasper, eh?"

"Yeah. He acts okay," Elmer mutters.

Ignoring Caleb's continual fist-clenching proves difficult. "What's on your mind, Caleb?"

The big man rubs the back of his hand before he answers. "Jasper says he lives at Merlon's Place. Guy and me, we lived there before we came here. We didn't like the outfit much."

"He's contented enough, Caleb."

"He almost ran outta money and he can't stay here for free because he don't need serious care. Hard times for old guys when you're forced into livin' at Merlon's." He straightens out the crib board and prepares for their next game.

Nick approaches and takes Kiki from her arms. "The ladies on the couch placed a request for the dog."

"Okay. I'll fetch Jasper and we can leave soon." She makes her goodbyes before she trots along the wide corridor toward Miriam's.

She discovers Jasper has moved Connie into Miriam's room and the three of them are deep into a discussion about Merlon's. "I wish you could come back here, Jasper. We miss you. Caleb and Guy never liked Merlon's," Miriam reminds them. "Why did Maura recommend the place, I wonder?"

"Don't worry. I'm okay. Once I need more help, I can stay here for free."

Miriam and Connie titter as Stella knocks on the door. "Ready, Jasper? Nice seeing you both." She nods to the two women.

****

The frozen earth provides little comfort. Tufts of grass scatter across the field like dead birds buffeted in the wind. The shivering crowd huddles together for warmth. Feet stamp. Today is the coldest she has seen this fall. Winter isn't official for another three days. No preacher officiates. Theodore Gorman stands erect at the head of the grave, his loose charcoal topcoat pulled from his gaunt frame by icy grabs of wind racing from the ocean. Stella leans into Nick. Mallory was not her friend, but the loss grips her, nonetheless. The coffin is lowered by a machine that crunches and hesitates on the way into the grave. Otto King and Luther Greene, both dressed in black suits with Nero collared shirts, hover nearby. Red hands extend below white cuffs. More people are gathered than Stella expected. Curiosity, because of the body found at the bottom of the pit last week, has driven them here. Her feet are ice cubes. She shuffles and pulls her cloche tighter over her ears. Support for Theodore in his grief is paramount, but the merciless gale tormenting her shoulders, and the seeping chill through her boots, make sympathy and solace a challenge.

At a distance, in an unobtrusive spot, Stella can see the truck and trailer with the backhoe parked alongside, ready to complete the job once the attendees scatter.

"Please join the family at the Harbour Hotel for light refreshments. Thank you for your comfort on such a blustery day." Theodore jams chapped hands into his pockets, gazes at the people assembled, and trudges toward a Royalty Funeral Services sedan.

"Do you plan on attending the reception?" Trixie hisses in Stella's ear.

"For a few minutes and a cup of tea. Where's Val?"

"We're off in one of King's cars. I thought I'd check with you first."

"Are you and Val still coming for dinner Saturday night?"

"Oh, yeah. Talk later." She trots off on heels dangerously high for such uneven terrain.

Pepper has the largest dining room prepared for the gathering, with chairs arranged around a light lunch buffet. Stella makes her way toward the urn marked "tea." Her thoughts are focused on the truck idling in the gully, waiting to load the digger before returning to the storage compound. There must be a record of the unit assigned to transport equipment on December 15, 1979.

****

After supper, they stretch out in front of the fire. "Funerals exhaust me," Nick grumbles as he pats Kiki and sips his wine.

"Me, too. I'm sorry for Theodore and Val, but happy for Mallory. She suffered a long time." She pauses. "Did you see the truck and trailer in the distance?"

"Yup. Waiting to load the digger after the grave is filled in."

"I bet there's a record of where the funeral home's machine was delivered on December 15, 1979. I'm gonna contact Aiden tomorrow and suggest the police ask the company for their records." Before she expands on her suspicions, the telephone jangles. She races for the kitchen.

"Shale Cliffs RV Park…."

Del Trembly interrupts. "Hi, Stella. Del here. Caleb Hall wanted me to call you. We're back here in the office. Can you talk with him?"

"Sure. You asked Olive Urback if you could use the nurse's station office because Caleb wants a conversation?" Clarification seems necessary.

"Right. Here he is."

The phone clatters in Stella's ear. She hears encouraging mumbles from Del.

"Are you Stella, Norbert Kirk's daughter? The one with the little dog?"

"I am, indeed, Caleb. What can I do for you tonight?"

"Sorry I'm botherin' you. I don't use phones much anymore."

"No problem." Stella sits on a kitchen chair. Nick appears in the doorway and motions he's on his way outside with Kiki.

"Elmer and me, we were talkin'. We're pretty sure we know the man they found in the hole."

"Shall I come for a visit, Caleb?"

"No. Guy can get upset."

Stella squints into the receiver. "Okay. Go ahead."

"Me and Guy, we both lived at Merlon's." He clears his throat. "We moved in here two years ago the end of this month."

"Yes. Go on."

"Guy clobbered another fella with one of his weights, and Merlon's said they wanted Guy out." The words tumble in a sudden rush. "He was admitted here, and I came, too."

"And the person he hit, Caleb?" Stella's heart thumps.

"Ira Gold. Elmer first met him when they both lived in the seniors' apartments and their wives were alive. Ira liked overalls and putterin'."

"When did this happen?"

"The middle of December, two years ago. Don't know the exact date. Before Christmas."

"What happened after the altercation?"

"Elsie called for Helga, and she took him to the hospital."

"And you never saw Ira again?"

"We wondered if he died, but Elsie said he moved into another home. We assumed Harbour Manor, but Guy came here first, and me soon after. No Ira. They don't appreciate you askin' a lot of questions at Merlon's."

"Caleb, I'll tell Detective North about our conversation tomorrow, okay?"

"Will I go to jail? Will Guy go to jail?"

"No, Caleb. No one will go to jail. This is a big help. We need identification of the man we found in Mallory Gorman's grave, and you've provided solid information. May I suggest Detective North talk with you and Elmer?"

"Sure, but not Guy."

"Why not Guy?"

"His memory comes and goes. Sometimes he figures he's lived here at the manor since the day he was born. There are days his brains are porridge, Stella."

"Okay. I'll do the best I can. Will you thank Del and Nurse Urback for me? I appreciate your call, Caleb. You've been a big help."

Once off the phone, she returns to the living room where Nick and Kiki are settled in front of the television. "The identity of the man at the bottom of Mallory's grave may no longer be a mystery." She sits with a thud and repeats Caleb's information for Nick's benefit.

He twists in his spot on the couch. His mouth hangs open for a moment before he regains his composure. "Stella, you can't expect that two middle-aged staff members from Merlon's Place rented a digger and buried a dead resident in a field."

"You're right, but what happened? Did the man die at Merlon's Place, and they buried him in what is now the graveyard expansion? Did Luther Greene borrow the machine from the funeral home at the time? Does Ira Gold have family? Caleb said they were told he was hospitalized but never heard more."

"His relations took over, Stella." Nick's response is blunt.

"Okay, smart fella. If you're right, how did he end up in the grave?"

"Good point." He shrugs. "Could the body not be Ira Gold? Maybe Caleb has the circumstances, or even the dates, wrong."

"I need tea." She wanders into the kitchen. Nick and Kiki trail behind. As she plugs in the kettle, she frowns. "Here's what I know: December 15, 1979, is the date Dewey Laird gave us when he heard machinery noises."

Nick nods as he places their empty wine glasses on the counter, and then reaches for Kiki before he sits at the table.

"Luther Greene borrowed the digger on the same day."

"Okay. Could be coincidence, or he did a job for a relative and Dewey heard the machinery noises from the manor."

"Fair enough. Miriam Sylvester hired a guy named Ira who wore overalls, and he stopped appearing late in the fall of 1979. Caleb and Elmer were both acquainted with a man named Ira Gold, who lived at the seniors' apartments followed by Merlon's, after his wife died." She pours hot water over black currant tea bags. "He liked overalls. Caleb and Guy Boucher lived at Merlon's, along with Ira Gold, until December 1979, when Guy hit Ira with one of his weights." She peers at Nick over her cup. "I didn't ask why the incident happened. Guy and Caleb both moved into the manor in late December 1979, after the altercation. Exact dates shouldn't be hard to find."

"Still, lots of missing pieces, Stella. And your theory is…?"

She hesitates. "No theorizing until I toss the idea around with Aiden."

"But one's bubbled to the surface. I can tell."

Chapter 12

Don't Dead Bodies Haunt You?

Icy air pierces her consciousness. She snuggles against Nick, who rumbles beside her. The comforter covers her chin but exposes her toes. She rearranges the puffy whiteness, to no avail. Nick stirs.

"Your feet are frozen," he mumbles, eyes still closed.

Stella sits, moving the duvet further away from her face and toward the end of the bed. She turns and throws herself against his shoulder. "How do you manage to stay toasty?"

"Younger," he quips, before he shields himself from an expected assault.

"My age? The old lady feels the temperature in her bones?" They wrestle, but the result of their teasing ends in warm, rumpled sheets and lazy lovemaking.

In the kitchen, showered and contented, she makes coffee and toast while Nick builds up the fire. "We'll soon be comfy."

"I turned on the baseboard heater." She checks his expression for an argument and sees none. "Power's expensive, but I couldn't rid myself of the chill this morning." She slams her hands into the pockets of her hoodie.

"The heaters will take the edge off. When your father moved from oil to electric, the cost was much cheaper. He made a good decision at the time. We should explore hot water heat in a year or two."

More money. "We'll see. The fireplace does the trick for now. Ready for breakfast?"

"Yeah. Kiki, too, if I judge the dance."

Stella gazes with fondness at the dog who wiggles around her feet. "Don't let her fool you. Miss Kiki has eaten. She wants your toast, thanks to Duke." She sits. "What do you have planned for today?"

"Here's a thought. Housework. I'll vacuum and polish the floors. We can clean the kitchen counters, dust, scrub the bathrooms." His eyes widen with faked enthusiasm.

She bites into a slice of bread. "I miss the staff, but if I consider company invited tomorrow, a scour is a good idea. I need to telephone Aiden first, and share the discussion I had with Caleb Hall."

In her office, Stella reviews her notes made after the call from Caleb. Her hesitancy doesn't stem from the particulars, but from Aiden's preoccupations. She decides she'll invite him for dinner with Trixie and Val tomorrow night. Nick won't mind. Rosemary arrives on Sunday. She expects the investigation will be riddled with additional challenges for Aiden once she's home.

"Detective North, please. Stella Kirk calling."

"One moment."

He's in Port Ephron. She guessed correctly.

"Good morning, Stella. How was the funeral?"

"No suspicious behaviour, but a chat with the company that loads and delivers the digger might be wise. I saw them at the other side of the graveyard. I suspect they documented where they delivered on December 15, 1979."

"Agreed."

"I'll interview if you call first. The name is Port Heavy Equipment Rental and Storage. I glimpsed part of the logo on the truck at the funeral, and Otto King mentioned them. Heavy equipment transportation isn't why I called, though."

"Oh?"

"Nick and I took Jasper to Harbour Manor for a visit."

"Great. Your father and Del Trembly were probably delighted when they learned he's okay."

"We met many happy people. Later that evening, I accepted a call from the manor, because Caleb Hall from the bridge group wished to provide the investigation with information. He gave me the possible identity of our victim."

"What? We came up empty when we interviewed him and the others."

"Once they found out Jasper moved into Merlon's, Caleb and Elmer decided cooperation might be a good idea."

"Details?"

"Elmer lived in senior's apartments with his wife, at the same time as a fellow named Ira Gold, who did odd jobs and wore coveralls. Ira moved into Merlon's because he wanted someone to make his meals after the missus died. He met Guy Boucher and Caleb at the home. I assume he worked for people like Miriam Sylvester, because he had little money after he paid his room and board."

"Why didn't Caleb and Elmer share this information before?" Aiden's tone has sharpened with annoyance.

"Fear of consequences, I imagine. Caleb told me how Guy and Ira fought, Guy hit Ira on the head with one of his weights, and Ira was hospitalized. They never heard news of him again."

"He's no longer at Merlon's, for sure?"

"No. He isn't hidden like Jasper. Social Services assessed Guy for Harbour Manor because of his unpredictability and potential violence. Caleb followed soon afterward. Elmer relocated directly from his senior's apartment to the manor after his wife's death."

"Okay. I still don't understand. Where did Ira go?"

"Caleb assumed Ira went to the hospital. Records need verification, but I bet he died the same night, and someone buried him in the empty field before the area became a legitimate burial ground. Can you find out who owns JanlonNS?"

"Yes, but the task will take a few days because of the time of year."

"I'm convinced Hector Greene and his wife, Maura Martin, own Merlon's and Jane's."

Quiet weighs on the line for a moment. "Interesting theory, but why?"

"She never admitted a connection, Aiden. If I operated a successful guest house, I would admit my ownership when asked. If she and her husband encourage personally funded Harbour Manor residents to move into one of their facilities with a goal of obtaining control of their affairs, there's an issue."

"I'll assign a detective to check current Nova Scotia corporate listings and see what they can find—and request hospital records, too. Good work," he offers, in what Stella assumes is reluctant praise.

"Tomorrow night is your last evening before Rosemary arrives and you'll be out of circulation for a while. Trixie and Val are coming here for supper. Please join us. The tree will be decorated," she adds, for extra enticement.

"I should stay in town and help Mary Jo and Toni, but they'll see a lot of me over the next two weeks. Besides, your invitation sounds better. You and Nick are too kind."

"All we can do is feed and support you, my friend. Six o'clock. Okay?"

****

Best tree ever, she admires. Cut on the property and trimmed earlier in the day. The old house sparkles. The wood fire crackles. She returns to the kitchen to finish their preparations.

"Might there be an issue with Val attending your pre-Christmas supper this year?" Nick asks.

"Trixie said Val sees me as a cop and wasn't comfortable when we investigated the Owen Ellis-Thomas case. I hope he'll come around once he's here for a meal." Stella measures brown sugar and cinnamon then mixes in peeled and sliced apples.

"Could Aiden's attendance make matters worse?"

"Val isn't involved in the current mysterious dead body investigation."

"Except they discovered the corpse in his sister's grave plot."

"True." She pauses to measure and add frozen cranberries. "But he has no vested interest. He wasn't operating the digger. He doesn't work for any of the relevant companies. Besides, after tonight there's Christmas Eve, followed by our New Year's Eve celebration of the sale of Trixie's shares. Surely he'll be desensitized to me after all the socializing."

"Fair enough." He surveys their accomplishments—a lasagna plus a cranberry/apple crisp, both ready for the oven, and a loaf of garlic bread purchased at the hotel the day before—a contented grin lighting his face. With one arm around her shoulder, he adds, "Let's take a walk through the park before dark. We can make the salad when we get back."

"Good idea." She leans into his flannel shirt for a quick touch of his warmth. "Let me grab my jacket."

They wander the roads, cleaned of snow for now. Nick has completed the winterization tasks requested by their seasonals. The septic system will move forward in the spring, and their partnership is official in twelve days. She purrs her contentment as they meander. Kiki trots in front of them. The little dog runs a few feet, turns around, determines they're still behind her, and skips ahead again. *What a family.*

Trixie and Val arrive near five-thirty. "Wow! Your veranda could be a picture in a designer magazine, Stella. Where did you find the white lights?" She picks her way up the stairs in leather boots and tight red jeans, not interested in an answer. Her rabbit fur jacket doesn't hide the short creamy angora sweater underneath. "And your door." She points. "Did you make this yourself?"

Stella turns and studies the broom wreath she fashioned from pine boughs, wired together, and decorated with a plaid ribbon. "Indeed. I'm not a total klutz."

A pat on the arm by her sister indicates no offence was meant. Val mounts the stairs after Trixie, and they muddle inside. He holds a bottle of wine in one hand and a six-pack of local beer in the other. Nick rushes over and takes the offerings, places them on a side table, and welcomes Val. The wind rustles the spruce trees. Kiki, in her green turtleneck, wiggles her hellos.

"Well, here's the bug. You bought her a new sweater." She winks at Stella. "You did, didn't you?"

"Her special little treat for Christmas, since Duke isn't around. Did I tell you he went to Florida with Cloris?"

"Not very fancy." Trixie frowns at the dog.

"Never mind my taste in canine accoutrements. By the way, Aiden should be here any minute. I told him six."

Nick and Val open beers while Stella pours wine for herself and her sister. They regroup in the living room when the door opens. Aiden stands on the threshold, ladened with Nick's favourite brew, as usual.

"Hi, Aiden. There's time for a beer before dinner. Let me take that." Nick, the consummate host, hangs Aiden's coat in the front closet. Stella pours the beer.

Although Val fades into Trixie's wake for the better part of the meal, conversation flows. "Found an identity?" Trixie asks in between crunches of her Caesar salad.

Aiden hesitates. Stella is convinced the slight shake of his head is imperceptible except to her. "No information has been made public yet, Trixie. We've developed a theory, although we can't share."

"How's Rosemary?" Trixie addresses her next question directly to Aiden. "Stella said she'll be home for Christmas. I'd love to see her."

Focused on his dinner, Aiden mumbles, "Social engagements are iffy. She isn't well."

"Maybe we can visit later, after the excitement of the holidays." Trixie won't take a hint. "Rosemary will soon acclimatize to life outside a hospital, right Aiden?"

He nods.

"Don't dead bodies haunt you?"

Val's remark might be construed as accusatory and random given the current discussion, although Stella relates. "Are you haunted, Val?"

"I see the guy's body on the floor in the basement of the community hall every day. Can't use the stairs without rememberin'."

"Not unusual." Aiden's kind tone chimes in. "Most people who discover a dead person are left with the effects. Eventually, your brain will find a storage space, so the experience and the memory won't tumble out any time you see a staircase or recall the writers conference."

Stella fidgets. She's never heard Aiden sound so thoughtful. He's more a "get over it" kind of guy. She notices Nick, leaned forward, eyes squinted as he watches her. Lorraine Young, Lucy Painter, and Paulina McAdams wander the crevices of her thoughts every day. The reason Owen doesn't occupy real estate in her mind as often is because they weren't personally acquainted.

"Someday, I'll cope with the fact I found a dead kid at the bottom of the stairs?" Val toys with his napkin and avoids Aiden's gaze.

"Yes, you will."

They linger over tea. Trixie offers to help clean-up, but Stella declines.

"Thank you for a great meal, but we'd better be on our way, then. The weather looks iffy and Brigitte worries." She leans and brushes her cheek against Stella's—an unusual behaviour—and mutters a Christmas Eve reminder. "Don't forget."

"Not a chance! The special dress for Mia, remember?"

After they leave, Aiden, Nick, and Stella settle for more tea in the kitchen while Nick puts the dishes in the sink. Aiden says little but makes no move to go home.

"Tomorrow must worry you," she begins.

"If I'm honest, I'm terrified. A repeat of Thanksgiving would be devastating. Mary Jo should be the one scared, but she's oddly optimistic."

"Rosemary's visit is for how long? I can't remember what you told me."

Nick returns to a spot beside Stella.

"Until January fourth, for sure. I'm scheduled back at work on the fifth.

Her psychiatrists will re-evaluate on the third before further plans are made."

Stella leans over and touches Nick's arm. "Bring Rosemary for dinner on the second, Aiden." Nick tenses under her touch. Stella hopes Rosemary won't make another pass at him in their kitchen, but support for Aiden is her main goal. "We'll hold a celebration since our full-fledged partnership will be one day old!"

"I can't commit. You understand."

She swivels toward Nick. "Because Aiden's off for the next two weeks, are you okay if we discuss the case for a few minutes?"

Ever gracious, Nick stands and bows. "Pay no mind to the dishwasher."

"Your contributions are always helpful. Join in if you want." Aiden has always appreciated any analysis on Nick's part.

"A question?" she asks.

"Why am I not surprised?"

"If we determine Ira Gold is the person whose body they found, and he died at Merlon's, what happened after his death? Who did notifications? What about his cheques?"

"More than one question, but I agree. We need answers. He lived at the seniors' apartments before Merlon's. I'll have a detective speak with the manager regarding the victim's move—forwarded mail—those details."

****

The phone jangles as Stella prepares lunch. Nick made cinnamon buns yesterday, and she happily anticipates seconds after they enjoyed them right out of the oven on Sunday. She reaches for the wall-mounted unit by the kitchen door. "Shale Cliffs RV Park. Stella here. How may I help you?"

"Hi, Stella. Moyer. Detective North asked me to call."

"No problem, Sergeant. What's new? The graveyard case?"

"Yeah. Couple of items. Forensics confirmed the body is Ira Gold. Once a possible identification was presented, they used his lack of teeth and a birthmark. The pathologist determined the dent in his skull matches a hand-held weight."

"Great. Now we can verify Ira Gold died after Guy Boucher hit him in a fit of anger."

"The report says there's a chance he didn't die immediately, but they can't be conclusive. The body was buried a long time."

"Two years."

"Right." Sergeant Moyer huffs and continues. "You're ahead of me. North asked that you contact Merlon's. The manager of the senior's apartments said when Ira Gold moved, his mail was transferred, and he organized the process himself because he had no money for the fee."

"Which is the reason the manager remembers." She nods to herself. "Did Aiden ask that I touch base with him after I interview Elsie or Helga at Merlon's?"

"No. He showed an hour ago, gave me details, said to ring you, and left."

"Okay. I'll call Merlon's first and Aiden afterward. If I can't reach him, I'll leave a message with you."

"Sure. Sergeant Social-Secretary," he mumbles.

"Now Sergeant," she pacifies. "Talk soon."

After lunch, Nick returns to the machine shed. The plow attachment for the old truck needs work. The part won't turn the way he expects, which makes the prospect of future snow removal a challenge. Other than the skiff of white stuff they experienced Saturday evening, the weather calls for cold and clear—no storms for now, but she doesn't envy him in the workshop. She takes advantage of the quiet to make a call.

"Merlon's."

"Hi, Elsie?"

"Yup. Who's this?"

"Stella Kirk. We talked on the phone, and I visited with a police officer named Detective North."

"Okay."

The woman could be hesitant or forgetful. Might as well jump right in. "The body we discovered has been identified as Ira Gold, a former resident of Merlon's. Do you remember him?"

"What if I do? Listen, I'm busy cleanin' after lunch."

"Will you tell me about Ira?"

"He don't live here anymore."

"Did he fight with Guy Boucher?"

"Can't recall."

"You told me you've worked at Merlon's for years, Elsie. Surely you remember Ira Gold and what happened."

"Listen," the cook spits into the phone. "The rules are clear for staff. No gossip. I don't know nuthin'."

"What did you do with his mail, once he left Merlon's, Elsie?" Stella's convinced the woman knows more.

"Letters ain't delivered straight here. Somebody collects at the post office. If there's somethin' for me, I get an envelope in the box by the back door; same with the residents."

"Okay. Who brings the mail?"

"I can't talk no more. Lotsa work. Ira left. Alls I can say."

The phone clunks. Stella sits and stares at the receiver. She should call Aiden, or will he call her because he wants to find out what she's discovered? *And my discovery is...?*

She takes a big breath and telephones Rosemary's sister, Toni. Mary Jo answers. "Hi, Mary Jo. May I speak with Aiden for a minute?"

"Sorry, Stella. He took off with Rosie for a drive, not ten minutes ago. He said we needed a break. I expect he drove her home for a walk-around, but don't call his house and add more upset."

"Her visit isn't going well?"

Mary Jo guffaws. "The three of us can't manage her. We're makin' a hash of the job. Toni wants her back at the hospital. Aiden insists she should be with him. Rosemary spends much of her time crouched in the closet and I'm at the end of my rope. Shall I tell Aiden you called?"

Chapter 13

You Are Too Suspicious

One wing of Harbour Manor is devoted to administration offices. She walks past a small meeting space where the Board of Directors congregates on a regular basis, before she reaches Patsy's office. Stella hasn't seen Patsy since she made the arrangements for her father in late 1978. In Norbert Kirk's case, he was assessed by the provincial government as requiring care. He is responsible for a monthly room and board charge equivalent to his Old Age Pension. Stella receives an invoice each month, which includes an extra amount for his private room. He has no other income sources. The necessary funds are taken from his meagre savings and, in the end, will come out of Stella's own pocket, and Trixie's, as well. Today, she wants to learn how accounts are managed for people with minimal resources and who are not subsidized by the province—Jasper Nunn, for example.

Light spills into the corridor from Patsy's office. Considering the length of the hall and the absence of humanity in the shadowed space, Stella appreciates the comptroller's wish for openness. She taps on the door casing. A halo of Shirley-Temple-style red curls bobs from across the room.

"Hi, Patsy. Stella Kirk here. Remember me?"

"Absolutely. Norbert Kirk's older daughter. Problem with the bill?" Her expression is open and welcoming.

"No, Patsy. I'm here as part of the investigation into a body found when crews dug Mallory Gorman's grave."

"Yes. Caleb Hall often wanders this way for a visit, and he told me. Said you think you've identified the man in the hole, now."

Avoiding direct chatter about the case, Stella jumps straight to the topic at hand. "Can we discuss financial options when someone chooses residency at Harbour Manor? My father was assessed as needing nursing home care, but what about people in similar circumstances to Jasper Nunn, who don't qualify but live here anyway for the food and the company?"

"Can't be specific." She sweeps an arm through the air. "Perch someplace." The boxy space is piled high with file folders and papers. Keeping this office in business has required the sacrifice of a forest of trees. Patsy's desk and the credenza behind her are stacked a foot deep. "Bad time." She gestures at the chaos. "Year-end on the horizon. Filing has no advantage." She points at a chair in the corner and snickers. "Hand me those files and I'll explain the concept of private-pay."

Stella does as she's told and positions herself in the now empty chair. Patsy drops the paperwork on the floor. The top folders slide sideways. She ignores them, plops plump elbows on her desk, and meets Stella's eyes.

"Private-pay residents move into Harbour Manor for different reasons, although they must be over sixty-five to qualify. Men come because their wife died, and they can't fend for themselves or live with family; women more often because they need the company of others. They may sell their house and the nest egg covers their care. Once they become infirm and are unable to manage without help, or they lack mental capacity, Maura organizes an assessment by the government, and they're switched into the public-pay column. The province subsidizes them, except for their Old Age Pension, and they are billed for any extras—the private room, in your father's case."

"And if they run out of funds before their health deteriorates to the point where they become eligible for financial support?"

Patsy's red curls tremble. "My heart breaks. Residents arrive in my office frantic—no clue what's next. We're discouraged from recommending options. I keep a list of four boarding homes for seniors and I provide the names when someone asks." She adopts a stern expression. "I don't show favouritism and I don't discuss money. I'm also aware of a few people who take in one elder at a time. They're on the list as well."

"You never suggest a spot."

"No exceptions." Her gaze challenges. "And I make a point of not documenting what different places charge. I supply the names on the QT, if you understand." She closes her eyes for a moment.

"Jasper Nunn, or any resident in such circumstances, could receive a copy of the list from you and choose based on his resources and the boarding home fees."

"Correct, although Jasper closed his account but required no information from me."

"And Willy Saunders?"

"This conversation is out of bounds, Stella, but Willy paid her bill and left, same as Jasper. She never mentioned financial issues. I assumed she was in dire straits, though. She refused an assessment when I asked if we should request the government be involved. I expected she would qualify for subsidization." Patsy removes her tortoise shell reading glasses and tosses them toward a pile of papers nearby. "I shouldn't answer your questions, but I'm worried. Willy was fading."

"What about her mail? Her cheque came here, right? No other relatives?"

"Correct. She signed over her Old Age Pension and wrote another cheque for the difference."

"Who collects the Harbour Manor correspondence?"

"Jack Lawson drops off mail most of the time. Maura employs her on a shoestring for other errands, too."

"Ira Gold never lived at Harbour Manor?"

"Never."

"The information you've shared today is much appreciated, Patsy, and I understand the sensitive nature of what you do." Stella stands. "I needed clarification of the process. I've spoken with Jasper, and he explained the details once he moved into Merlon's."

Patsy's chubby face clouds. She doesn't respond.

"I'll check with Maura. Maybe she re-directed mail straight from the post office."

Harbour Manor's comptroller retrieves her glasses, adjusts them on the end of her nose, pats her curls, and studies a piece of paper in front of her. "Good luck, Stella. Great chatting with you."

****

"The Family and Friends Christmas Party is tonight, and I can't make time for you today. You didn't call."

Stella refrained from announcing her arrival on purpose. She wanted to catch Maura off guard. The nurse runs from reception into the lounge, then toward

Dewey Laird's room where she asks him for help with the lights. She dashes to answer the door where she accepts packages for a resident, then she runs back into the staff room to corral Lulu, and finally off into the corridor again.

"One or two quick questions, Maura," Stella puffs as she follows. "I visited with Patsy…."

Maura stops in her tracks and turns. "Why did you interview Patsy? She doesn't involve herself with residents."

"I want a clear picture about how payments work for people without a government assessment—the private-pay guests."

"They are given a bill and they pay. Stop your search for problems where none exist." She bustles along the hall again. "Will you be at the party later today? Your father won't care one way or the other."

The slur doesn't go unnoticed, but Stella soldiers on. "Stand still for a moment, Maura."

Nurse Martin stops. "Ask your questions. Food must be organized, and staff given directions. Our Christmas gathering is a big event. I'm busy." She crosses her arms and taps her foot.

"Patsy said Jack collects the mail."

"Correct. Why?"

"People in situations comparable to Jasper and Willy no doubt need help when their personal resources are depleted. You help." A statement, not a question.

"Oh, Stella. You make the financial part of our job sound sinister. We often assist residents with their banking. Many private-pay guests receive help from family, who are forwarded the invoice and cover the monthly bill. Others sign over their Old Age Pension cheque and write the manor a cheque for the difference. I sometimes took Jasper and Willy into the Savings and Loan, myself." She juts her chin in Stella's direction. "It's kindness, Stella… helping people with no support. You are too suspicious." Her tone becomes one of someone focused on a person with challenges in comprehension. "I'm in a helping profession. I help people."

Maura resumes her mission and immediately bangs into Dewey when she rushes around the corner. "Dewey, for God's sake, careful. You almost bowled me over."

"Sorry, Nurse Martin. I'll finish my exercises before I hang the lights. Running late." He glances at Stella. "I reviewed my diaries in case I found more machinery noises."

Stella lifts her brows in response.

He frowns. "No luck, but I tried." He pats Maura on the shoulder and races off, resembling an Olympic power walker preparing for the next games.

"Are we done here? I hope your sister and her family drop in for fruitcake and a visit with your father. I don't suppose you'll bother before you leave."

Is my lip bleeding? I must've bitten through it by now. "Maura, please be patient. Since you receive the mail from Jack, and Patsy never saw cheques for Willy or Jasper after they left, did you, in fact, forward them? Jasper moved to Merlon's, and I believe you were aware, but didn't tell me when I asked."

"Confidentiality." They are now stopped in front of Eula and Addie's room.

"Stella, do I hear your voice?" Eula sings out her question.

Maura trots in. "What can I do for you ladies today?"

"Addie and I want a visit with Stella. We see you all the time, Maura." A wave of the old lady's arm dismisses the nurse.

"There are a couple more questions I have for Nurse Martin. I'll come back, Eula." Stella catches Maura on her way along the hall toward the nurses' station.

"I thought we were done." She focuses on the tile floor. "Yes, I forwarded Jasper's mail. Willy obviously handled her own because I never saw hers. No more, Stella. I must work, and your questions are inappropriate in the first place." She glances at the date written on the blackboard in the hall. "Thank God. Only two shifts left and I'm on vacation until January 4th." Her smile is weak. "Time for a break."

"Who covers for you, Maura?"

"Olive works days. Deal with her." She turns with a swish and disappears.

Back with Eula and Addie, settled in their matching gliders, she assures them she will be at the party later in the afternoon.

"We loved seeing Jasper the other day. Addie and I thank you for your help. You found him and brought him for a visit." Her smile could light a room. "I hope you can drive Jasper over here again soon."

"He wasn't lost, Eula. He moved into Merlon's Place," Stella reiterates, with patience.

Addie's hands flounder in her lap before she turns to Eula.

"Your father has been pretty good the last week. Did you see him today?"

125

"No. I'll pop in before I go home, Eula, but he doesn't know me."

"You know him." Her soft voice settles in the quiet room.

****

"Hi, Norbert. Ready for the party tonight?"

The old man turns in his chair and squints. "What party? Is Nick throwin' a party?"

She swallows. "The manor's Christmas party is tonight, and Nick and I are invited. Trixie, Brigitte, and Mia will be here, too."

"Right. Any presents?"

"I think Santa might bring one for you from your family." She attempts a tease.

"Okay. What did they buy me?"

"Not a clue, Norbert."

"See ya later." The swivel recliner spins toward the window.

On her drive home, she focuses on payments, cheques, and residents' mail. What happened with Willy's mail if Harbour Manor never forwarded it? Maura lied about Jasper, where he moved, and his money. Maybe her lies continue. Recollections of Eula's soft voice and the sympathetic expression on Addie's face derail her theorizing. Poor Addie. She's unable to express herself with words anymore, but she understands. Eula's remark had a kernel of truth, and Addie pushed her into voicing their thoughts. Norbert is her father, and the fact he can't remember her doesn't mean she doesn't remember him. Lessons learned today.

She pulls into the back lot. Time to get ready.

****

Trixie calls before Stella has finished dressing. "When will you be at the nursing home?"

"The invitation said after four." She checks the clock radio. "Ten of, now. Nick's downstairs. We'll leave in a few minutes. You?"

"Yellow House is open until four-thirty, but we're organized. I'll see you soon. And his present?"

"Wrapped and waiting—a brand new bathrobe in Nick's favourite colour, plaid."

"Good. Gotta go." She disconnects.

Stella adds a pair of gold hoops and makes her way downstairs toward the kitchen. Before she enters, she hears Nick in deep conversation with Kiki.

"Okay, little one. You stay here in your bed tonight. We won't be gone long. I turned on the electric heat. You ate your supper, and we went out for a quick pee."

She can see the Pomeranian cock her head and gaze at Nick.

"You'll be cozy in your new green sweater." He gives her another pat and stands. "Oh, hi. You're here."

"Didn't want to interrupt," she giggles. "Trixie will arrive after four-thirty. Brigitte has the shop open. We'll take Dad's present, since he won't be with us for Christmas Eve dinner at Yellow House. Trixie told me he'd rather stay at the manor." She shrugs. "Makes me sad, even though Dad's in a place he likes, his bills are paid, and he's happy enough. I should be satisfied."

****

Harbour Manor shines and twinkles in the fading light as they park the Jeep. Christmas music floats through the open door while they wait for another family, who arrived before them, to squirm their way inside. With her father's present under one arm, and holding Nick's hand, they enter the foyer. "I want Trixie and her girls here before we give Dad his parcel. Let's leave his gift with Del."

"Hi, Del. Party time."

"Not to sound ungrateful, but I hope your package isn't for me." Del is decked out in her signature Breton hat, only this one is bright red with a white feather in the band. Her dress is long, black, and covered in tiny sparkles. Her shawl matches her hat. "Eve came in earlier, helped me dress, and left me a stack of stuff. She's on holiday from school and said she'd be back later with her mother."

"No, the present is for Dad, but Trixie hasn't arrived yet. You look stunning, by the way."

"Just drop his present on the bed and return whenever. Thanks for the compliment. I think I can still turn a head or two. Mr. Cochran," she titters, as she looks at Nick and winks. "Can you escort an old lady into the lounge?"

"With pleasure, Mrs. Trembly." He holds her arm as she stands. Stella walks behind them.

The total population of the nursing home seems to be crowded inside the common room. Addie and Eula, in Christmas corsages, sit together on a sofa. The bridge club members are each in V-neck sweaters over white shirts and sport holiday-themed ties. Dewey, adorned in a lighted contraption which resembles antlers, buzzes around with his camera. The tree reaches the ceiling. Connie Gee and Miriam Sylvester are both in wheelchairs in one corner. Miriam snuggles under a colourful Christmas throw.

"Miriam, your coverlet is gorgeous," Stella swoons.

"William sent it from Alberta." She pats her gift with a crooked hand.

"You remember my sister, Tess Boone?" Connie introduces Tess to Stella.

Stella nods. "We met not long ago, right here, and you were at the writers retreat, correct?"

"Yes. I'm a friend of Frances Ellis. Known her for years." She waves in a dismissive gesture. "I fancy myself a writer but never accomplish much more than a paragraph or a poem."

Connie's head rolls behind the scarf, which holds her upright, as she focuses on Stella once more. "Tess is a fabulous author. I told her, if she wants a story, help me tell mine." She stops for breath. "Alas, she won't be bribed or enticed," she gulps.

Tess pats her sister's leg. "I can't document your struggles, Connie, and we've discussed this before. Now, shall I find a few sandwiches for you two girls, or do I make for the sweets table?"

"Sweets," they sing, in unison.

Tess waves at Stella as she elbows her way toward the buffet.

Stella leaves the two women and heads for the bridge club, but Trixie grabs her sleeve. "We're here. Where's Dad?"

"Still in his room. You guys go while I find Nick and fetch the present."

As Nick and Stella enter Norbert's room, he has his arms wrapped around Brigitte while he holds Mia on his knee. The child plays her part and prattles away. Neither pays the least attention to what the other says. Stella hands the parcel over to Trixie.

"You made the purchase. Give it to him," she hisses.

"No. Better you."

"Here's your present from Santa, Dad."

Brigitte lifts Mia off Norbert. He tears into the paper, rips open the box, and discovers a red plaid flannel bathrobe. He struggles to his feet and asks Nick for help to put the garment on.

"Perfect fit," Nick compliments, before he offers his help to take it off.

"Not a chance, my boy. My new robe is comin' with me. He leaves his family in his wake as he struts toward the lounge with his new bathrobe over his clothes. Carols waft along the hall.

"An especially successful gift, Aunt Stella." Brigitte giggles as she leads Mia closer to the music.

Each staff member is decked out in a holiday sweater. The kitchen did a fabulous job with the buffet enjoyed by all. By seven o'clock, residents and their families are drifting toward their respective rooms.

Nick and Norbert return to Norbert's room. Trixie, Brigitte, and Mia have already said their goodbyes. Stella putters along the corridor, having a quiet exchange with any familiar resident she passes. Patsy approaches and touches her elbow. "A quick word?"

"Sure. Here?"

"No. There's an empty room near your father. Most people won't pay the up charge for a single. As a result, the manor has vacancies. Here we go." She leads Stella inside and shuts the door with an unnerving firmness.

"I withheld a piece of information today and have since reconsidered. I won't become involved, though. Please understand, I can't lose my job." Her red curls wobble. "After Willy Saunders approached me and paid her last bill, her government pension arrived with the others. With no forwarding address, I held it until Maura returned the next week. When I asked her for an address, she said she would send the cheque to Willy."

The quiet of the empty room provides clarity. Maura has lied again and knows where Willy Saunders lives.

Chapter 14

Too Many Questions

Copies of their partnership agreement, plus the related documents for the sale of Trixie's shares in the company, litter her desk. Their lawyer, Andrea Picard, sent the papers by messenger yesterday morning while Stella visited at the manor. Andrea requested they review the file in preparation for the formal signing and transfer on New Year's Eve. Nick scanned the lot and said he saw no problems, suggesting she should do the same. Trixie's money rests in trust with Andrea, which makes December 31, 1981, a mere formality.

Responsibility weighs heavily as she peruses each piece of paper, aware of how stressful the task became before she sorted her finances—but her thoughts stray. Rosemary has been home for two days. A final debriefing between herself and Aiden is scheduled for later today. She jots a list of loose ends: what did the police discover regarding hospital admissions from Merlon's on or about December 15, 1979? Who owns JanlonNS? Has N. S. Social Services been contacted? Do they report assessment requirements for residents at Merlon's and Jane's? She rubs the back of her neck. Too many questions.

At least she made progress on the backhoe puzzle this morning. Once she located the Port Heavy Equipment Rental and Storage phone number, she called. The owner, identifying himself as Lonnie, confirmed he stores a small digger for Royalty Funeral Services, as he did for the previous owners. He agreed to see her.

"The papers appear fine, Nick." He's in the kitchen with Kiki, making bread. The smell of the activated yeast tickles her nostrils. "I'm off to the Port for a quick interview with Lonnie from Port Heavy Equipment Rental and Storage. Do we need more flour?" She leans against the door casing and watches him while she teases.

When he turns, he has a swipe of the white stuff on his nose. "I think I've made enough for Christmas. I wanted a few extra buns for Brigitte." His face is flushed. "She and her mother do a masterful job for their Christmas Eve spread and I wanted to contribute."

"Great idea." She sidles across the kitchen and kisses him goodbye. "I'll be back for lunch. Before I go, do you know Lonnie, the guy who owns the storage yard?"

"Not a clue."

"He sounds cooperative enough, but if he's good friends with Luther, I might encounter resistance." Her jaw is set. "I'm off."

"Be careful. Want company?"

"Always, but I'll be fine."

She jumps into her coat, shoves her feet into boots, grabs her shoulder bag, and makes her way along the slippery veranda. The Jeep sits near the stairs. Wind whips the vehicle when she motors over the isthmus. She finds Port Heavy Equipment Rental and Storage at the edge of the community—a ramshackle two-story metal-clad warehouse erected in the middle of a large gravel parking lot. Machines of various descriptions, from trucks with flatbed trailers to graders, front-end-loaders, and backhoes, sit scattered around the perimeter, framed by an eight-foot chain-link fence. The tall overhead garage door stands open and Stella parks off to the side.

Stepping into the murky interior, she's confronted by a dilapidated dump truck, the hood pulled forward far enough to rest near the cement floor. "Hello. Lonnie?"

"You found me," Lonnie chuckles, as he pops out from deep within the motor compartment. He must be forty but stuck in the 1960s with a full-on Beatles haircut and a tie-dyed T-shirt. "Give me two secs." The garage owner crawls over the side of the truck and slides along the fender until his feet connect with the cement. He wipes his hands with a greasy rag and makes a slight bow in Stella's direction. "I'd shake your hand, but...," he smirks and flutters his filthy mitts. "You said on the phone Royalty's machine has come up in an investigation?"

"Right, Lonnie. I work as a consultant for the RCMP, and we want confirmation of the whereabouts of Royalty Funeral Services' equipment—it would have been owned by Port Ephron Funeral Home at the time—on December 15, 1979."

"Follow me." He leads her into a cluttered and dirty office, which contains a scarred wooden desk, a Coke machine, and access to a bathroom. The scent of urinal cakes, their disinfectant properties soon to expire, permeates the confined space. "I'll go upstairs and find the file."

Happy she chose jeans for the occasion, Stella perches on a brown metal chair. He returns, dressed in a grey hoodie, with a manila folder clutched in damp hands. She expects he washed while in his private quarters above. No surprise he didn't use the office bathroom.

"Here we are. Port Ephron Funeral Home, now Royalty Funeral Services, December 1979. Did you say the fifteenth?"

She nods.

"We parked their machine at the edge of the new graveyard. Two years ago, they called the area 'the field behind the Shale Harbour Graveyard'."

"Did the driver wait?"

"No. The work-order directions state: off-load and go back on the seventeenth for a reload and return delivery. Before you ask, the job occurred as requested. The extra day happened because the sixteenth fell on Sunday. Luther Greene came in on Monday and paid the bill in cash."

"I assume your employee never saw Luther operating the machine."

"He took the digger to the site, unloaded, and fetched it two days later. No Luther." He replaces the papers in the file. "Are we done? Gotta finish that truck so I can lock up by noon, and my vacation can start."

"Yes. I appreciate your cooperation."

"Vic Staples found a body out in the new graveyard the first of the month, right? Did Luther Greene bury someone back two years ago?"

Stella swallows a gasp. Lonnie has expressed aloud what she believes. "No idea, Lonnie. A witness heard machinery noises on the evening of December 15, 1979, and the digger you delivered might be the culprit." She glances toward the line of limp, and flickering, coloured lights framing the lone window. "Not long before the big day. Happy Christmas, Lonnie, and thanks again."

****

She answers the kitchen phone while she sips rooibos tea. She wrapped Nick's new book, Ken Follett's *The Key to Rebecca*, while he and Kiki walked around the park. Mia's dress snuggles in a box full of tissue and she can't wait for the expression on her great-niece's face.

"Stella."

"Hi, Aiden. Rosemary's visit working out thus far?"

"No."

"Tell me." She frowns.

"We've failed to entice her out of the front hall closet most of the time."

"You guys should call someone."

A dull cough rattles in her ear. "Everyone is exhausted, but her sisters think it's important she spend Christmas with them, and we'll decide afterward. We initially planned she would visit until the third, but I'm doubtful." His words tumble on top of each other. "Honestly, Stella. I found a dog on the side of the road, once. Hit by a car. The incident happened years ago. I tried to pick him up and take him to the vet. He used every ounce of energy in his battered little body to bite me. I sat beside him while he died. Rosemary fights us the same way that poor pup struggled. She can't see we desperately want to help her."

Stella remains quiet. He doesn't need kind words. He needs a listener.

"I told them I wanted a shower and a change of clothes. I thought I'd talk with you before I go back. This call will be the last time you hear from me until Rosemary leaves."

"You've decided on readmission?"

"No choice," he sputters, before changing the subject. "Any updates?"

"Did you find any information on JanlonNS?" She answers a question with one of her own.

"No one's proceeded with that line of inquiry. Expect more after the holidays. We determined no Ira Gold was admitted to hospital on or around December 15, 1979, though. Hospital administrative staff were cooperative. They said they treated no head injuries the month of December 1979."

"I interviewed the owner of Port Heavy Equipment Rental and Storage, Lonnie, earlier. He could be a leftover from the era of the Beatles before Sergeant Pepper." Stella giggles. "He found the file and confirmed Luther scheduled the funeral home digger for a delivery on December 15, 1979, and retrieval on December 17. The driver off-loaded the machine at the edge of the field, which has now been turned into the graveyard expansion. His instructions were on the work order, and he noted he didn't see Luther. On the seventeenth, Monday, Luther stopped at the garage and paid the bill in cash."

"Perhaps Luther Greene buried Ira Gold after Guy Boucher whacked him in the altercation at Merlon's, although how did they carry the body out of the house? If my memory serves me, Caleb has no knowledge of what happened after the incident. Staff told him Ira was admitted to hospital, and he believed them. Correct?"

"Yes. We met another resident at Merlon's who has his faculties and has been a boarder since before December 1979. Do you remember Horace? I should make a Christmas visit with homemade cookies for the old guys. What do you think? When Elsie took us around, she did the talking."

"Do what you're able." His breaths are shallow. "I won't be much help until January. Sorry. Must run. Mary Jo and Toni will wonder why I've been in the shower for an hour. I'll call if I can."

Left holding the bag again, after the RCMP relieved her of her duties at the end of the last investigation, Stella pauses and reassesses whether she should become more involved while Aiden remains on leave. Curiosity wins. When they visited Merlon's, Horace peered at her as if he had more on his mind. With a plate of cookies and Nick in tow, she might secure an opportunity for a chat with the old man.

She hears the door bang before Nick and Kiki make their way into the kitchen. "Good walk?"

Kiki answers with grunts and wiggles, excited for a dog cookie, ultimately proving her worth.

"Great, but windy. You?" He bends and kisses her cheek.

"Aiden called. They're in trouble with Rosemary, but I have a question—two, in fact. Will you fix an electric clothes dryer on Christmas Eve eve, and is there butter and icing sugar in the house?"

Nick plugs in the kettle before he sits beside her at the table. "I can repair most dryers. Even kept a few spare parts for any work in our camp laundry. Do you remember, when I first arrived here, you owned four washers and four dryers in your laundromat, and one of each worked? They run now. And the pantry is full of baking supplies. What's your scheme?"

"The dryer over at Merlon's Place for Gentlemen was out of commission when we completed interviews a week ago. With luck, the unit still doesn't work. I'll take the old fellows a box of shortbread cookies while you keep Elsie and Helga busy in the laundry room."

"You think I can keep the help occupied?"

"If you wear those tight jeans you said were too small," she hoots.

"Oh! Pimping is part of your investigation?" He attempts a pout, before he admits with reluctance, "I admire your style."

****

Making shortbread cookies can't be difficult. Her mother made them every Christmas when they were children. She scrounges in the pantry for the stained and chipped recipe card box used by Dorothy Kirk many years ago. Her mother wrote each set of instructions, in her cramped hand, on an index card and filed them in alphabetical order. Although a baker of the basics and not much else, Stella treasures the box—sentimental? Regardless of the current circumstances, she continues to consider this space to be Dorothy's kitchen.

The butter sits on the counter and softens. She assembles her ingredients—icing sugar, white flour, salt, and baking powder. How complicated can the process be? She sets the oven to three hundred and fifty degrees.

"Need an assistant or two?" Nick and Kiki wander in from the living room.

She takes a breath. "Your company works. Tool kit ready?"

He nods. "What's wrong with the dryer?"

"No idea. Helga said the dryer didn't work and Elsie needs to hang the clothes outside." She creams the butter with her hand mixer and adds the icing sugar, a quarter of a cup at a time, while Nick steps in and holds the bowl.

"Maybe an appliance guy fixed their machine by now. You could call and ask."

Waving the buttery beaters in his direction, she exclaims, "Ah, but we require the element of surprise. Elsie never provided the opportunity for us to talk with the men alone when Aiden and I visited. In hindsight, I believe she was afraid we'd discover Jasper Nunn bunked in one of the rooms. My goal is resident interviews without staff present. Horace has been at Merlon's for five years." She mixes the flour, salt, and baking powder in a metal bowl.

"No need for your involvement, Stella." His eyes are dark.

She nods and elevates her voice above the rattle of the mixer while she blends the dry ingredients with the butter and sugar. He continues to hold the bowl. "I've missed a piece of information, Nick. I can't tease out the problem, but the hospital says they never treated a man named Ira Gold for a head injury on the dates suggested, and there's no death record." She stops and turns off the mixer for a moment, lowering her voice back to normal. "Luther Greene borrowed the funeral home's digger and instructed delivery to the edge of the field—now the new graveyard." She resumes beating.

"You assume Luther Greene buried Ira Gold, and for two years no one noticed him gone? Explain why Luther sticks his neck out and performs an illegal act for Merlon's Place?"

"Someone ordered him. He's Hector Greene's nephew. Hector and Maura Martin are married." She stops mixing, satisfied with the consistency, and surprised the dough resembles her mother's version.

"Didn't you say Ira Gold never lived at the manor?"

"Right. Will you find the cookie cutter in the junk drawer—the tree-shaped one?"

****

The cookies, baked to golden blond perfection and nestled in a small box lined with both wax and tissue paper, are secured on the back seat. Nick's toolbox is loaded. After they settle Kiki, they're off to visit Merlon's Place for Gentlemen.

Three separate knocks are required before Helga answers. "Good afternoon. Stella Kirk, right? What do you want? I am supervisor for next four days and busy, busy."

"Hi, Helga. Wonderful to see you again. Merry Christmas. My partner Nick Cochran," she nods at Nick while he beams his most infectious smile, "and I are here with cookies for the men and assistance for you."

"Help for me?" She glances at the toolbox.

"Miss Helga, I understand your dryer is on the fritz. I'm kinda handy and thought I might fix the problem for ya."

Her eyes widen. "You can repair appliances? Why do this for Merlon's Place?"

"Christmas." Stella hastens to add, "May we come in?"

"Please. The weather is cold and hard for hanging out clothes."

"Show me the way, Miss Helga." Nick turns and winks at Stella.

"I'll take the cookies upstairs for the men." Helga doesn't hear or notice. She's too busy as she bustles Nick toward the laundry facilities.

****

She discovers the four residents—Cecil, Fred, Horace, and Jasper—in Horace and Cecil's room. Fred is telling a story and describing how funny his wife was. As she peeks inside, Fred's eyes are brimmed with tears. Jasper notices her first.

"Good afternoon, Miss Kirk. How did you creep up those stairs before Helga caught you?" He chuckles and glances at the other men.

"Helga and my partner, Nick, are deep in the throes of clothes dryer repair. She'll be busy for a while."

"I hoped you might come back. Elsie doesn't let us talk." Horace peers at her with milky eyes.

"What's in the box?" Jasper isn't shy with his questions.

"Shortbread cookies. I made them fresh today." She hands her efforts to Jasper, who opens the lid with exaggerated care, and stares inside.

"They are almost too pretty to eat." He lifts one out of the box for himself and gives a second to Cecil before he passes them to Horace and Fred.

Each man enjoys a cookie before Horace clears his throat. "I lived here when Guy Boucher hit Ira Gold with one of them exercise weights. Those stupid barbells. He carried one around with him and put it on the table when we ate."

"Tell Miss Kirk the entire story," Jasper encourages.

"The reason I'm here." Stella nods her encouragement in Horace's direction. "Take your time."

"Crazy Guy. He picked fights. Caleb could keep him under control, but not that day. They lived in the room next door and came in here one afternoon before Christmas. Ira asked Guy to leave his weights in his own room because he was scared of Guy's temper. Guy flew off the handle and lambasted Ira upside his head. Poor old Ira dropped like a stone." He nibbles on his second cookie.

"What happened afterward?"

"Elsie said Guy knocked Ira out."

"We wanted her to call an ambulance. We saw blood on the floor." He glances down. "The spot stained the boards. Covered by a rug, now. She sent Caleb and Guy back to their room and shut the door. She called someone who came and helped her with Ira. They took him to the hospital."

"Who arrived?"

"Two men—one younger and one older. Elsie shuffled me off into Caleb and Guy's room, but I flat-out refused because of Guy. She put me in the empty room where Helga sleeps now. I watched with the door ajar. Helga's only worked here a year," he clarifies.

"Elsie told you they took him to the hospital?"

"Right. They boxed his stuff. Guy left and Caleb soon after."

"Do you remember other residents?"

"Sure. Lloyd and Weldon both lived here. They were sick in the night. Elsie said they went to hospital, but they never came back." He reaches over and pats Cecil's veined and chapped hand. "Cecil here's good company."

"And Fred and me, we're both in fair health. The four of us will be around for a few days yet," Jasper adds, in a soft voice.

They hear heavy thuds on the stairs as Helga thumps her way toward the second floor.

"Thanks, fellas. Enjoy the cookies. Don't broadcast our conversation," Stella whispers.

Jasper and Horace both put fingers on lips while Fred gives her a thumbs-up sign.

"My dryer works, Miss Kirk, because of your handsome partner. He said the machine needed a new on and off button. The old one didn't catch?" She shrugs. "What did he do? I don't know." She shrugs again, her indifference palpable. "No more frozen clothes to drag off the line, though. He's putting his tools away now." She surveys the four men.

Stella imagines she sees a glimmer of affection.

"Only family allowed visits with residents alone, but you brought cookies." She displays a forgiving and toothy grin. "Okay, I guess." She helps herself and drops crumbs on the carpet as she munches. "Good. Very good."

Chapter 15

The Tide Sneaks Its Way to High

Snowflakes the size of a puppy's paw take their time floating toward the ground. Even the light breeze doesn't knock them off course. Stella stands by the kitchen window, a pottery mug of cranberry tea held near her nose, watching. Storms approach, rain pummels, heat rolls off the land, wind whips—the norm for a coastal dweller. Today, the gods grace her with a magnificent spectacle: her image filled with white one-of-a-kind miracles.

"Are you ready for a play with Mia, Kiki?"

Kiki pricks her ears and tilts her tiny face.

"We'll go in the car to Mia's house for Christmas Eve supper." She bends and pats Kiki before she rinses her mug and taps her leg for the dog, who follows her upstairs.

As she trots along behind, Kiki's nails click on the floor.

Nick emerges from the shower, damp and flushed from the hot water.

"Aren't you a sexy sight? We should skip dinner and stay home." Heat floods her cheeks. She's succeeded in embarrassing herself, as usual.

"Whatever you say, my love, but I imagine one Trixie Kirk will turn up and fetch us in a matter of minutes, if we don't arrive at Yellow House on time."

"Correct. Clothes." She opens her closet door and peruses the various options inside. "I'll miss Dad tonight."

"Your father is drifting further out to sea, Stella. I noticed another change on Monday when we visited. He doesn't mention the park anymore, and I know his recollection of Trixie is vague now." As he dons a plaid shirt, he adds, "Norbert still has room in his poor, withered brain for Brigitte and Mia, though."

Stella reaches for black palazzo pants and a creamy cotton sweater with black polka dots. There are few occasions when she wears pretty clothes. She almost forgets how. The red crystal drops—her mother's—will work in her ears tonight. "Let's encourage Brigitte to take Mia for a visit with her great granddad more often." She turns toward her lover, while she blinks the mist from her eyes.

They stand opposite and survey each other. "We present well enough to leave the property," Stella giggles. "And you, Miss Kiki? Does your new green sweater fit the bill?"

Kiki chases her tail in response, at which point Nick scoops her into his arms. "We're due by four. We might be punctual."

She has assembled their gifts on the dining room table, ready for loading into the Jeep—Nick's homemade buns, the box with Mia's dress snuggled in tissue, and two bottles of Trixie's favourite white wine. They unplug the tree lights, turn on the porch light, and begin the short trip.

Fat and fluffy snowflakes continue floating down, contacting the windshield as splats of slush. They take their time crossing the isthmus. The tide sneaks its way to high.

****

Yellow House shimmers with electric candelabra in every window and the bushes in the front sparkle with coloured lights. Mia and Carter answer the door. Brigitte has followed instructions. Mia, dressed in play clothes, holds Carter's hand, and squeals with delight when she spies Kiki under Stella's arm. The old banister dazzles, wrapped in garland and ribbon, and smelling of pine.

"Come in, folks. Gonna turn into a nasty night." Carter pushes the door open and widens the space as they struggle inside. Once Kiki's paws hit the floor, she dashes with Mia into the kitchen. "Let me take your coats—and the wine," he blusters.

Nick hands Mia's present to Stella and they follow Carter through the bookstore to access the family room at the back. "I brought you and your mother buns, Brigitte. Made them yesterday. Hi everyone," he adds.

Stella surveys the gathering.

Trixie glitters in a sequined shell paired with a floor-length midnight-blue velvet skirt. Her silky strawberry-blond hair, which Stella has coveted throughout their lives, sits piled on the top of her head in contrived disarray. She sports a Christmas apron wrapped around her still small waist. The

Gothic letters spell Christmas Glammy.

Struck by the change in her sister, Stella attempts quiet analysis. Trixie has hosted Christmas Eve dinner since Stella moved home to Shale Harbour. Despite her financial ill-fortunes, she insisted she prepare and present the complete meal—no offers of help accepted. She showed she could be the one in control, the one in the giving position, once each year. Now, her demonstrations of her capabilities will be limitless if she desires. She won't be forced to depend on a low-wage job and a cheque each month from Shale Cliffs RV Park.

Trixie turns toward Nick and accepts his offer with a flourish. Light from the tree reflects in the glitter of her tank top. Her face flushes with excitement and confidence. "I hope you people brought your appetites. I think we've assembled enough food for Main Street."

Brigitte giggles at her mother. "We don't need introductions, do we?"

"No way," Carter shouts from the back porch, where he's taken the wine to chill in Brigitte's second fridge.

Val Reguly, settled on the kitchen couch, stands, and shakes Nick's hand. "Nasty storm comin'."

"Aunt Stella, you and Mom take Mia upstairs." She winks.

"Good idea! Mia, this is a present for you. Let's go find out what's in this box."

Mia turns toward her grandmother.

"I'll come, too, munchkin."

They scramble into Mia's room. Stella absorbs the space. She will not be side-tracked by recollections of Paulina—how she and Hester searched closets, touched clothes, and snooped inside the drawers of her bedside tables. She blinks and focuses on her great-niece.

The child's eyes widen. "Can I look?"

Stella sets the box on Mia's bed, opens the top, and peels back the layers of tissue. "What do you think?"

Mia lifts one pudgy hand and touches the soft folds.

"Aunt Stella brought you a party dress, Mia. Let's take off your play clothes and check the fit."

Mia struggles with her shirt, complicating the act of undressing as any four-year-old can manage. Trixie finds white socks and black patent shoes.

Mia holds both arms in the air while Stella lowers the dress over her head.

Mia wiggles around so the buttons in the back can be fastened. She stands in front of the mirror, eyes wide.

"Fabulous, little one." Stella swallows back tears.

"Thank you, Aunt Stella." The little girl surprises both women when she pulls *The Velveteen Rabbit*—last year's gift—from her bookcase. "Read?" she asks as she approaches Stella. "Let's read."

"We'll take the book downstairs, Mia. You model your new dress for Mommy and eat your supper. We'll read later, okay?"

Mia pouts, but not for long. She's not a child given to dramatics. Stella stands on the top step and watches her hold the banister in one hand and her book in the other while she navigates the stairs. Trixie lifts the child's skirt to prevent a fall. By the time Stella re-enters the kitchen, Mia is twirling in the middle of the floor as Kiki spins and barks beside her.

Not to be outdone, Trixie steps forward with a parcel wrapped in tissue. "Hey, Bug, what's in here?"

Kiki pricks her ears and trots toward Trixie.

"Such a plain green sweater," she simpers. "You need more fashionable attire." From the paper, she reveals a pure white turtleneck, covered in sequins and matching her own top, if one were inclined to compare.

Everybody claps while Trixie manhandles the little dog out of one sweater and into the other. She leans back and admires the result with a crisp nod. "Perfect fit." She turns toward Stella. "Has she eaten, or may I give her turkey tonight?"

"Oh no. I put kibble and her dish in my bag." Stella lifts her brows at the group. "Never thought you'd find me with dog food in my purse."

****

The evening proves exhaustingly wonderful. Stella observes how Val helps Trixie at every turn; how Carter focuses on Mia while he keeps Brigitte within sight. They eat, drink wine, and relax with tea. Brigitte sits in the rocker by the tree and reads to Mia. The three men discuss cars, since Carter has traded his truck for a new gold Pontiac Grand Lemans. They parked behind the vehicle on the street when they arrived and wondered who the owner could be. Stella overhears Carter tell Nick and Val how he accepted delivery in Halifax because the car required a special-order. He wanted an option better suited for Mia than the middle of a bench seat in a pickup.

Trixie and Stella return upstairs. Stella assumes they'll discuss the business deal scheduled in a week. "I'm not interested in the share transfer, Stella. The process is well in hand. Carter said your lawyer in Port Ephron has the documents, and you and Nick will sign them New Year's Eve before dinner, right?"

"Correct. Two trips to the Port in one day. We meet Andrea at two o'clock and the reservations are for seven-thirty."

"Great." She brushes additional business discussion aside with a flick of her wrist. "About your investigation—I might have info." Her eyes twinkle in the light of the bedside lamp.

"Information, Trixie? What do you mean?"

"Old Age Pension cheques come earlier in December than other months. The post office was a madhouse on Tuesday. I waited until people moved out of the way before I could access our mail."

"And?"

"Jack Lawson grabbed the mail from three boxes. She took forever. I never liked her. I paid attention. There were cheques in each one. She stood at the table by the window and sorted them before she left."

"Whose mail, besides her own, did she retrieve?"

Trixie shakes her shiny curls. "I do not know," she replies, giving each word emphasis. "I will find out. Renée Tait works at the wicket, and we were in the same grade through high school. I recall the box numbers. I'll ask her."

Stella touches her sister on the arm. "Best Christmas present yet."

"You suspect whose mail she gathers, don't you?"

"If Renée won't cooperate, call me. There's another way to test my theory."

"Okay. We'd better rejoin the party."

****

Domestic bliss infuses the family room—except for Carter. Brigitte reclines in the rocker by the tree, Mia on her lap, and *The Velveteen Rabbit* open in front of them. Val and Nick are comfortable on the big kitchen sofa. Carter perches on a chair at the table. Stella notices how his knee pumps as if he can't wait, but for what, exactly?

"Hi, everyone. Stella and I needed sister time. Can I fetch anyone another drink? More tea?"

Carter stands. "Have a seat, ladies." He sounds formal. "Mia, come over here for a minute and help me surprise Mommy, okay?"

Mia scrambles off her mother and trots across the room, straight into Carter's arms. He reaches into his pocket and withdraws a small blue box. "Will you take my present to Mommy and tell her Uncle Carter has a question?"

The child toddles toward Brigitte, whose face has turned the colour of her daughter's dress. "Mommy, Uncle Carter," she turns back from where she came. Carter nods. "Uncle Carter has a question."

"Give her the present."

She holds the box in her pudgy hands.

"Stand beside her, okay?"

Stella is convinced Carter and Mia have rehearsed.

Mia twists around and clutches the arm of the rocker.

Carter approaches Brigitte and drops on one knee.

Although riveted to the scene which plays out in front of her, Stella takes a quick glance at her sister's face and sees a cloud reflected in her eyes.

"Brigitte Kirk—and Mia Kirk—will you marry me?"

"Yes!" Mia claps her hands. Kiki barks. Everyone cheers. The spell breaks while Brigitte bends and whispers "yes" in Carter's ear.

She caresses the box in anticipation. He opens it for her, removes the pear-shaped diamond solitaire, and slides his present on her finger. A perfect fit.

They spend the remainder of the evening in admiration of the ring and in congratulations for the happy couple. Mia, overtired and fading, fusses when her bedtime comes.

After a trip upstairs to tuck Mia in for the night, Brigitte returns to the kitchen. "She was asleep the minute her head touched the pillow. Thanks, everyone." She wraps an arm around Carter's shoulder while he sits in the rocker. "A memorable Christmas, for sure."

Ever the host, Carter walks Nick and Stella to the door as they prepare to leave. The snowstorm had worsened over the course of the evening. With Kiki's spare sweater and dish stashed in her handbag, they wave goodbye and dash toward the Jeep parked on the street, behind the Grand Lemans. Before they left, she whispered in her sister's ear a reminder to talk with Renée after the holidays. Carter's last communication unnerved her. He mumbled a request—for her to discuss with Trixie that the time is right for her to move out when he moves in.

****

The drive to Shale Cliffs RV Park is far worse than they anticipated. Conditions have deteriorated to blizzard proportions. Navigation of the isthmus proves not for the faint of heart. Even with the tide on the wane, water laps the sides of the road for most of the crossing. Nick swerves off the highway into the driveway which leads to the park, struggling to keep the Jeep between the ditches. Snow has drifted six inches deep near the house, and he comes to a stop as close as possible to the veranda without sliding into the steps. He turns off the ignition and faces her. Without a word, he wraps his arms around her, while Kiki remains snuggled under Stella's coat, and emits a long sigh. "I am thankful we're home, my girl. I had doubts."

"Not me." She pats him on the back. "Unshakable faith." Not true, but the right comment at the right time.

They climb the slippery stairs after Kiki takes a minute out of the wind. "Maybe a maple liqueur before bed," he puffs, as he closes the doors and turns out the porch light while she plugs in the tree lights once again.

"I'll find us a drink while you tackle the fire."

A quick five minutes pass before they curl together on the sofa. Snow whips around the house and the trees creak under the weight. "I hope no limbs fall on the house tonight," he worries out loud.

By eleven o'clock, they're snuggled in bed. Kiki snores on her pillow on the floor beside Stella. "Carter's proposal was fabulous."

"I'm pleased for him she said yes. Tough on a guy if he has an audience and the plan goes sideways."

"Trixie's face clouded for a second before she put on her best smile. Circumstances will change once Carter moves in. Did you hear his remark when we left? He's charged me with convincing Trixie to move."

Nick rubs his thumb along her shoulder. "Trixie always lands on her feet. Once she has her money, she'll decide what's best for her."

His touch distracts her, preventing a reply. She cuddles deeper under the covers and inhales the scent of him.

****

They mark their third Christmas as a couple with the exchange of books, a tradition they began in 1979, the first winter Nick spent in what was the manager's cabin at the time. They were on the edge of involvement, around the periphery—hesitant, tentative. With confidence and comfortability now, she can reflect on her reluctance in the beginning while Nick expressed his eagerness. They tried secrecy through the summer of 1980, but Alice saw through their ruse and Duke soon figured out the lay of the land as well.

Here they are on Christmas morning, curled end-for-end on a couch in front of the fire, Kiki under a blanket between them. They sip coffee doctored with more maple liqueur and thumb through books which smell papery and new. Piles of snow reach the second step on the veranda, but neither hurries to plow or shovel. No need.

The Key to Rebecca, by Ken Follett, his book from Stella, has absorbed Nick's attention. Her favourite cinnamon buns will be warmed in the oven for a mid-morning breakfast. They'll make lobster chowder for an early supper—a perfect day. She opens Carol Shield's *The Box Garden*, but her brain struggles to focus.

Trixie knows the numbers accessed when Jack Lawson collected the mail. With Christmas on a Friday, the post office is closed until Tuesday. She doesn't know if she possesses enough patience. She glances at the clock. Ten. Breakfast is finished at the boarding homes. She scrambles to her feet and trots into her office. "I'll be back in a minute," she says over her shoulder, although Nick has already dissolved into his book.

"Merlon's."

"Good morning, Helga. Stella here. Merry Christmas!"

"Same. What do you want today?"

"I need your mailing address for our records."

"Box 212. Why now?"

Stella can sense her palm, wrapped around the receiver, sweat. "Well…I wanted to wish you a Merry Christmas and wish the men the same. I thought I would find out," she babbles, "since I forgot to ask on the day I delivered the cookies."

"Your cookies were good. Happy Christmas. I'll tell the men you called."

The phone clunks in her ear, but she doesn't care. Box 212.

When she calls Jane's, the telephone rings for ages. As she decides to hang up, May answers.

"Jane's. What?"

"Hi, May. Stella Kirk, here. Merry Christmas."

"I guess. I'm awful busy. What do you want today?"

She tries creativity. "Thought I might send a thank-you card for the residents. I need your post office box number."

"Okay. Where's that letter from Flora's sister?" Paper shuffles in her ear. "Oh, here. Box 113. Now I gotta go, Stella, and don't bother with a card. Most of the girls won't give a rat's ass."

Stella frowns at the dead receiver in her hand. Although the rudeness annoys her, mission accomplished. Boxes 212 and 113.

Nick trudges into her office. "Ready for more coffee and a cinnamon bun? Thought I'd scramble eggs, too."

"Perfect. I want to talk with Trixie, but I'll come help in a minute."

"Good morning. Yellow House. Merry Christmas."

"Trixie. Hi."

"You sound excited. Did Nick present you with a diamond for Christmas?"

Stella ignores the tinge of jealousy in her voice. "No, a book. We exchange books, Trixie. You know our tradition. What did Val give you?"

"A clip for my hair." She inhales. "A nice enough gift, but I guess Carter wins the prize."

"You don't sound pleased."

"What about me? I will not, repeat—will not—move into Val's basement suite with him, and I can't stay here anymore."

"Buy your own place and visit Yellow House when Brigitte needs help with Mia. After the end of the year, you can afford whatever you want. Your best friend works as a realtor, don't forget."

Silence. "Why did you call, Stella? We never talk on Christmas morning."

"Did you write down the box numbers Jack Lawson accessed on Tuesday?"

"Wait a sec. I jotted them on a slip of paper after we talked. Here: 212, 113, 422 and 100."

Her insides vibrate as she pants her response. "Trixie, 212 and 113 are the post office boxes for Merlon's Place for Gentlemen and Jane's Retirement Home for Ladies. Box 100 is the manor. Jack collects the mail for those two boarding houses as well as Harbour Manor." She gasps and her voice elevates. "Someone delivers personal mail to both residences, but not cheques. Elsie, from Merlon's, told me someone leaves personal mail at the home. She never mentioned cheques, and she never identified the person. Where do the cheques go? Where does Jack take them?"

"Relax, Stella. Let me guess. I suppose you think following her is a good idea."

Chapter 16

She Wasn't Confident

Snow sits in piles on both sides as she twists and cranes to manoeuvre the Jeep into the narrow driveway of Yellow House. The art of backing into a parking spot is not her area of expertise. She's early, in the faint hope coffee will be courtesy of Trixie.

From Christmas Day on Friday until yesterday—Monday—she and Nick bathed in the privacy and quiet of a house closed to the public, and a business shuttered for the season. They plowed and shovelled—the snow has been relentless. They walked around the park with Kiki, slept in, baked bread, ate whatever pleased them, and talked, talked, talked.

She snuggles into her long winter coat and settles behind the wheel. The post office opened at eight-thirty, but the mail isn't sorted before ten and Jack arrives each day between ten-thirty and eleven. Her watch says near ten.

Conversations focused on their new partnership, joint ownership, and the future. He mentioned marriage. She joked. One wedding in the family at a time, please. She studies the intricacies of the ice-crystal-covered windshield. His sincerity is unmistakable, but she struggles, yet again, with commitment. Soon, the park business arrangement will include Nick as her equal. *Has a marriage certificate become a big issue? What difference does a piece of paper make?*

His parents called. She accepted the receiver for long enough to express Season's Greetings. Nick held the phone with one hand while he clenched the other into a fist. His neck and jaw tightened. His voice escalated before he glanced in her direction and lowered his tone. When he returned to his spot at the kitchen table, he said little. She didn't ask any questions. The incident was the low point of their four quiet days. She has no concerns. A Florida visit, for quality time with Tobias and Yona Cochran, won't happen in the foreseeable future.

People materialize on the post office steps. The poor postal workers will be forced to sort mail while the lobby fills with the impatient. When she called yesterday and asked if Trixie might join her on what can be described as an amateur stake-out, her sister scoffed but said yes.

"Why can't we wait in the children's library at the front of the house? We can pull back the curtains. At least we'd be warm," she whined.

"You're right, Trixie, but I want a view from every angle. No one expects to see us sitting in my vehicle, in your yard. We can observe, and once she comes out of the post office, we'll follow her and determine where she takes the mail."

"The boxes might be empty."

"Understood, but an insurance cheque for a guest at Jane's normally arrives at this time of the month. If I'm correct, she'll drive to Harbour Manor because she's collected cheques."

"Okay. I'll come out at ten with coffee. You'd better not be late," she threatened. "Don't leave me stranded in the driveway."

Arriving ahead of schedule, Stella waits in the Jeep for her sister.

The passenger door creaks when Trixie bends into the cab after she sets the mugs on the hood and frees her hands. "We could be inside, Stella. Here's your coffee." Stella notices the tight jeans and short coat—not ideal attire for a stake-out in a chilly car.

"Jump in. If Jack collects the mail today, she'll be here soon, right?"

"She often arrives at ten-thirty. Will you come back every day until she appears?"

"I'm not sure. Thanks for this." She lifts her cup. "Are you grumpy?"

Trixie places her mug on the dash while she adjusts her bunny fur jacket. She takes a sip. "Strong. Good when describing both my coffee and my men." She sneers a laugh.

"You're not grumpy?"

"Brigitte suggested I should find a place for myself and come take care of Mia when she needs me. Mia has one more year at home before kindergarten, but after she starts, Brigitte will have no more use for me."

"Another baby?" Stella stares out the window at the post office and doesn't turn toward her sister.

"What?" Trixie's hot breath touches her cheek. "You can't be serious."

"The girl is young. Could be lots of babies. Who knows?" She keeps eyes front. No sign of Jack Lawson.

Springs object when Trixie throws herself back against the seat. Stella senses a shudder run through her. "I never imagined more children." She grunts. "She'll need me for sure."

"Considering a house purchase?"

"Yeah." Her tone sounds defeated. "I'll call Cavelle when we're through with your wild goose chase. What do you hope to accomplish today, anyway?"

Stella turns toward her sister, whose focus is across the street, and ignores her mood. "A woman who lives at Jane's, Flora, told me she receives insurance settlement money besides her Old Age Pension. The government sends cheques earlier in December, but others arrive on their regular schedule, which means today or tomorrow." She's explained part of her plan before. "We've confirmed Jack gathers the mail for Merlon's and Jane's." She holds her mug in one hand and points a finger toward the windshield with the other. "Someone takes personal mail to the homes. The person may or may not be Jack. Jane's and Merlon's access residents' assets directly for services rendered. Jasper Nunn said he signed over his pension and his savings account."

"Crazy, Stella."

"Agreed, but if people have no family, the boarding houses ensure they're paid regardless of the resident's mental capacity. Where does Jack drop off cheque mail? The answer is not Merlon's or Jane's. I already asked."

"You want to follow Jack Lawson today." The statement lacks enthusiasm.

"Yes."

"And Aiden's aware?"

"No. He's too busy with Rosemary. They take her back to the city on Monday, the fourth, and he returns to work on the fifth."

"She's here, Stella, as expected." Trixie gulps her coffee and points out the frosted window.

Her heart pounds. She wasn't confident of her scheme, but Jack's on her way up the post office steps. "We wait until she comes out and follow her."

Trixie opens the Jeep door.

"Don't leave now."

"I'll find her car. She drives a green clunker sedan." Trixie gallops off and returns in a minute. "Brr. I need more clothes."

Stella muffles a giggle.

"She's parked two doors away and will drive past us before she can leave Main. Turn this beast on and take the chill off. We'll be ready to follow her when she goes by." Trixie leans forward. "Jack's on her way out of the post office now." The urgency in Trixie's voice is a surprise.

Jack's car whizzes by the Yellow House driveway. Stella shifts the Jeep into drive and creeps out into the street. She allows one vehicle between them. Before the two women can relax, Jack turns into the Groceteria lot. Stella parks on a side avenue nearby.

"She might have half a dozen errands. We could be behind her for hours," Trixie whines.

"Possible, but she'll deliver the mail, too." Stella doesn't turn off the Jeep, in the hopes Trixie's mood improves if she's not cold. "I can drive you back, if you prefer." If Trixie says yes, Jack may leave the store and she'll have no idea where the green monster goes next.

"No. You'd lose her. Besides," she teases, "you'll need a witness if your hunch plays out."

Jack climbs into her vehicle and sets off toward the outskirts of town, past the expanded graveyard, and straight for Harbour Manor.

"Right!" Breathless and light-headed, she slows the Jeep and gives Jack ample opportunity to park and enter the nursing home. She hugs the icy shoulder, but little traffic means less risk of someone nearby paying attention.

Once Jack lopes inside, mail in hand, Stella pulls into a space reserved for staff at the far end of the lot. She maintains sight of Jacks' car via the rear-view mirror.

"What now?"

"I can see her vehicle and the front door, but I don't expect she'll notice us. Duck, Trixie, in case she recognizes your hair."

Trixie doesn't react to the sarcasm.

They wait. In ten minutes, Jack retraces her steps and navigates away from the manor. "Will we follow her?"

"Yes, but we won't stop. My Jeep is obvious at either boarding home. We can confirm she goes into one of them before we quit."

"She must collect and deliver the Harbour Manor mail to the finance person."

"Jack collects mail for Harbour Manor. There's a good chance she delivers cheques for Merlon's and Jane's to the manor as well."

"Does the finance person keep the books for the boarding homes?"

"Nope. Patsy isn't involved in the finances of Merlon's or Jane's. I'm sure."

They follow Jack's green monster until she pulls into the yard at Merlon's Place for Gentlemen.

****

At the Harbour Manor Christmas party, Maura Martin told her she would be off until the fourth of January and Olive Urback was assigned day-supervisor duties. Today might be the ideal time to give her new friend and ally, Olive, a call.

"Harbour Manor. Nurse Urback."

"Hi, Olive. Stella Kirk here. I guess the appropriate greeting is Happy New Year."

"The same to you, Stella. Are you popping in for a visit with your father?"

"Trixie and I will come by soon, Olive. Today, I need a favour."

"Depends." Hesitation sounds in her response.

"Maura may have received mail since she went on vacation, and I wonder if you could check on what has been delivered."

"Stella, your request is unethical. You shouldn't ask me to examine someone's correspondence. Besides, I told you before, I refuse to become embroiled in your issues. I need my job."

"I'm not asking you to open and read letters, Olive, or even tell me the names, if you're uncomfortable. The question is: does Jack Lawson deliver pension cheques, addressed to Merlon's and Jane's boarding homes, there to Maura?"

"She brought mail earlier." Stella hears Olive take a deep breath. "Wait a minute."

After an interminable five minutes, Olive returns. "Jack came in on the twenty-second, too. I was busy after the Christmas party—my first day shift in ages. I count twelve Old Age Pension cheques and one other. Do not, and I repeat, do not ask for names of the recipients, Stella. They're stacked on the corner of Maura's desk, and I have no reason to be in the office. I work out here at the station."

"Shouldn't money be Patsy's domain?" Manipulation of the woman is underhanded, but she wants confirmation they weren't sent directly to the nursing home.

"Stella. Honest to God. The addresses are people who live at Jane's Retirement Home for Ladies and Merlon's Place for Gentlemen." Her voice sputters. "Don't ask me for help again."

"Sorry, Olive. You know details, right?"

"I'm suspicious, but I will not, and I repeat, will not, become involved in whatever you are investigating." Her voice is barely above a whisper. "With a sick husband, I need my job. I can work during the day over the holiday because my daughter takes time off. She stays with her father when I'm on nights. We have no life. Now you've heard my tale of woe. I refuse to risk what little I have, okay?"

"Olive, my apologies. You're afraid and I understand. I appreciate your help and I won't ask again."

"Goodbye."

Jack delivers cheques for residents at Merlon's and Jane's directly to Maura Martin. Three women are in residence at Jane's right now and four men at Merlon's. She nibbles on her thumbnail. *One extra cheque for Flora makes a possible eight. Five additional cheques?*

****

The next day, Stella contacts Aiden. "Hi, Mary Jo. Might Aiden be with you today?"

"Yes, Stella. I'll fetch him for you."

"Before you run, Happy New Year, by the way. How's Rosemary?"

"Not great, but they've made plans for an evening supper with you and Nick on the second. Good luck," she snickers. "Aiden!"

"Hi. I expected to touch base after New Year's. You must be busy because of the big share transfer." His titter sounds nervous when he adds, "Almost a marriage."

"Nope. We completed the paperwork. I've been investigating. Can you request a warrant for examination of someone's mail?"

"The government does not react kindly when the police interfere with the mail. Why?"

Undeterred, she tries another tact. "Will Old Age Pension Services tell the RCMP who receives cheques sent to Merlon's and Jane's?"

"Stella, what in the world for?" His impatience bleeds through the connection. "The process involves approaching a judge with an Affidavit to

Obtain a Search Warrant, which must state each step we've taken to find the information required. Since your snooping doesn't count, when you act alone and unsupervised, we don't have sufficient cause."

"I have a hunch."

"One of many. Just ask me." His mockery borders on ridicule. "I expect you've uncovered a nugget, but I can't access a warrant."

"Right," she mumbles, holding back a caustic remark of her own. "Your office has authority to research who's behind JanlonNS, though. Then we can produce enough information for a warrant."

"I must go. Listen, we identified the man in the grave. We've found no family," he lectures. "Our focus, after the holiday, will be to determine what happened to Ira Gold and if Luther Greene dropped him into a hole in the graveyard expansion."

"Luther Greene used the funeral home's backhoe and buried him. There's no other plausible explanation. I have more questions, Aiden. The issue is bigger than Ira."

"I must go," he repeats, heightened anxiety in his voice.

She can hear Rosemary. "I understand. How's the visit?" She can be magnanimous if she tries.

"We hope she'll stay until January fourth, but who knows? If I'm out of sight for five minutes, she yells. She's not herself anymore, Stella. Dinner on the second might be out. We'll wait and assess her mood then."

As her call ends, Nick strolls in with coffee for them both. Kiki trots along behind, cruises around the desk, and plants her front paws on Stella's leg.

Shoulders slumped, she whispers, "Hey, little one. Need a hug?" And to Nick, "Thanks for the coffee, Love."

"You've enjoyed a busy morning and my watch says barely ten." He never asks.

"Enjoyed might not be the word. When I called Olive Urback and asked if she would rifle through Maura Martin's mail, she was annoyed. No surprise. I hope I haven't alienated her. I talked with Aiden about warrants. He said he couldn't obtain permission based on my 'snooping'." She strokes Kiki with one hand and holds her coffee cup with the other.

"You're determined not to take offence, correct? You accepted involvement in the current investigation as a favour, remember? You agreed."

Her expression is resigned. "He asked for my help because Essie

Matkowski has family problems and took leave. I shouldn't be considered a snoop, though." She pouts. "There are more elements involved besides an unidentified man in a grave. He lived at Merlon's, and another resident assaulted him. Aiden's ensnared in Rosemary's issues—I don't blame him—his work should be reassigned," she pants.

Nick leans forward and meets her eyes. "Your role would be reassigned as well."

"True, but I might be heard first. Aiden brushed me off and his preoccupation is bound to hurt the case. Maura Martin and Hector Greene are involved, but, so far, I can't find solid proof about how or why." She frowns until Kiki pokes her with a paw because she stopped petting.

"Let's go visit your dad this afternoon. We can take Kiki and wish everyone a Happy New Year."

"Good idea. I need more practice snooping." She lifts her brows when she peers at him over the rim of her mug.

He closes his eyes for a second, no doubt in exasperation. "Kiki and I are off outside for a few minutes. Consider what you want for lunch, okay?"

She nods, while her mind visualizes Harbour Manor and the location of the office behind the nurses' station. With any luck, Patsy will be at her desk and may cooperate in a small investigation. *I want to verify to whom those cheques are addressed, besides the current residents. By my math, there are five more cheques than people.*

When the veranda door opens, she hustles toward the kitchen and decides, on the way, that a call to alert Olive of their visit would be ill-advised.

Chapter 17

Nervousness Proves Unfounded

The fibrous smell of warm paper wafts through Patsy's open door as Stella makes her way along the empty hallway to the finance office. A photocopier hums. Nick and Kiki are entertaining her father. Olive, the dog lover, was last seen trotting toward Norbert's room. Stella allowed the nurse to assume she would visit Del Trembly.

"You're in time to hear the good news firsthand. I've been busy copying a letter from the Board of Directors for residents and families."

"Good news, Patsy? I guess prices aren't increasing?"

"On the contrary." Patsy reaches a chubby hand across the desk and snatches a piece of paper from the pile. "Here. Read for yourself."

Stella accepts the offer and scans the document. The charge for single rooms is reduced by twenty-five per cent per month, as of January 1, 1982. "You mentioned a high single room vacancy. The board expects a drop in the price will help? May I keep a copy?"

"Sure. Save me a stamp." She responds to the second question first. "As for capacity, yes, we hope the lower cost encourages." Patsy turns in her chair and grins at Stella instead of focusing on the photocopier. She clutches her mug of tea in both hands. "What can I do for you today?"

"I need your help. Olive is occupied with Norbert and Nick for the moment. I'm told there's a stack of government cheques on the corner of Maura's desk. They were delivered by Jack Lawson."

Patsy's eyes narrow.

Maintaining her nerve, she soldiers on. "Will you list the names of the addressees?" Before the financial officer can argue, Stella continues. "They were collected from the boxes for Merlon's and Jane's. You don't manage their finances, but there are more cheques than residents, and I'm curious." She stops for breath, prepared to fortify her argument.

"Okay."

"What? I thought you'd tell me to mind my own business."

"The smart answer." She stands with effort and squeezes around her desk. "I think I'll check your father's admission papers. Now aware of the lower fee agreement, you asked for a calculation of the differences. You say the reason is tax purposes, which I don't understand, but I agreed to find the information and write the pertinent details out for you. We strive to support familial requests."

Stella's mouth hangs open while she listens to the finance clerk as she concocts, at a moment's notice, a viable excuse for entry into Maura Martin's office.

"You are good." She tilts her head in mock respect. "We won't have much time. Nick will keep Olive occupied with Kiki for a few minutes, but not for long."

Patsy grabs a pad and pen from her desk, and they rush along the still-empty corridor together.

The first person they meet is Lulu, who bustles past the office as Stella takes a post beside the hallway entrance. The nurses' station is in full view. She'll be alerted if Olive approaches. Her heart pounds and she breathes in short gasps. Her nervousness proves unfounded. Patsy can enter the supervisor's space if her purpose is as she recited with such ease. Lulu materializes again.

"Are you on guard?" She stops.

"Waiting for Patsy. I asked for Dad's admission information and what we need is filed inside."

"Your father has been well. He and Del spend time together in the lounge."

Lulu seems in no hurry. Stella glances through the open door. Patsy scribbles on her yellow pad. She addresses Lulu. "My partner is with Dad now. We brought our Pomeranian for a visit."

"Oh? I must find Kiki before I deliver afternoon treats. You folks can stay, you know. Families are always invited."

"Thanks, Lulu. We'll see how the time goes." The nursing assistant sprints toward Norbert's room. "I think Olive is on her way." Stella hopes Patsy heard her.

As her stomach churns, Patsy's voice drifts into the corridor. "Hi, Olive.

Stella Kirk is in the building. I mentioned the price reduction in single rooms. She asked to review Norbert's admission forms and note the original contract—which has changed over the last few years." Patsy gushes and adopts a more confidential tone. "Family members make the most absurd requests. One person wanted a count of the days since their mother's arrival. Now, why in God's name does anyone need those calculations?"

Relief punctuates her breathing as she wanders the hall in the other direction, turns the corner at the end, and makes her way into the lounge. She sees Del, in a recliner, fiddling with the television remote. As her heart rate calms, Stella directs her attention toward her friend.

"How are you? Can I help with the TV?"

"Stella. Wonderful to see you. No sign of Willy, eh? I suspect you haven't come to report you found her."

"Sorry, Del. Nick and I brought Kiki for a visit with Dad. They'll be here anytime."

"Most residents show their faces around three. I'm here first because Lulu helps me. What's new in the investigation?"

"Aiden's back at work on the fifth. We've made little progress. You know as much as I do, since you were in the office with Caleb when he called me." Stella keeps information superficial. She has discussed the basics with Del in the past. The woman's memory is on the decline.

"Hey, Del. Look who the cat dragged in." Norbert points at Nick and Kiki as they arrive at the common room.

"And here's Stella, too," Del adds. "I call this a party."

Residents appear. Once her father settles, she and Nick greet many others before they make their escape.

"Give me a minute. I want to check with Patsy. Meet you in the car."

Before she arrives at Patsy's door, she hears voices and stops. "Listen, Olive. The cat will be out of the bag in no time. I trust Stella Kirk."

"We could lose our jobs."

"No. She can't fire us without cause. Staff dismissals go before the board, and she doesn't dare. We could report her ourselves, but I prefer we stay at arm's length. I wish I understood the woman's game, but I'm sure the list will help Stella. I'll call her after supper and give her the names."

Patsy and Olive both suspect an issue. Stella returns the way she came.

****

Back at the house, they prepare a quiet dinner—a ginger stir fry Nick is concocting from Christmas Eve turkey provided by Trixie and kept in the freezer. Stella chops broccoli and boils water for rice. She expects Patsy to call her later with the list of names she collected. Did Patsy say she would contact her? Well, no, but she overheard her discuss the cheques with Olive. They both know more, although reluctant to share specifics.

"You're quiet," Nick remarks as he makes the sauce.

"I expect Patsy, from accounting at the manor, to call after supper. She and Olive both suspect someone of something."

When the phone on the kitchen wall jangles, they're seated with wine and supper. "Shale Cliffs."

"Hi," says Trixie, much to Stella's disappointment. "Tomorrow is our big day, but I wanted to tell you about my conversation with Renée Tait at the post office. Are you eating?"

"Not yet." She glances at Nick and shrugs. "What did Renée say?" Her curiosity piques.

Trixie's voice lowers. "Don't let on to Brigitte that I've helped you. She thinks the reputation of the business might be in jeopardy."

"I disagree. She's being unreasonable. Who will be aware you gossiped with Renée and reported your conversation?" She frowns. "Between us, then, what did Renée say?"

"Jack Lawson collects a pension cheque for her mother, too. Obviously, that's the fourth box number."

"Flora told me Monica Lawson died at Jane's. Jack visited every day when Monica lived at the boarding home, but now, not so much. She couldn't care for Mrs. Lawson at home, which is why she was at Jane's in the first place. Renée's information makes no sense. Will you introduce me? Post office people are busybodies—valuable busybodies." She chuckles.

"No problem. Let's meet her after the share transfer. With Aiden off work, you're the only one in a dither to solve these questions: who is dead? who is where? and who spends the money? Aiden still not involved?"

"Nope. I guess the security of old people isn't sexy enough for a detective, although I need patience until he returns." Bitterness has invaded her tone. "Talk soon. I expect another call any minute. Good night, Trixie, and thanks."

The phone rings as she replaces the receiver. Nick points his index finger at her plate in mock frustration. "Shale Cliffs."

"Hi, Stella. Sorry to telephone at supper time." The tenseness in Patsy's voice betrays her impatience. "Grab a pen and paper."

"Right, and I appreciate your help."

"Here are the names: Wilhelmina, Ira, Lloyd, Weldon, Minerva, Roxanne, Flora, Ethel, Horace, Cecil, Frederick, and our dear friend Jasper. I counted two cheques for the same Flora, by the way."

"Thanks."

"Don't ask again, Stella. I support you and the police uncovering the truth. I've suspected an issue for ages."

After she says good night, she studies the list while Nick serves more wine, and she finishes her tepid meal. A frown defines her mood. She notes the identities of the residents at both Merlon's and Jane's, which count for eight cheques, including Flora's insurance. In addition, she reads five other names: Wilhelmina, Minerva, Lloyd, Weldon, and Ira.

"Do those two boarding homes collect pension money for people who live off-site?"

"Ira doesn't live off-site. Ira is dead."

"If the person identified is the same Ira. The cheque might be for a different Ira. You don't know."

"No. You're right, but with such an uncommon name, it would be a curious coincidence. I'll call Aiden tomorrow and see what he suggests we do next."

"What do you suspect?"

"I have a couple of ideas."

****

New Year's Eve arrives, and a busy day awaits. Nick and Stella are scheduled for an appointment with Andrea Picard at ten. The papers for transfer of the shares were signed by Trixie yesterday. Today marks the formalization of the partnership agreement, and a representative from the law firm of Stephens and Stephens will deliver the cheque to the Shale Harbour office for Trixie. By the time they're due for supper at the Purple Tulip, the deal will be completed. She presses a hand against her chest, fingers splayed. This conclusion was impossible to foresee in 1978.

Stella stares at her closet. How does one dress for a New Year's Eve changing of the guard? The temperature has dropped below zero. She opts for comfort over fancy—her normal decision. Warm dark blue trousers and a grey cotton sweater fit the occasion. She trims her ears with crystal drops. A haircut is in order. She claws wisps off her face and hopes anyone doing an assessment will notice the jewellery and not her hair.

Nick has taken Kiki out. The little dog won't be pleased, left to her own devices, but she'll enjoy a walk when they return from Port Ephron.

"Are you ready? Let's not be late." His voice floats toward the second story.

"On my way."

The highway is icy. Nick takes his time when he navigates the causeway. Throughout the holiday season, dependable roads are a rare commodity. He pats her hand while he drives.

"Excited?" She knows his answer but craves his response, regardless.

Despite the tricky driving conditions, he makes eye contact for a moment. "I can't wait for our official partnership, Stella. Our future is here, you and me, and your family welcome the idea with open arms. From the time my aunt died and left me money, I knew the life I wanted. You and your family are the bonus. I am a lucky man."

She blinks. The windshield blurs. "I'm happy, too. When I came home to help Dad, I thought I forfeited my future. I never imagined the universe unfolding this way." She reaches over and touches his thigh. "We make a good team."

Andrea Picard's office, on the third floor above the Royal Bank in downtown Port Ephron, exudes simple elegance. She works alone, with an administrative assistant and a law clerk. The reception room furnishings are soft, lemon-coloured leather chairs paired with teak accent tables. They are five minutes ahead of schedule. Before they settle, Andrea rounds the corner, extends her hand to each of them in welcome, and leads the couple along a hallway lit with modern sconces, into her space at the end.

Since she has not met in Andrea's office before today, Stella admires the generous surroundings, the leather furniture, the feminine teak desk, and the classic shelves of law books. Andrea Picard has arrived. She assumes the size of the bill.

"We've completed your paperwork and will finish two different transactions. The first notes the share sale from Trixie Kirk over to each of you. The second is for part two of the loan agreement required for your septic project."

"And the documents are in order?" Stella needs to contribute.

"Yes. The bank requires your signature on the agreement and the share transfer document. The money currently sits in our trust, and I expect a representative for Stephens and Stephens to collect the cheque for your sister soon. Once I deliver the paperwork, the loan will be deposited into your business account. The official date of transfer is tomorrow, but finalization won't be until Monday. Banks and their holidays." She slides two documents and a pen toward Stella. "Little green dots mark the spots for your signature."

The end creeps nearer. As she signs the pages, Nick becomes her fifty percent partner. The extra money for completion of the septic system is secured, and the bank gets paid the one thousand dollars a month Trixie once received. The cool fountain pen caresses her fingers. She can't remember the last time she used a real fountain pen. Scratchy sounds punctuate the silence. She finishes and emits held breath.

On their way toward the Jeep, Nick wraps his arm around her shoulder. "Celebration lunch?"

She meets his gaze. "Let's go home, spend the rest of the afternoon with Kiki, and take a walk. We can celebrate tonight."

"Are you okay?" He leans closer, brows furrowed.

"I'm perfect, Nick. Let's go home."

****

They return to their park and enjoy a long walk while they check on the security of each stored unit. Curled on the couch in front of the fire with Kiki under a blanket, they drink tea and talk. Before time drifts away, she calls Aiden, with the goal of running her thoughts regarding the boarding homes and the five extra cheques past him.

Toni answers. "Oh, I don't know, Stella. Rosemary has been good, but if Aiden talks on the phone with you, she might react badly. They are due at your place for supper the day after tomorrow. Talk with him then."

She acquiesces with reluctance. Under normal circumstances, the opportunity for suspects to leave the area or destroy evidence is a concern. In this case, Ira's cheque sits in plain view on Maura's desk. Ira is dead, and Patsy has seen the name. Although not stated, she is convinced the piece of mail is addressed to Ira *Gold*. Whatever the scam, and she is determined to sort out the details, clues won't be hidden or resolved by January fifth when Aiden returns.

The act of deciding proper attire has been her lifelong burden, and here she stands, for the second time today. For the New Year's Eve celebration, she decides to leap out of her comfort zone. In the back of her closet are creamy white palazzo pants with a Chinese dragon motif in red, cranberry, and pink hues. They are loud and funky. She has a short, red angora sweater handed down because the shade clashed with her sister's hair. She skips downstairs in search of approval she's confident she'll receive from her partner.

"My, oh my." His mouth falls open and his eyes widen. "No one will notice *you* at the Purple Tulip tonight." He takes the necessary two steps and wraps his arms around her. "You, my love, are beautiful."

"Thank you, Sir. You're not too shabby yourself in khakis and a fisherman's knit. Quite preppy."

"Old man preppy." He chuckles as he reaches for their coats and helps her into hers. "I'm excited. I hope Trixie doesn't second-guess herself."

"Won't happen. Trixie's primary issue has become Brigitte suggesting she find a place before Carter moves in. She's afraid she'll be useless once Mia starts kindergarten. I suggested more babies, and she freaked."

"I vote for more babies."

"Me, too."

****

The Purple Tulip glows with twinkle lights, Christmas trees, and holiday-themed accessories. Val and Trixie haven't arrived. Mitchell, the maître d', shows them to their table, near a modern gas fireplace installed in the wall at eye level. Stella orders a house white wine while Nick opts for one of their local brews. They are holding hands and giggling over Kiki and her craziness when Trixie and Val are led into the dining space.

"Well, you two act like partners, for sure. What are we drinking?" She drops her rabbit fur jacket on the back of her chair, revealing a black and clingy jumpsuit with a caramel sash. Her stiletto heels match, and she found a coordinating sparkling ribbon for her hair.

Val touches her arm—a confident and possessive gesture—while he assists her.

They enjoy a superb meal. The restaurant serves a prix fixe menu—citrus salad on Romaine lettuce, stuffed pork tenderloin with a red wine demi-glaze, and roasted vegetables, plus Baked Alaska for dessert. They drink, laugh, and indulge. Over post-dinner tea, Trixie surprises them.

"Cavelle placed an offer on a property for me."

Stella sits straighter in her chair. "Good for you. Where?"

"Russ' house."

Stunned, Stella leans back and takes a breath.

Trixie smirks, enjoying the reaction. "Cavelle told me Russ instructed his lawyer to sell his assets and put them in a trust until he's out of prison. The place is a steal. The price doesn't even cover the upgrades. Cavelle thinks I can take ownership by the middle of January."

Russ Harrison (AKA Harry Russell) renovated a Craftsman cottage when he first moved to Shale Harbour. He spared no expense, and the result is an extraordinary example of the style, situated five minutes from the park. When they dated, Trixie dreamed of moving in with Russ; of being mistress of his home. Once he was identified as the hired hit man who killed Paulina McAdams, her dream vaporized.

Recovered from her initial shock, Stella stands, moves around the table, and hugs her sister. "Congratulations. I hope the place doesn't remind you too much of Russ."

Trixie accepts the hug and pats Val's hand. "No. My affair with a murderer ended, thanks to you." She meets Stella's eyes. "Val and I will live in the house, and I'll help Brigitte in whatever way I can."

Nick hoists his tea. "New beginnings." He clinks his mug with Val and Trixie before he turns to Stella. "And family. Thanks for welcoming me into yours."

Chapter 18

Summer is Over

"We should trade the Jeep for a new pickup—one of those Datsun compacts. What do you think?" Nick and Stella are curled in bed, wrapped in musky sheets, while the cool morning sunshine inserts itself through a separation in the bedroom curtains.

She curbs an instant retort as various arguments dart through her mind. Nick has money. She doesn't want more debt. Equality of investment is her goal. She's afraid if they take on too much, they'll lose the gains made until now.

"Those Datsun mini trucks are perfect. We could test-drive one in Halifax."

He hasn't noticed her lack of response. "The books need reviewing, Nick." *Be honest*. "The idea of another loan scares me. What's wrong with the Jeep?"

"No specific issues, but time for a trade." He runs his fingers along the inside of her arm. "I could buy us a new vehicle."

She covers his hand with hers. "Once we go through our year end, we can make a wise decision. I know the money from your aunt burns holes in your pockets." Although a tease, she compresses her lips. A churlish response would sound unappreciative. "I guess you could purchase whatever truck suits you, but pace yourself. Don't forget unforeseen expenses and emergencies."

"You're right." Nick acquiesces. "We can scan the accounts today and get a jump on the new year. I'll make coffee." He kisses her on the lips before he climbs out of their bed and turns toward the bathroom.

In the stillness which remains, she questions her nervousness. Should she let him spend his money and forge ahead with investment in the park regardless of her ability to fulfill her fifty percent obligation? The obvious answer is an emphatic "no." Although he means well, their agreement is fifty-fifty, and his expectations will require management.

While in the shower, with the smell of hazelnut coffee wafting from below, she reviews the list of names on cheques where there are no obvious recipients. Her thoughts turn to Horace, a resident at Merlon's for five years or more. Arrival on the boarding home's doorstep on New Year's Day for an interview would be inappropriate. She can't imagine Elsie or Helga admitting her.

Breakfast, or brunch since the clock said past ten, consisted of a decadent pairing of thick slabs of brown bread toast with scrambled eggs. Stella's senses twitched in the quiet that followed. "Let's review the books." She holds her index finger in the air. "One call, first."

"Sure. Trixie?"

"No. Merlon's Place. I want to contact Jasper."

"Whatever for? He hasn't lived at Merlon's for long."

"Horace has resided there at least five years. He might remember if anyone on the list of names besides Ira ever boarded there. I thought I'd ask Jasper for help."

"Good idea." He leans across, coffee cup in both hands, and squints. "You've figured out what happened to Ira Gold."

"Possibilities, but I need a conversation with Aiden."

"I'll clear the table. You go make your phone call and we can peruse the books afterward. The bank didn't have an issue with our loan. We must be on the right track."

Her pulse quickens, although her resolve remains intact, enhanced when he grins.

In her office, she finds the number and calls.

"Merlon's. Elsie speakin'."

"Good morning, Elsie. Happy New Year. This is Stella Kirk. How are you?"

"Busy." Silence balloons.

"I called for a quick chat with Jasper."

"Okay, but don't be long. This telephone is for emergencies."

"Understood. Thank you."

"Hello, Stella. Jasper Nunn here."

"Jasper. Happy New Year. I need your help."

"Certainly. Problem?"

"Maybe. Will you visit with Horace and ask him if he remembers any more details about the Lloyd or Weldon he mentioned, or other information like last names?"

"Sure, Stella. I'll call you tomorrow."

"Perfect. If I'm out on the grounds, leave a message, okay?"

"Don't much appreciate phones or answerin' machines, but I can ask Horace for you. Lloyd and Weldon, right? You and your father are fine people."

His words warm her. "Yes. You're a good guy, too, Jasper. Talk later."

Back in the kitchen, Nick has finished the dishes when she rounds the corner with the ledger and relevant paperwork from the bank. She knows they experienced a successful season, but as Norbert often said, the tourism industry parallels farming. Success depends on the weather and the equipment. In Shale Cliffs' case, the third element is staff. They are blessed with great employees, but Alice graduates university after one more year. If Eve works in reception, they'll need a replacement for her on the grounds. It takes a special person willing to clean public bathrooms, weed flower beds, and mow lawns. Eve loves the machinery. Although studying for a commerce degree, she might not want the office job.

"How did your call go? Did my friend Helga let you talk with Jasper, or do you need to elicit my charms again?"

She giggles, reminded of his assistance with the boarding home dryer. "Elsie's back on days, but no problem. Jasper will quiz Horace about the two mystery male names on my list. He said he'd ring tomorrow. I brought the paperwork."

"I see." He approaches and wraps her in his arms. She drops the ledger on the table. "I didn't mean to push. I'll contribute whatever is necessary for our success. I want what's best for us. Perhaps we can save each month until the end of the season."

"For a new vehicle instead of buying now?" Relief ripples through her.

"Right. We'll gauge how our reservations go and reward ourselves if we make any money."

She leans back and separates herself from his blue denim shirt. "Good grief! We'd better see a profit after what we've plowed into septic, electrical, and water."

He hugs her. "Shale Cliffs will be fine, as long as the weatherman doesn't give us rain every day, or a hurricane for good measure."

****

While they sip tea after lunch, Stella realizes, with a start, their dinner with Aiden and Rosemary is tomorrow night. "They could still cancel. Lasagna? Spaghetti? There's salad in the fridge, and bread in the freezer."

Nick frowns. "Rib-eye steaks, too. The veranda's protected. Why not barbecue? A treat for January second."

"Great, but the stores aren't open until tomorrow. I think grocery shopping will be in order." She smirks. "We can't do much with a few carrots and a potato or two. Not enough for a pan of roasted veggies."

"Maybe we can find root vegetables at the Groceteria."

"Wait." Stella slaps the table, which wakes Kiki from her lunchtime nap. "I'll call Hester. Haven't spoken with her in ages. She has a cold cellar full." She taps Nick's hand. "Problem solved."

After clearing the dishes, she reaches for the kitchen wall phone and telephones the Painter farm.

Cavelle answers. "Happy New Year."

"Hi Cavelle. Same to you. I expected Jewel."

"We gave Jewel and Ken the day off. Jacob, Hester, and I decided we could manage our New Year's Day dinner."

"Good for you, but I'm surprised Jewel followed orders."

"Jewel devotes herself to Kenny and Hester. She never spends a full day away." Cavelle's voice holds admiration for her staff. "If she has an appointment for Kenny, Hester often goes with her. Jacob and I want them to have their own life, even though they live in the bungalow next door and work for us."

Jewel and Ken Winslow moved into the house originally planned for Jacob and his new wife, Lucy. Opal Painter killed Lucy. Family secrets were revealed, and in the end, the Winslows were hired to help with Hester, and work on the farm. Cavelle maintains her realtor position, Jacob manages the land, and Hester is supported. Although tragedy battered the Painter siblings, they survived.

"Commendable. I am in desperate need of a favour."

"Sure, Stella"

"More Hester's department, but I invited Aiden and Rosemary for supper tomorrow night. Nick wants barbecued steaks, and I thought to pair them with roasted root vegetables."

"Your cupboard is bare, and the Groceteria will be little help."

Facts are facts. "Correct. Do you have a spare variety pack?"

Cavelle's soft laugh allays her concerns. "I'm sure we do, but I'll let Hester be the judge. She has our complete inventory memorized, as you might expect. She's right here."

"Hello, Stella. I understand you created an inadequate dinner party plan."

Suitably admonished, she replies, "Can you help me with enough root veggies for four people, Hester? Nick wants to cook steaks on the veranda."

"It's January. Someone should remind him summer is over."

Stella chuckles despite herself.

"Cavelle, may I invite Stella over, or is such an invitation inappropriate because of the holiday?"

After a muffled response, Hester uncovers the mouthpiece. "I will fill a box. Please come for tea. No charge for the vegetables or the tea. You are my friend. Are you permitted to recount aspects of your current case? Cavelle said you are in the midst of an investigation. Shall I assist with analysis?"

"Okay." Stella fumbles with her response. "Sure. Thanks." Did Trixie reveal basic investigative details to Cavelle? No matter. She doesn't know much.

"Perhaps I can help."

"I'm at a standstill until Aiden returns on the fifth. See you at three."

Nick wanders outside with Kiki while she watches from the open doorway. "We're set," she shouts. "Off to the Painter farm for tea." He waves as Kiki leads him along the cottage driveway.

****

There's little traffic on a holiday, which means a quiet drive. Most people are smart enough to stay home and off icy roads. She left Nick cuddled in a chair by the fire with Kiki, his new book, and a cup of tea. Meanwhile, she does her best to navigate the Jeep between the ditches.

"Welcome, Stella. You are five minutes early—an improvement."

Stella knows Hester has waited since two-thirty. "Wonderful to see you. The house smells good."

"Cavelle and I made biscuits. I set eight aside for you."

"Aren't you generous, Hester?" She attempts a feather touch on her friend's shoulder, but Hester dips and avoids the personal contact.

"Come into the kitchen. The tea is ready, and you can inspect the produce I chose for you."

"Lead on."

When they reach the back of the house, Cavelle is standing in front of the sink, clad in an apron, and washing baking dishes. Golden biscuits cool on a rack nearby. A cardboard box rests on the floor by the door.

"I found you a butternut squash, a turnip, three small parsnips since the big ones can be woody and are better in stews, red potatoes, and carrots. Do you know how to roast them?"

"Hi, Cavelle, and yes, Hester, I believe I do."

Hester ignores her and continues. "Jewel's recipe calls for garlic, salt, pepper, and olive oil. She says you must let the vegetables sing, but rosemary enhances the flavour. I added a package of mine, and two bulbs of garlic. Again, no charge."

"Hester, come on. What do I owe you?"

"Our gift. The matter is settled. We made your favourite black currant tea today."

"Special treatment, Hester."

The slimmest of smiles emerges.

"I think I'm done." Cavelle removes her apron. "Your call inspired us. We put a stew in the oven and baked biscuits. Hester was a big help."

"Jewel lets me take part in kitchen activities when I'm not busy with my research. Sometimes, she plays with Kenny and tells me the steps. I learn new tasks and never forget."

Cavelle sets her cup on the table. "Were you surprised Trixie placed an offer on Russ' house?"

"Yes. I didn't know he wanted to liquidate, but I guess property ownership in prison is a challenge." She wrinkles her face.

"Trixie loved his Craftsman. It will be perfect for her."

"Let's hope, because a maudlin Trixie creates a problem for everyone."

Clearing her throat, Hester makes eye contact with Stella—a rare behaviour. "Houses are not the reason for bad deeds or bad people. A house can give you solace and refuge, regardless of its history."

"You are wise. I've missed you. Life has been busy since the writers retreat case concluded."

Hester mumbles a response. Cavelle and Stella both nod.

"Trixie tells me you're involved in another investigation with Aiden; the one with the man they found in Mallory Gorman's grave?"

"Yes, but Aiden has been wrapped in domestic challenges with Rosemary and the pace is slow. I'm certain Merlon's Place for Gentlemen and Jane's Retirement Home for Ladies are tangled in the issue somehow. There are many lines of inquiry. I need Aiden's help with the research into JanlonNS to identify the actual owners."

"Hector Greene and Maura Martin."

"What, Cavelle? How do you know they own the boarding facilities?"

"I sold them both properties ten years ago. They didn't finalize the offers until they obtained municipal licences for boarding homes, so I assume they run them, but they might lease to someone else."

****

Unsettled. Apprehensive. Stella checks her watch for the umpteenth time and the evening has barely started.

Earlier, Nick and Stella placed the dining room table in front of the fireplace in the living room. Aiden and Rosemary arrived on the veranda at five, as planned. Nick brought in a platter of steaks, fresh off the barbecue. Stella arranged the roasted vegetables in a matching serving dish. The biscuits were warmed in the oven. Rosemary refused wine. Stella opted for ice water, too. The men nursed beers. They took their places—Stella and Nick at either end; Aiden and Rosemary together facing the fire. The atmosphere and surroundings could be warm, cozy, and oozing friendship, if not for the dread racing along each nerve. Nick served.

She expected a vacant and flat Rosemary, the product of a medication load designed to muffle her mood swings and provide balance. The woman's current behaviour makes no sense. When medicated for her manic phases, Rosemary's eyes are dull. Her communication is sullen and often unresponsive. Tonight, she appears normal, dressed in slacks and a sweater set—no outlandish shoes, no low-cut dress. She wishes Trixie were here. Trixie can handle Rosemary regardless of her condition. Stella tries, but success is a rare commodity because Rosemary sees Stella as a threat.

Aiden and Stella were high school sweethearts—lovers, if the truth be told, and the truth has not been told. Rosemary suspects her husband carries a torch for Stella and won't accept there is no spark between them now. One of her psychiatrists identified Stella as Rosemary's nemesis.

"Not many changes around here, Stella." Rosemary peers at her with squinted eyes.

"You're right. I lived here as a child. The furniture and the dishes belonged to my parents." She adds, in a lighter tone, "But…you saw the upstairs. Nick did a renovation, and now we enjoy a private master suite." She pops a carrot into her mouth. The herb helps, although the name doesn't. "That was a big change."

"And we've upgraded the electrical and water systems and the septic installation is ready for spring. There's progress for you, Rosemary." Nick's distraction attempt fails.

Her eyes never leave Stella and continue burning black. "You work with my husband, even though he fired you. No change."

Aiden squirms. "Come on, Rosie. There are extenuating circumstances, and Stella agreed to help in a pinch. We talked. You understood."

"Yes. I snoop, Rosemary. Aiden returns on Tuesday and the case will be well in hand." *Facetious? Maybe.*

The evening progresses through various degrees of discomfort. For whatever reason, Rosemary focuses her attention on Nick and bombards him with vivid details regarding the deteriorating circumstances between her sisters and herself. Aiden takes the unexpected opportunity to listen to Stella's latest findings.

"We can talk on Tuesday, but I've followed the money, which leads straight toward Maura Martin." She pauses and checks Rosemary, who continues to occupy Nick. "Cavelle told me she sold the two original houses to Maura and her husband, Hector Greene. Based on her information, I think JanlonNS could be a corporate entity owned by them. Your office will confirm, I assume."

"Okay, but what difference does ownership of the boarding homes make?"

"Jack Lawson collects the mail for both, which she drops at Harbour Manor." Aiden furrows his brows. "Never mind. I'll explain the details on Tuesday. Simply put, there are five more cheques than residents and one of them is addressed to an Ira."

"Ira Gold?"

After she glances once again toward Rosemary, she gains sufficient confidence and continues. "Long story. I expect the cheque is for Ira Gold, but I was told only first names." She leans back. "Let me clear the table and make tea." She rises. "Nick, you entertain our guests, okay?"

She gathers the plates with enthusiasm and dashes into the kitchen, a fruitless attempt to escape the discomfort she has felt throughout the evening. She plugs in the kettle and fills the sink with soapy water. She braces herself before the return trip to grab the serving dishes. Her route is blocked by Rosemary, now occupying the doorway.

"I thought I might help." Her face has no expression, but her eyes flash. She clutches the sides of her cardigan. Although she stands, her ankles are crossed. The posture gives her an unbalanced appearance, both physically and psychologically.

Stella swallows. "Hey, Rosemary. You startled me. Nick and I are pleased you and Aiden came for supper with us tonight."

"I've learned tricks in the psyche ward, Stella." She stabs the name.

"Hopefully, they help."

Rosemary laughs, purposefully hushed, toneless, and insincere. She steps closer. "You ignorant woman. Let me give you the details. They taught me about managing my inclinations." She tilts her head. "The doctors call it habit reversal therapy. My behaviours—when I wear clothes from the fifties and channel Annette Funicello—are impulses masking my truth. I stopped my medication over a month ago and now you can see the real me." She glares at Stella. "Under control, of course. I hate you and always will."

She sidesteps the woman and stands nearer the door. "I believe you." *Off her drugs? Aiden never mentioned this change.*

"Stay away from Aiden. He fired you once—for me. He loves me."

"Yes. I agree he loves you. I accepted the contract because Essie has a family issue. I think her mother's sick. You stopped your medication." She makes a statement, avoiding any justifications or defensiveness on Rosemary's part, but curious for more information.

"They're stupid at the hospital. One of the other patients taught me to pretend to take the pills but spit them in the toilet later. My sisters and Aiden don't know, either."

"Why tell me?"

"Because my 'lack of stability' the shrinks call my manic phase, means I could hurt you."

Careful with her tone and words, Stella watches Rosemary for sudden moves. Other than a dirty dish as a missile, she assumes she isn't in any physical danger. "Rosemary, I want the case solved as soon as possible. Aiden hasn't been involved. He's been busy with you. I am no threat."

Her hollow cackle rattles off the cabinets, no longer tempered to insure privacy. Stella hopes Aiden or Nick hear. "I act. It works. Aiden's so scared he won't leave me alone. It's great."

Stella backs out of the kitchen. "Nick, will you come and help me with the tea?"

Chapter 19

Aiden is Doomed

Stella and Nick check the doors and turn off the downstairs lights before they make their way to bed.

"She seemed fine—intense, but better than before her hospital admission."

At one point, ages ago, Rosemary made a pass at Nick. Although he was shocked, Stella persuaded Nick to overlook the manic behaviour. Aiden, mortified, apologized. Upon reflection, the episode began this most recent phase.

"Rosemary received habit reversal therapy—a new treatment which focuses on awareness of her actions when the spiralling starts. She's learned self-control."

Nick stops in front of the closet. "Sounds as if she performs."

Nodding, Stella continues. "Rosemary stopped her pills. She said I deserve a warning because I'm the person in danger."

His face blanches. "Does Aiden know? Tell Aiden."

"No need. She's back in hospital tomorrow."

"After dinner, while you were talking to Aiden, she told me how her sisters meddle in her affairs and that she wants to slap Toni. According to her, sometimes bad behaviour happens. She winked." He frowns. "Man, I don't trust her for one minute."

They ready themselves for bed. After what seemed like an endless evening, she aches to close her eyes. Five minutes after his ruddy cheek touches the pillow, Nick's gentle rumbles indicate he's asleep. She pats Kiki as the dog settles, and stares at the ceiling. Nick is right. She should reveal Rosemary's secret, but Aiden and her sisters aren't in serious danger. There's no urgency to blow the whistle. The woman has threatened her, and if she thinks Stella has told Aiden, her agitation will increase. She comforts herself in the knowledge Rosemary goes back to hospital tomorrow.

Reaching again for Kiki, she breaks a cardinal rule and lifts the little dog into bed. Kiki curls into a ball and cuddles in response. Aiden is doomed.

****

"Miss Kiki was beside you this morning." He winks. "I thought we made a rule."

"Rosemary tormented my thoughts most of the night. I needed company." She giggles. "You were no help."

"As I've mentioned in the past, you can wake me," he teases, as he opens his arms to her.

Trixie calls before they finish their Sunday breakfast. "Hi. You're up early."

"I live with a pre-schooler for a few more days." She groans. "Listen, I spoke with Renée Tait yesterday. If you go to the post office for a talk tomorrow morning, she'll be there. She works at the wicket on Mondays. Come here first and we'll walk over. The best time is early, before the mail's sorted."

"Okay, I'll be at your place by nine. Thanks."

"How was supper with Aiden and crazy girl?"

"Could have used your company. She's off. Normal outfit, but her eyes were angry. She told me they taught her habit reversal therapy."

"What?"

"Yes. Her psychiatrists and therapists coached her in the idea of reversing her habits instead of masking her truth with anti-social attitudes—the way she treats Aiden, the clothes. You know." She avoids any medication discussion with her sister. "She sounded like the shrink when she explained."

"So did you right now. I'll miss the old Rosemary."

"She's not gone. I don't think Aiden's aware her therapy has backfired. She returns tomorrow, and I'm not disappointed."

"You sound surly. Leave your attitude at the park when you come into town."

Stella replaces the receiver on the wall and ponders Trixie's comment. Revealing Rosemary's secret to Aiden is the cure for her dark mood.

When the phone rings again, she's busy as Nick's assistant while he makes brown bread and a batch of hot milk buns.

"Jasper Nunn here." His tone is deep and melodic.

"Good morning, Jasper. I'm happy you called. Did you talk with Horace?"

"As you asked. Horace remembers Lloyd Gurney and Weldon Beck. His memory ain't as sharp as mine, but he figures they were here three years ago."

"Did he tell you more?"

"Yup. He said—gimme a minute."

The line quiets. Stella waits.

"Hi again. Helga came into the kitchen, and I waited until she left. I told her Horace needed help." He chuckles. "We cooked up a diversion. Smart, eh?"

"Smooth, Jasper." Impressive.

"Okay. I'll be fast. Both Lloyd and Weldon were sickly men. Lloyd had two heart attacks while he lived here. Weldon had cancer and they couldn't operate—in his brain, I guess. One after the other, they moved away. Weldon left first. Lloyd thought he was admitted to the hospital. He stayed alone in a room before he disappeared, as well. Horace assumed he found a bed at the manor. He never heard from either gent again. Ira—you already know his story." He pauses. "I don't think anyone found a bed at the manor, do you?"

"No, Jasper. You've been a colossal help. Your assistance is very much appreciated."

"Here comes Helga," he whispers. "Gotta go."

"Off the phone, Jasper. You said you'd be a minute," are the final words Stella hears before the line goes dead.

Lloyd Gurney and Weldon Beck. Neither were well men. She will bet her share in next season's profits that the three male last names on those cheques in Maura Martin's office are Gurney, Beck, and Gold. She turns toward the pantry and retrieves more flour for Nick, while hoping chatty Renée reveals surnames.

****

"Come on in." Trixie answers the door at Yellow House as Stella lifts her knuckles and raps. "We've time for coffee." With her mug clutched in one hand and the other holding her ratty red cable-knit sweater closed, she hustles Stella inside.

"None for me, thanks, but I'll buy you a cup at the café after our visit with Renée."

"Fair enough. Monday is croissant day. Tiffany says there'll be hot blueberry sauce for dipping."

Stella admires Trixie's ability to eat whatever she wants without repercussions. The elastic-waisted pants she chose this morning prove she doesn't enjoy the same advantage.

"Come say hi, before we go." She leads the way through the children's library and the dining room, now the bookstore, to the back of the house where Brigitte and Mia are reciting nursery rhymes and eating a leisurely breakfast, both still in pyjamas.

She hugs Brigitte and pats Mia's soft curls before Trixie wriggles into her rabbit fur jacket and they leave. On their walk across the street, Stella looks for logic where none seems to exist. "I'm curious why Renée agreed to answer my questions. Gossip must put her job in jeopardy."

"Lobster," Trixie replies with a flick of her strawberry curls.

Eying her sister's frown, Trixie adds, "She wanted a feed for New Year's Eve. I used my contacts and found what she needed. The task was a favour, but at delivery time, I traded the lobster for whatever she knows. She said she'd speak with you, but the information can't come back and risk her job. I agreed on your behalf. Alright?"

"You've somehow gained deal-making ability, but okay. Good job, by the way," she adds, in the hope she hasn't insulted her sister.

Renée Tait pushes through the saloon door between the mail room and the public space. Her stature is minuscule. No one has natural hair that black. Her eyebrows are painted on, and she has a dollop of rouge on each cheek matching bright red lips—a real life Betty Boop. Stella wonders how she sees over the counter. In response, Renée steps on a box, positioned in front of her wicket.

"Good morning, ladies. Trixie, you must be frozen after your dash across the street. Hi Stella. I don't see you often. Your handsome boyfriend runs in for the mail." She swivels a hip in Stella's general direction and smirks. "Aren't you the lucky duck?"

"More than a boyfriend. He's her partner in the business, now." Trixie puffs with pride. "I sold my shares the end of last month. Oh, and you might as well know a change of address will cross your desk any day. I bought a place outside town."

"Duly noted—the murderer's house, right?"

"How did you find out?"

Renée leans closer. "The wicket knows."

Trixie soldiers on, which leaves little room for Stella to insert a word. "My sister needs information regarding Jack Lawson, Monica Lawson, and the mail Jack retrieves."

The postal clerk peers past them toward the door. "Move over for a minute. One of my regular customers has come in. He buys stamps from me on Mondays." She waves them to the side. "Hi, Charlie," she simpers. "Ten today?"

With no other choice, they wait. After Charlie leaves with his purchase, she motions them back. "This place will start to jump soon, but I'll help as best I can. Here are the names of the people she collects cheques for: Minerva Gardiner, Wilhelmina Saunders, Ira Gold, Lloyd Gurney, Weldon Beck, and Monica Lawson." She offers her verbal list, which also includes the seven residents at Merlon's and Jane's, and she mentions the extra cheque for Flora. "I must admit, I'm surprised she takes care of her mother, because she dumped Monica at Jane's when the work became too much before. The neighbours hate Jack. Mrs. McKechnie, who lives next door, complains the most."

Stella finishes jotting the names on a small pad retrieved from her purse. "What kinds of complaints?"

"I can't talk for long, but I called Mrs. McKechnie and asked her if she would meet you this morning. Buy her coffee." She hops off her step. "I'm off out back. Stock needs replenishing. She'll be here any minute. She's made police reports at least twice. A cement planter caused no end of concern." She wiggles ringed fingers at them and uses a stage whisper when she repeats, "Buy her a croissant, too. The old girl will answer whatever you ask."

Obviously, the two women are alike, if the lobster is any indication, Stella muses in silence.

Renée disappears as an older lady, bent at the waist and carrying a wicker basket, hauls open the plate glass door. Stella and Trixie glance at one another before Stella nods and addresses the entrant. "Mrs. McKechnie? I'm Stella Kirk and let me introduce my sister, Trixie. Renée suggested we speak with you."

"Yes. Renée said you're interested in my terrible neighbour. We can't talk here—too many big ears."

"Couldn't agree more, Mrs. McKechnie. Why don't we pop over to Cocoa and Café? Trixie tells me Tiffany and Andrew make croissants on Monday."

The elderly woman shuffles a turn and pushes the heavy door out into the cold without replying. Stella and Trixie hurry to keep pace.

"Renée was right. The old girl will go through hoops for a croissant," Trixie whispers.

"Let's hope she'll talk. She sounds like a chronic complainer."

"We'll see."

Mrs. McKechnie stands with obvious impatience on the front deck of the café. "Shake a leg, you two. I might freeze out here and need coffee."

****

Stella watches Tiffany lift an eyebrow as the three of them muddle through the doorway. The bells finally stop tinkling. "Find a seat anywhere. We're quiet today."

"Thanks." Trixie waves. "Word on the street is you planned croissants and wild blueberry preserves in celebration of your first day of business for 1982."

"Your sources are correct," she chuckles. "Coffees?"

Echoes of yes bounce off the polished antique pine floors.

Mrs. McKechnie removes her knitted hat and wriggles out of her plaid-lined trench coat.

Since a conversation starts best with acknowledgement of the other person, Stella opens with the classic, "Tell me about yourself, Mrs. McKechnie."

"Please, call me Eunice." She accepts a mug of brew from Tiffany. Steam spirals between them. "Listen." She points her finger. "I filed two police reports related to unusual occurrences in the area, and they treat me as if I'm some kind of kook. Renée said you help the police, Stella. How are you different?"

"Eunice, I contract with them and we're investigating the body found at the bottom of the hole dug for Mallory Gorman's grave. The location is in the new section opened by the municipality in the late fall. As a result, we are following up on other reports in the past months."

"The local detachment didn't show any interest, but I'll tell you about both my experiences." She quiets when Tiffany returns with two croissants and a small bowl of hot wild blueberry preserves for each of them. "My oh my, how yummy. A feast for the eyes and one for the tummy." Her guffaw at her own rhyme seems out of character. She breaks a piece of the pastry, dips it in the jam, and places the morsel in her mouth.

Stella watches in fascination as she inserts the food with her thumb and index finger, closes her lips, and chews. Eunice tears off another chunk, dips, and inserts the same way once more. She holds both fingers between her lips while she enjoys the initial bite. She catches Trixie's eye. Her sister has noticed, as well.

"I'm happy the police are paying attention, although this is a rather convoluted approach for an interview."

"A more personal touch is my preference. Shall we start again, and you can tell us more about yourself?"

"First, I am a retired practical nurse. I left work because of my late husband, sick with Parkinson's." She dabs her navy lips and fingers with the paper napkin. "Lots of illness around. Take care of yourselves, girls. You can't count on men to be there to help."

As she struggles to recall the last time she saw a doctor, Stella asks Eunice to tell them more.

"I'm a night hawk. I often don't settle until three or four in the morning. Miss my husband. Can't be helped." She waves her hand and brushes away her grief. "I quilt. I read. I walk my poodle, Brutus, and I visit Mr. McKechnie at the graveyard. Most people are never aware of late-night events because they're tucked in their beds. Many say no good comes from activities after dark."

"Will you share your observations with us, Eunice?" Stella's croissant remains untouched.

"I sit with my husband late at night."

"At the graveyard? Don't you find the place creepy?" Trixie has never mastered the art of thoughtful silence.

After a quick glare in her sister's direction, Stella pushes Eunice for additional information.

"Two years ago, I heard a machine when I visited Mr. McKechnie. Brutus noticed the noise, too. In the part of the field where you found the man's body, there was a big digger with lights on and I could see everything despite the snow coming down. I sat beside Mr. McKechnie, with Brutus in my arms, and watched." She stops and breaks her second pastry into bite-sized pieces. "I went to the police station the next day. A husky man named Sergeant Moyer wrote my information on a slip of paper, but no one called me back."

Stella's voice catches. "Eunice, do you remember the date?"

"Mr. McKechnie and I communicate every Wednesday and Saturday.

This was Saturday, December 15, 1979. I can double-check my calendar when I return home, but I confirmed before I came out, and am sure I'm right."

"Thank you. What was the second report you filed?"

"Horrible Jack Lawson lives next door. I thought, when she dumped poor Monie into Jane's Retirement Home for Ladies, she'd sell the house. No such luck. Jack has never worked at a normal job. I expected a real estate sign, but she must've tapped into Monie's savings. Makes me mad."

The act of information retrieval from Eunice McKechnie challenges Stella. "What did you report, Eunice?"

Eunice removes her fingers from her mouth. "Will you ask Tiffany for more coffee, please? The pastries make me thirsty."

Trixie swivels in her chair and waves.

With her cup filled, Eunice continues. "Around six months ago, Jack built a cement planter in the middle of the night. Any civilized person hires a contractor who works from eight until five. On the same night, I assembled my quilt frame in my living room." She glances at both women before she explains. "I don't entertain many visitors. The contraption sits where there's the most space, the biggest window, and the best light." She shakes her white curls. "Anyway, Brutus decided he required a stroll at two in the morning. I saw her mixing cement in a wheelbarrow. She huffed with the weight of the stuff. She built the ugliest monstrosity you can imagine in the front of her house. Jack's no mason."

"You told the police Jack Lawson built a cement planter in the middle of the night? When?" Stella's mind dashes in ten different directions.

"Six months ago." She pushes a piece of dipped croissant into her mouth with two fingers, drawing out the action for as long as possible, in Stella's eyes. Her nails have turned blue. "I didn't report Jack because of her hideous masonry. I reported her because she told people she brought her mother home from Jane's, but I've seen no sign of her. Such circumstances should be suspicious enough for the police." She sniffs her indignation.

"Perhaps the details are confused, Eunice, a common occurrence when we don't know the facts. You're sure you saw heavy machinery, in what is now the graveyard, on December 15, 1979, around ten o'clock, and six months ago, Jack Lawson built a cement planter at her house."

"Yes. And Monie never came home from Jane's. May, the housekeeper at Jane's—I attended school with her—told me Monie died. I assumed a modicum of interest from the police. Now you know everything I told them."

"It has been a pleasure to meet and talk with you."

"I appreciate a kind ear. I spend most of my days alone and I understand old women can get muddled, but I don't think I'm wrong." She stands and hauls her cap over her curls before she lifts her coat from the chair.

Stella jumps and assists her on with the heavy garment.

"Appreciated, dear. I must go. Time for Brutus' walkie, and I need a nap. Nice meeting you both. By the way, Trixie, your daughter has done a fine job with Yellow House. Paulina would be pleased." She pushes open the door, the bells tinkle, and she's gone.

"Tiffany," Stella motions across the empty café. "I'll take the bill."

Chapter 20

Second Thoughts Niggle

"After the twenty-plus years I've lived with and managed her illness, I can't put my finger on the problem, but this time her behaviour is different."

They're shuttered in Aiden's Shale Harbour office. Their purpose—review Stella's latest information and concerns. Preoccupied with his wife's status, Stella squirms in her seat while he describes the perpetual battle he endures when managing Rosemary North. "Somehow, regardless of her sisters' descriptions of her behaviour for the admission psychiatrist—the rants, the violence, the attacks—he authorized her return to Port Ephron." Aiden lifts his hand when Stella opens her mouth. "Not with her sisters. With me."

"Rosemary has moved back with you?" Her statement becomes a question. *Do I tell him about her threats?*

"Yes. Much to my surprise, she's her old self. We arrived home, and she prepared supper—supper, Stella. I can't remember the last time the two of us ate a meal she cooked."

"And Toni and Mary Jo? Are they happy with the arrangements?" He sounds better than he has in months. She opts to keep quiet.

"The three of them fell out over Rosemary's unpredictability. Toni told me she hoped I'd handle her better. I need Cloris now—to stay with Rosemary when I'm involved in a case."

"She's away with Duke."

"I gathered. I can't reach her. If they call you, will you request she contact me?"

"They'll be back at the end of the month. They drove to Florida. Cloris, or a friend of hers, has a place in Fort Meyers."

Aiden grits his teeth and forces a smile. "Guess I wait. Not many options." He stares at his desk surface. "On the topic at hand, my superiors conclude we've identified the old man and his cause of death. They aren't too preoccupied with how he landed in Mallory Gorman's grave."

"No family and no media pressure, but once we go through the information I've uncovered, you might disagree with the idea of closing the investigation."

"Rosemary must come first, Stella, and I'll reserve the long hours for a real murder. You understand." He studies her reaction.

She curbs the tension in her voice when she replies. "This death may not be an intended murder, but I'm sure there's a cover-up of one sort or another."

He acquiesces for the moment, and she launches into a detailed description of the indicators she's uncovered—she clarifies how Maura Martin and Hector Green, spouses, own the properties which are now Jane's Retirement Home for Ladies and Merlon's Place for Gentlemen. She describes, in significantly more detail than he appears interested in hearing, how the finances for both boarding homes are managed. She reports Jack Lawson's involvement, which includes her prior volunteer work at Harbour Manor, her employment by Maura Martin, and notes the woman questioned both Norbert and Del regarding their financial affairs. She lists the names on the thirteen cheques Jack retrieves and delivers to Maura Martin each month and stipulates the five addressees who are not guests, or are no longer guests—Willy Saunders, Ira Gold, Minnie Gardiner, Lloyd Gurney, and Weldon Beck.

After a short break while they scrounge for coffee, she begins again with little need to reference her notes, although he interrupts.

"Tell me how you found out whose names were on the cheques? What did you investigate when my back was turned, Stella?"

His tone holds no malice, but he hasn't made a joke, either. Second thoughts niggle. "I asked a few questions, Kiki provided distractions, and lobster helped."

"Lobster." He stares at her with his mouth open.

"Don't ask, Aiden. Trust me. The information is reliable." She ignores his continued expression of disbelief. "And I have suspicions regarding Monica Lawson. Her daughter, Jack, collects a cheque for her, as well, but I've been given to understand there's no sign of the woman. Her neighbour, Eunice, claims Jack says she brought her mother home, but she learned, from her friend at Jane's, that Monica died. Jack built a planter in her front yard in the middle of the night. The behaviour is curious."

"Do you understand why I'm worried?" His voice has developed a distinct edge. "You represent the police department and ask questions without authorization. You've interviewed people without proper supervision."

She stiffens to harness control and not overreact. "Didn't you prefer my unorthodox approach? Didn't you say my contract is temporary until Essie Matkowski returns? Well, I've discovered proof Maura Martin collects a cheque for at least one dead person, and from my conversations with residents at both Jane's and Merlon's, possibly more than one." She stops for breath. "And I'm convinced Jack Lawson's mother died. I won't declare she's in the planter—which might be far-fetched, even for me—but she sure as hell isn't in the vicinity."

"Tell me why you anticipate the people whose names are on the cheques aren't alive." His tone calms, but Stella has known Aiden most of her life. She misses the affection she often sees in his eyes when they work together.

"Flora, from Jane's, said Minnie disappeared in the night, as did Mrs. Lawson. And Horace, at Merlon's, told Jasper how both Weldon and Lloyd left for hospital and never came back."

Aiden stands. "Are you telling me you engaged Jasper Nunn to interview a witness in a disappearance case?"

"I knew getting back inside Merlon's again would be tough." She studies him and nods. "I took a chance. Horace has lived at Merlon's for several years."

"Stella, none of your information is valuable or usable in court. With no controls over your questions, you obtained facts without permission. What can I do with the details?" He slumps in his chair.

"Come with me and question Jack Lawson. Use your policeman's clout. Encourage her to admit she works for Maura Martin. Ask your staff to dig into JanlonNS."

"Your conclusions, Stella?"

"I refuse theorization until you're as suspicious as me," she huffs. "People collect pension cheques for other elders who aren't around, and I wonder why. One of those individuals is Ira Gold, and we know he's dead. The police don't seem to have much interest in protecting vulnerable old people. You can justify a visit as a follow-up on one of Mrs. McKechnie's complaints. Now, will you come with me to Jack's, or do I conduct another unauthorized interview by myself?"

"No. No." He closes his eyes for a moment. "Let's visit her after lunch. I promised I'd go home."

She scratches Jack's address on a slip of paper and plunks the information on his desk. "I'll meet you at two."

****

The 1940s Shale Harbour neighbourhood, called the "old-new" subdivision, has dual entrances east off Chestnut, and is named Chestnut Crescent—yet another example of the lack of originality by village managers and members of council. Ten houses comprise the group, four on the inside turn and six on the longer semi-circle rim. The little area was once considered ultra-modern, but after forty years, has lost much of its appeal. Many of the residences are rented to tourists in the summer and left empty throughout the winter. A drive along the street gives one the sense of abandonment. The Lawson home sports a hideous cement planter at the entrance and proves easy to locate, even if Stella didn't know the number. The dwelling resembles the others, with two narrow windows framing the door. The roof is peaked. In the Lawson case, the door remains uncovered, although some neighbours have added porches or extensions. Jack's house sits as constructed—a two-bedroom, one bath depression-era-style unit focused on the needs of the populace at the time.

Aiden hasn't arrived. Stella parks her car in front of Eunice's house. She suspects the property belongs to the chatty old lady because a picture window was installed years ago. She sits. Her watch says five to two.

Jack's home is unkempt. One drainpipe hangs askew. She sees loose shingles on the roof and the dirty white asbestos siding is chipped in many places. As she ponders her path to convincing Aiden to arrive at the same conclusions she has already reached, he pulls in behind her in an RCMP issue sedan.

She climbs out of the Jeep and waits. Aiden approaches with his shoulders slumped and his face a blank. She can sense his lack of interest. "Lunch go okay?"

"Rosie needs supervision when I'm at work, Stella. I want a successful fresh start." He squints at the house. "Ready? Let's put this interview behind us."

"I see her green car in the driveway. I assume she's here." Stella leads the way along the cracked and frozen walkway, ignoring Aiden's impatience.

"Stella Kirk? You're on the wrong side of the tracks this afternoon." Jack Lawson has opened the front door a scant two inches in response to Stella's brisk knock.

"Your crescent isn't on the wrong side of the tracks, Jack," she admonishes. "Let me introduce Detective North of the Port Ephron and Shale Harbour RCMP. I'm a consultant with the department," she adds, as a means of explanation.

"How do you do, Miss Lawson." Aiden remains on the second step. "We want a word."

"Give me a minute to find my coat. I'll meet you outside. My mother is asleep." The door clicks shut, and they wait. Jack reappears, her emaciated frame swallowed by a fur-trimmed car coat many sizes too big. She wraps the bulky garment around herself. "Now, what can I do for you?" She grabs her thin, grey-streaked hair and tosses a handful over her shoulder before she settles on the edge of the planter.

Aiden glances at Stella and begins. "I understand you collect the mail for two boarding homes in the community—Jane's Retirement Home for Ladies and Merlon's Place for Gentleman. Correct?"

"Yeah, I collect the mail for the boarding houses. What's your problem?"

"Who do you work for, Miss Lawson?"

"Maura Martin and Hector Greene. They own both places. I volunteer—and I work for money."

"Do they use a company name?"

"Yes, Stella." Jack's voice has developed an edge. "They own JanlonNS, a private company which runs the boarding homes. Not a secret, you two."

"Four men are currently settled at Merlon's and three women at Jane's." Stella's interruption is designed to lead Aiden in the right direction. "How many cheques do you collect and deliver?"

"No idea. I drop off whatever lands in the boxes. Now, my mother needs my attention, and I'm freezing out here." She stands.

"We could come inside, Jack." Stella inches her way toward the door. "I see you built a planter."

"I gather Eunice McKechnic blabbed. I confess, I worked on this baby in the middle of the night. Guilty as charged." She pats the cement unit behind her. "My mother needs lots of care during the day, and sometimes the only opportunity I have for property maintenance," she sneers, "is in the middle of the night. Eunice is a busybody who walks her yappy dog at two in the morning."

"May we meet your mother, Jack? Flora mentioned her when I visited at Jane's. The residents say you don't pop in as much anymore, since you moved Monica home with you. Lots of work, eh?" She studies Jack's face, finding evidence of strain, as she suspected. "I couldn't manage taking care of my dad." Stella remains wedged in front of the door. "Eunice says she's never seen Monica, or Monie as she calls her, even though your mother came back here with you."

"Let me in my house. No, you can't come in. I answered your questions. Now leave me alone." Jack shoves Stella aside. "Don't you police need a warrant? My mother is sick." The door slams in their faces.

On the way toward the street, Aiden says, "I'll apply for a warrant. Can you return to the station and write a complete report on what you've discovered and why we interpret entry into her house as necessary?"

"And her yard and the inside of her planter, too."

"Why?"

"There's a possibility Monica Lawson died at Jane's and Jack buried her in the yard or hid her in the planter so she could cash the government pension cheques."

Aiden blanches. "You're kidding, right?"

"No, my friend. Ira Gold represents the tip of a cheque fraud scam. Uncovering fraud won't be a problem." She waves at Eunice, partially obscured behind her living room curtains before she opens the door of her Jeep.

****

Jack Lawson's cement planter overflows with her mother.

Early the next day, Aiden called Stella and requested she be in the vicinity when the RCMP executed the warrant on Chestnut Crescent. The paperwork authorized a search of the house, the basement, the yard, and the outdoor planter, specifically for Mrs. Monica Lawson, once a resident of Jane's Retirement Home for Ladies. With Stella's report in hand, Aiden argued reasonable grounds based on the fact Mrs. Lawson had not been seen or heard from in six months. Reports of her demise conflicted with the lack of typical processes—no funeral, death certificate, or doctor's report from the hospital.

Stella parked in front of Eunice's and remained in her vehicle as requested.

Four uniformed officers entered Jack's, while Jack waited, perched once again on the planter. At one point, Aiden approached Stella's driver's side window. "Your suspicion of the planter intrigued me. Jack's mother isn't in the house. She said Mrs. Lawson went to the hospital, but we checked, and she's not a patient. Time for the mason, standing by, to open the planter before we destroy the basement floor."

"Good idea. Don't ruin the inside if not necessary."

"Especially with no signs of new cement in the house." He rested his hand on her shoulder. Warmth penetrated her coat. "I was out of touch on the case, Stella. Thanks for your diligence."

"We'll see if I'm right in a minute. Here comes the guy with the sledgehammer and pry bar." She climbed from the Jeep and leaned against the front bumper for a better view after Aiden returned.

Her stomach lurched as the second whack revealed a hand—dusty, mottled, and grey. Work stopped. Forensics arrived, and the police erected tarps around the entry, preventing curious neighbours from witnessing further progress.

****

Aiden bundles Jack into the back of his sedan. Stella follows him to the Shale Harbour detachment. She waits in his office while he completes Jack's paperwork. He rushes in.

"Forensics will be on Chestnut Crescent for the day, at least. We'll interview Jack and keep her here overnight while we assemble evidence. I could use your help."

"Let me phone Nick."

"Right. And I should ring Rosemary." His eyes dart around the room. "Let's break for lunch and talk with Jack afterward. You ask the questions."

She hesitates before she replies. "Sure."

Aiden departs for home while Stella calls Nick. After she assures him she's fine and will be back in time for dinner, she wanders over to Main and the café for a sandwich and a decent cup of coffee. She compiles her notes. They reconvene at one o'clock.

"I'll ask Jack for the details of her mother's death, Aiden. I'm convinced she died at Jane's."

Sergeant Moyer accompanies Jack into the interview room. Stella has taken her familiar post at the corner of the table. Aiden begins. "Miss Lawson, our forensics team will be at your home for a considerable time. Expect to be held overnight." He turns toward Stella.

"You built the planter six months ago, Jack. When did Monica die?"

"Six months ago. At Jane's."

"What happened?"

"Without income of my own, I needed Mom alive." Her voice shakes, but her slumped posture and closed eyes indicate relief to Stella. "She stayed for free because I worked for Maura and Hector. I was desperate for money and assumed if people were under the impression that I cared for Mom at home by myself, I could collect her pension. I didn't kill her." Tears run down weathered cheeks. She lifts her head. "Please understand, I didn't kill my mother."

Stella nods. "What did you do after she died?"

"Maura contacted her nephew, Luther, who came to Jane's with a station wagon from the funeral home. He loaded the body and brought her home. I needed three days to build the planter, and I kept her wrapped in a sheet in the living room on the couch." She clutches her chapped hands in her lap. "Maura was right. People made assumptions and I collected the money, although gross and scary doesn't begin to describe those three days. Since I don't have other family, there was nobody interested—except for nosy Eunice. I didn't kill her," she whines.

"Are you a scout for Maura and Hector?"

"A scout? What do you mean?"

"Do you troll for elderly folks with no family and no one who manages their affairs? Maybe people at the manor who are out of money and don't qualify for the nursing home subsidy—Jasper, for example?"

"Maybe," she mutters.

"You approached both Del Trembly and my father. You asked if they needed help with their finances."

"That was ages ago. Maura set me straight, though, and said I should only talk with people who are fit, running out of money, and have no family."

Stella nods toward Aiden.

"Miss Lawson, we're permitted twenty-four hours before we charge or release you. You are now held under suspicion. I expect a preliminary forensics report in the morning. Sergeant Moyer will accompany you back to a cell." He reaches for the phone and calls the front desk.

After they leave, his shoulders heave. "You understand how complicated this case could become."

Relief ripples through her. "Understood."

Aiden sits with both arms and legs crossed. "I'll call you tomorrow morning once I've heard from autopsy and forensics. I expect they'll be at work until the wee hours. Thanks for your report. At least you had a productive lunch break. No more work for us here." His face muscles sag. "You go home and spend time with your handsome boyfriend. I will take the opportunity and check in on Rosemary early for once."

She doesn't understand the snarky boyfriend comment, but rather than confront the issue, most often her preference, she does as he suggests. "I'll wait for your call. Have a nice evening."

He remains slumped, his body wrapped in his sullen frown.

On her way home, she wades through the myriad of emotions fluttering for her attention. Although vindicated, in reference to Jack and Monica Lawson, and convinced Maura and Hector are involved in a web of deceit around cheque fraud, she's mystified at Aiden's attitude. Part of her is pleased this may be her last case.

Chapter 21

What a Mess

Stella sits at her desk, elbows on the surface, index fingers massaging the bone between her brows. With five weeks of head winds, she still isn't sure Aiden will follow through and investigate the missing boarding home residents. She's convinced they'll discover more fraud and more players. Jack Lawson wasn't working alone, and her poor mother is likely not the only victim. Kiki snuggles deeper into her lap. Baggy sweatpants provide a nest for the little dog. The massage helps her think. Should she persist with the inquiry? When the phone finally jangles, she jumps and clutches Kiki.

"Shale Cliffs RV...."

"Good morning, Stella. Sorry for the wait. I received the preliminary report from forensics and autopsy."

"No surprises, I imagine." She muffles anticipated disappointment.

"You're right. Mrs. Dawson died of congestive heart failure—natural causes—six to eight months ago. Jack's confession is true."

"Fine. One problem solved."

"She's agreed to cooperate and take part in another interview. Carter Stephens said he would represent her as a legal aid rep., and he asked for a mid-afternoon appointment. Can you help a guy out?"

"Yes. I'm curious about what she says regarding other residents."

"Me, too. Shall we say two-thirty?"

"Perfect." She considers "me, too" a win.

****

Nick already has his afternoon planned. After spending the morning touring the park, he appreciated their warm lunch. She'll stop at the bank before she arrives at the detachment. "I'll be home for supper, Nick. Shall I buy us a treat in town? Fish and chips or a pizza?"

He slurps another spoonful of his tomato soup. "No need, my dear. I will make creamy chicken and mushroom linguine. There's a recipe in one of your mother's Italian cookbooks I want to try." His eyes widen when he looks at her. "You find poor old Willy Saunders, and I'll keep you fed."

His unwavering support encourages her to call Aiden and tell him he can run his own damned investigation. She prefers home. "Maybe I'll hurry the interview along." She blushes.

****

The Shale Harbour Savings and Loan sits at the town's entrance, on the corner of Main and the highway, facing south toward the ocean. The salmon-coloured Georgian structure, with the widow's walk on the roof, commands a presence when one approaches Shale Harbour from this direction. Although eighteen months have passed since Lorraine Young, a bank employee and resident of Stella's RV park, was murdered, Stella still steels herself whenever she enters the premises. The high ceilings and stone floors remain unchanged, although Lorraine's absence is palpable each time she enters. Mark Bell and Terri Price are behind their wickets. The manager's office is empty.

After a minimal wait, she exchanges pleasantries with both tellers while Mark counts the cash withdrawn from the chequing account she shares with Nick. By the time she's off the granite steps and begins the short walk to the police station, exhaustion and weak knees overtake her. Full recovery from Lorraine's death has been a slow process.

She finds Aiden leaning against the sergeant's desk, deep in conversation with Moyer. Once they see her, Moyer reaches for his paperwork and Aiden approaches.

"Let's talk in my office while we wait for Carter."

"Fine. Shall I ask the questions again today?"

"I'll lead, but chime in whenever you want. With a lawyer in the room, more formality is required."

"A circumstance which hasn't proved problematic in the past, if you remember Aloysius Fitzgerald, but you're the boss." She expects her surly sensitivities inserted themselves into her tone.

Once in his office, she enquires after Rosemary.

He shifts in his chair. "We've managed, but I'm impatient for Cloris' return. Mary Jo sent over food last night. She stayed outside, but Rosie flew off the rails. She took the casserole through the house and tossed dish and contents into the backyard. Mary Jo wasn't even out of the driveway."

"Maybe a medication issue?" Stella asks, in the faint hope Aiden will realize his wife has stopped her treatment.

"Rosie's annoyed with her sisters. After the incident, she settled herself and made us a nice supper."

"Her therapy must be successful," Stella mumbles.

Aiden lifts his brows but doesn't reply. His telephone rings. "Okay, send him into the interview room and fetch Jack. We're on our way." He nods at Stella. "Showtime."

Jack appears gloomier and more rumpled than normal. A night in cells can humble the most stoic and indifferent. The image of Meredith Tompkins, one of the owners of Grey Cottage Realty, who hired Russ Harrison, nee Harry Russell, to kill her friend Paulina McAdams, materializes. She realizes, with a start, how complicated her life has been in the last eighteen months, as she has assisted Aiden in the investigation of three murder cases. Carter Stephens, Brigitte's fiancé, marches into the room close behind Moyer and Jack. Decked out in a dark suit and white shirt, he carries the role of small-town lawyer well.

"Good morning, Mr. Stephens. For the record, you represent Miss Lawson who admitted, throughout the course of our previous interview, to pension fraud and improper interference with human remains. Here are the pending charges." He hands a file across the table. "You've met Stella Kirk. She continues as a consultant."

Stella acknowledges Carter with a nod.

"We will begin with the preliminary discoveries by our office. Mrs. Lawson has, indeed, been deceased for six months or more. We believe she died at Jane's Retirement Home for Ladies and was buried in a cement planter built by Miss Lawson at the time of Mrs. Lawson's demise. In our brief discussion yesterday, Miss Lawson revealed how Luther Greene assisted with the removal of Mrs. Lawson's body and its transport to Chestnut Crescent and the Lawson residence. In addition, she admitted to pension fraud and suggested Maura Martin encouraged her to conceal the death to enable cashing her dead mother's cheques."

Carter meets Jack's watery eyes for a moment. "My client stipulates to your report. She will also clarify details which may assist in your investigation. We expect leniency for Miss Lawson in return."

Aiden's expression remains fixed. "As you are aware, Mr. Stephens, we must analyze the information and determine value, but if Miss Lawson deserves credit for any revelations, you will be the first contact told."

"Go ahead, Jack. Tell Stella and Detective North."

Jack squirms. Her hands, although trembling, remain clutched in her lap. She focuses on them. "Minnie, that is, Minerva, Gardiner, and Willy, or rather, Wilhelmina, Saunders are both dead. I collected pension cheques for them when they boarded at Jane's as part of my volunteer work. Then they didn't live there anymore. The other residents asked what happened to Minnie, but May insisted she was sent to the hospital in the night."

"And Willy?" Stella's voice encourages.

"She turned up at Jane's after she ran out of savings—with her pension and nothin' else. They couldn't find space for her, so May let her stay on the veranda. They promised her a cat, and when she brought a tiny orange stray home from her wanderin's, they made them both sleep in the shed." She starts to blubber.

Stella offers her a tissue. "Please go on." Despite the horror, she craves more detail.

"The situation upset the night girl at the time, and she quit. After a while, Willy and the cat disappeared. I figured she died, but her cheque kept comin'."

"Can you explain the other cheques you collect, Jack? Ira Gold, for one."

Fat, sloppy tears coat weathered cheeks. "I saw his name on a cheque in the stack of mail, and when you found a guy in overalls in the hole, I assumed Ira was dead, too. He did some work at our place." She pauses and makes eye contact with Stella. "As for the other men, I'm not sure. I didn't volunteer at Merlon's."

Aiden leans across the table. "Do you believe residents died at Jane's and were never reported?"

"Yeah," Jack's whisper is hesitant. She hangs her head and doesn't comment further.

"Detective, I assume my client will be moved to Port Ephron and formally charged. May we expect consideration for her cooperation?"

Aiden nods. "I'll call Sergeant Moyer. After she returns to cells, arrangements for the transfer can be completed."

Once they leave, Aiden turns toward Stella. "We need a serious talk with Maura Martin."

"Indeed...and her husband and nephew...and the staff at both homes. Poor Jack. What a mess. Let me know when."

****

"I expect Aiden will close the case after we interview Maura today." Stella and Nick sit in the kitchen. Finished with breakfast, they enjoy more coffee because she's in no hurry. Warm sunshine spills across the floor. No one complains about the weather these days. Aiden expects her at ten.

"What happens with Luther and Hector Greene?"

"Good question. And conversations are necessary with everyone involved, which includes the staff at both boarding homes, but Aiden is pushing for a conclusion." She meets Nick's sympathetic gaze. "He should retire. The enthusiasm, the inquiring mind, have left him, through no fault of his own."

"Did you tell him what Rosemary said?"

She squeezes her lips together. "No. He thinks she's well-controlled on her medication, although there are still challenges with her sisters. Habit reversal therapy dictates her behaviour, for now. Hard to fathom continual success with the concept spread throughout a lifetime." She studies the bottom of her coffee cup. "He's described incidents where she slipped off the rails and, after a short time, magically returned to normal—self-knowledge from the counselling, I assume, and not her pills."

****

They meet with Maura in Aiden's office later that morning. She has been offered a lawyer and has declined. She told Aiden, when speaking on the phone, she has no secrets. Stella, comfortable in her spot at the side of Aiden's desk, stands when Moyer escorts the nurse in.

Maura Martin is a diminutive woman who enjoys a trim yet curvy figure, which explains why she prefers a traditional waisted nurses' dress uniform, as opposed to the scrub styles which hide your shape and are more popular with staff. She looks oddly out of place in starchy whites and a blue cardigan. Both her mousy hair and her nails are cut short and square. Her shoulders are rigid. She acknowledges Stella and Aiden with an abrupt nod.

"Hello, Ms. Martin. Our discussion today centres around Jane's Retirement Home for Ladies and Merlon's Place for Gentlemen. Can you confirm both enterprises are owned and operated by you and your husband, Hector Greene, under the business name of JanlonNS?"

"Accurate, Detective. And common knowledge, I might add." She settles herself on the chair opposite.

"You are licensed for three men at Merlon's and three women at Jane's."

"Correct again. You did your homework."

Stella frowns. "Four guests live at Merlon's now."

"Really?" She widens her eyes in exaggerated horror. "I must discuss the issue with my staff. They understand the rules, but sometimes the circumstances prove difficult—the act of turning away a person in need." She pouts.

"Ms. Martin, we are aware Jack Lawson collects the mail for both boarding homes on your behalf."

She opens her mouth, but Aiden cuts her off.

"And we are in possession of eyewitness evidence stating you receive five more cheques than registered residents in your establishments. Will you explain?"

Aiden and Stella are met with a blank stare. Maura's eyes glaze, as if she has no idea where she is or what has happened. Her reaction is the most bizarre Stella has observed, after interviews with many suspects. "Maura, cheques are delivered to your office at Harbour Manor each month."

"I receive no cheques. No one delivers my mail."

"Do you mean you don't understand, or do you refuse confirmation of our evidence?"

"Detective North, I am not aware of anyone who collects and delivers cheques."

"Maura." Stella struggles to curb her patience. "Jack Lawson takes eighteen cheques to your office at the end of each month. She remains in police custody, and we have her witness statement. Staff corroborated, and I observed Jack drop them off. The extra five addressees are Willy Saunders, Millie Gardiner, Ira Gold, Weldon Beck, and Lloyd Gurney."

Blankness continues. She focuses on the wall behind Aiden. "You two are settled on a non-existent problem. I will confer with Elsie and Helga, though, and insist Jasper Nunn be evicted. I'm sure you'll be pleased when we're back to our allowable three. You can take him home with you, Stella. He's light care, compared to your father."

"I think Jasper might afford Harbour Manor again, since the rates were reduced." She challenges Maura's stare with one of her own.

"What part does your husband play in your business, Ms. Martin? And your nephew, Luther? Do you pay him extra when he hides a body?"

"Detective North," she says, as she stands, "I came here of my own free will. I answered your questions as best as I am able. I possess no knowledge related to cheques or their delivery. My husband and Luther aren't involved in my profession." She retrieves her shoulder bag from the back of her chair. "I bid you good day."

"Aiden takes a moment and calls Moyer. He instructs him to accompany her out.

"I've never seen such total denial. Maura lives in a parallel universe."

"Here's what we'll do." He leans toward her. "I'll contact Hector Greene and Luther Greene. I want both here for interviews tomorrow morning. Once I secure warrants for Jane's and Merlon's, we can execute them at the same time. With our information on the additional cheques, especially Ira Gold's, and Maura Martin's abject denials, my superiors will approve a move forward, I'm sure." He reaches for his phone before she leaves, waves one hand and adds, "I expect the searches to consume the day."

****

"The case isn't closed yet." As they prepare dinner, Stella fills Nick in on progress. "I expected Maura would admit she's committed cheque fraud, but no such luck." She tosses the salad. "Patsy from finance listed the names she saw, and Renée, from the post office, filled in the blanks. Maura continues to act unaware; as if she has no clue."

"What happens now?"

"Scheduled interviews with Luther Greene and Hector Greene in the morning, and search warrants for both boarding home properties, executed at the same time. We'll talk with staff at the two residences, but I imagine they do as they're told."

"On a Saturday? I guess your case isn't closed, but shall we enjoy a quiet evening while we can?" He fusses at the stove, while she rummages in the fridge for salad dressing.

"Yes. You, me, and fur-face." She turns to tweak Kiki on the end of her nose.

****

The next morning, she reaches for the bleating phone on the kitchen wall while Nick, tousled and yummy in a T-shirt and pyjama bottoms, rustles silverware.

"Hey. Hope I didn't wake you."

"No, but I haven't drunk any coffee yet. Be on your guard," she snickers.

"When I called Otto King at the funeral home yesterday, he said Luther was a no-show for work. I instructed him to call the station the minute the guy arrives, if he arrives today, and we'll send a car to fetch him. On the positive side, Hector Greene will make time for us. Can you be here by ten, again?"

"No problem. What about a lawyer to accompany him?"

"I'm doubtful. I've asked for his cooperation in our investigation. I want him relaxed because the execution of both warrants begins at eleven o'clock when extra staff arrives from Halifax. Judging by his attitude, I don't believe Maura has spoken with him."

"Maura was in complete denial throughout our interview, although the walls are closing in now."

"Hopefully you're right. We got permission for searches of the boarding houses, out buildings, and the surrounding property. With the warm weather and the snow melted, a grid search at each location should be straightforward."

Her stomach churns. She hopes she's right. "May I observe the action, Aiden?"

"We can both attend the site, but after we interview Hector, and Luther if we find him. And I'll dash home at noon."

"Okay. As for Luther, call Vic Staples. They're buddies. Maybe he knows where Luther went."

"Great idea. See you later."

Once off the phone, Nick gives her one of his "I won't ask" stares, but she explains the situation.

"Let me drive into town and buy you lunch at the hotel. We'll enjoy an hour alone before you race around in search of bodies buried under the apple trees." He finishes his last bite of toast and retrieves Kiki from her bed in the corner. "I hope Duke calls," he mutters.

"What? Me, too. Aiden wants a word with Cloris. He's counting on her assistance again with Rosemary—respite during work hours. I expect their days are numbered before she goes off the rails for the umpteenth time."

"Will Cloris stay all day? She was back-up before."

"Not sure if she would want such as assignment, but Toni and Mary Jo are no help now. Rosemary's therapy is an act."

"If she tries to hurt you...." He pats Kiki, perhaps with excessive enthusiasm, leaving further words unsaid. His anxiety for her is written on his face.

"I think you might be over-reacting a titch." She holds her thumb and forefinger an inch apart. Her expression softens. "I'll tell Aiden when the case wraps. I know I said 'soon' once, but I'm sure now. Do we need Duke for help with more work when he comes home from Florida? What's the urgency to speak with him?"

He rocks in the chair with Kiki in his arms. The tiny dog, dressed today in a navy-blue fisherman's knit sweater, relaxes in pure bliss with her eyes closed. "To say we want to keep her." He leans his cheek against her fur. "I mean, he's here when we're open. He can visit with her, walk her, even spend time with her at his trailer, but she'll be ours. What do you think?"

"Do we need a dog underfoot? Do we need vet bills?" She watches Kiki with a barely disguised grin.

"Be practical. She's around all the time, now. You agree, right?" He holds his face against Kiki's and they both plead with mournful eyes.

"We'll talk over lunch." She attempts a stern tone. "The hotel at noon."

"Call if you can't meet me."

"Oh, no problem. Aiden flies out the door when twelve o'clock hits. Rosemary insists he come home. Alright, my two cute friends," she pats them when she passes the chair, "I must dress for my sojourn into town."

Chapter 22

Maybe She's Nearby

Hector Greene's stature impresses. He stands well over six foot four inches and holds himself upright and contained, presenting at the Shale Harbour RCMP detachment in a black pinstriped suit with a vest and bow tie. Stella watches him remove his black felt fedora. The action reveals his bald and shiny dome. He tosses both the hat and his wool topcoat across a chair in the interview room and sits, albeit with considerable caution.

"Thank you, Moyer. Mr. Greene, my name is Detective Aiden North and let me introduce my colleague, Stella Kirk."

He nods.

"Do you know why you've been asked here today?"

"Not for sure, Detective, but I'm happy to cooperate with local law enforcement."

"We understand you and your wife own JanlonNS, which is the holding company for Jane's Retirement Home for Ladies and Merlon's Place for Gentlemen."

"You are correct. Merlon is my middle name and Jane is Maura's." He smirks. "I suggested the names were too cliché, but Maura liked the concept." He leans toward them. "An issue at one of our establishments? Maura handles the day-to-day activities—staff difficulties, collections, and such."

"JanlonNS, as you call your company, collects money for dead people." Stella's goal is to knock Hector off guard in the hope he'll reveal the scheme he and Maura run.

He throws his head back until his nose points toward the ceiling, and crows. His guffaw continues until Aiden intervenes.

"Mr. Greene, your response is exaggerated."

Hector pulls himself together. "Sorry, Detective. Money for dead people. Why in God's name do the deceased require funds?" He reveals large horse-like teeth at Stella. "An inside track with the other side?" He titters at his joke.

Stella may well bite her tongue in half before their interview ends. She doesn't appreciate Hector Greene's humour. "Let me rephrase. We gathered evidence which shows more cheques are collected for residents of your two boarding homes than there are people who occupy them."

"Miss Kirk." Hector covers his mouth in mock horror. "I don't for one minute believe you are a member of the force and I possess no knowledge of cheques or numbers." He pauses and glances upward again. "Oh yes. Maura mentioned a man at Merlon's will be evicted because we are over our quota for an unlicensed facility. Is Mr. Nunn your concern?"

Aiden's eyes narrow. "Stella Kirk consults for the department and her input is valuable beyond measure. Jasper Nunn is not our focus. Your business receives thirteen cheques instead of an expected eight each month. Unless you secretly house more residents than Jasper Nunn, we want the location of the other four people—and bear in mind we found Ira Gold, the fifth person, at the bottom of Mallory Gorman's grave."

He widens his eyes and hunches forward. "Can't help, I'm afraid. I am a partner of JanlonNS in name and little else. My beautiful wife is the work horse in the company." He leans in on one shoulder. Stella is reminded of news anchors engaging with their viewers. "And I mean my remark in the nicest way," he whispers.

"Your statement will stipulate how you are not involved and possess no firsthand knowledge of how the boarding homes are run? Is this the case, Mr. Greene?"

"Couldn't say the words better myself, Detective. Now," he glances at Stella before he returns his attention to Aiden, "may I go for my walk? I suffer from an injured back and spend two hours in the morning and two in the afternoon walking. Our current weather is a godsend. If I sit for long periods, I experience excruciating spasms." Without waiting for a response, he places both hands on the table and lifts himself erect. He retrieves his hat and coat before he makes his way out the door.

Aiden jumps up to escort him to the exit.

"I could spit tacks," Stella suggests, when Aiden returns. "The man is a phony."

"Tell me how you really feel," he mutters, while he scratches notes.

"He's as involved in JanlonNS as Maura. He knows they collect extra cheques. And his back isn't as serious as he claims," she huffs.

"Right on every count, Stella." He checks his watch.

"No sign of Luther, eh?"

"Nope. I'll call Vic Staples again before I run home for a few minutes. Are you off to the café?"

"Date with Nick at the hotel. See you at one. I imagine we are in for a crazy afternoon."

****

"Hi, Pepper. Nick must be here. I saw the park pickup."

"Oh, Stella, hi." The ponytail swings. "He's waiting for you in the rear dining room. I expect you two prefer the quiet," she adds, acknowledging their relationship with a soft smile. "We are hosting a half dozen accountants in town for a weekend seminar, and I'll seat them in the front."

"Thanks, Pepper. You're a star. Has Eugenie promoted you to official manager status?"

Her pretty face clouds. "Not yet, but she will. She's been busy."

Stella makes her way along the narrow hall and into the last dining room at the back of the main floor. There he sits, notepad in hand, with a list of one sort or another on the go. She takes a quick moment and observes his hands—broad and square with long fingers. His nails are trimmed, although the edges show signs of a person who works with machinery. She loves those hands. "Hi."

Nick lifts his attention from his notes and smiles. The room seems warmer. "Hi. Pepper said we might enjoy lobster chowder and cheese biscuits. Good for you?"

She slides into the seat across from him. "Sure. Standard Shale Harbour fare. Whatcha workin' on?"

"Winter work projects—paint the living room and clean the brick around the fireplace. Okay with you?"

"Those jobs haven't been done in thirty years. And you expect Kiki's assistance, right?"

He snorts. "Subtle, my love. Duke can help and visit with Kiki while he's at the house."

"Okay. Duke will assist with the renovation of our living room and his incentive becomes visits with his own dog. If you cajole Duke into giving up Kiki, you are the man!" She smiles. "Here comes Pepper. Any blueberry grunt for dessert?"

****

Her Jeep remains in the detachment parking lot while she drives with Aiden to Merlon's Place for Gentlemen. The large property is located at the edge of town, surrounded by more modern homes on smaller lots. She sees police vehicles, forensic trucks, and several unmarked cars.

"You stay here. I'll find the site commander for an update before we drive over to Jane's."

"Fine." She opens her window. Aiden's standard issue sedan, like most law enforcement units, smells of sweat and dirty socks. The view, from her vantage point, consists of a hodgepodge of cars and trucks. Neighbours assemble—a woman with a baby in a stroller, a man with his dog, and two older fellows who stand close together. She waits and checks her watch. Aiden's been gone ten minutes.

She wanders into the back yard for a glimpse of any progress for herself, despite Aiden's instructions. She picks her way along the gravel driveway, soggy and pot-holed from the thaw. As she rounds the corner, she sees a line of uniformed officers walking shoulder to shoulder through the garden. A few traipse over rhododendron bushes and spirea as they maintain positions. She stops at the edge. With no sign of Aiden, she holds her position.

"Over here," someone shouts, and two men in white coveralls race toward the searcher near the centre.

The forward movement of the line has stopped. She waits.

"They've found a depression in the ground." Aiden approaches her from behind. "I recall I asked you to stay put. You can be uncooperative." He nudges her shoulder with his own.

"Sorry. You were gone for a long time—curiosity. What happens now?" She clenches her fists in her pockets, waiting for his answer.

"Suspected spots are taped off and once they've walked the total property, they dig. I expect any excavations will take the day. The ground might be frozen below the surface. They'll tent the area first and warm the earth."

"They dig by hand?"

"Yes, by hand."

"Shall we interview Elsie and Helga?"

"No need. Detectives are assigned, and social workers will assess the residents in case anyone needs more care."

"Did you alert the manor? Most will need more care."

"Not yet. I'll contact Olive Urback if we find a body because moving every resident will become necessary then. If not, the social workers will follow their reassessment protocols and I understand most will require relocation."

"I suppose our next stop is Jane's." She expects depressions in the back yard at Jane's, too.

By the time they reach Jane's Retirement Home for Ladies, the street of Victorian houses and early twentieth-century two-stories swarms with police cars. Aiden parks away from the activity and they walk toward the residence together. A white tent has been erected at the foot of the rear lawn. Aiden, once again, approaches the person in charge while Stella stands aside.

A forensics worker emerges from a garage-style building with plastic evidence bags. The yard is littered with garbage bins, a mower, rusted paint cans, and lengths of wood. She watches him speak with a team member, who accepts both bags and writes notes on each one. Stella covers her mouth with her hand and closes her eyes. She recalls her conversation with Charlotte, now the night staff person at Cliffs Guest Residence, who told her she took food to a woman who stayed in the shed at Jane's. She called the structure a workshop, although Stella considers the description generous.

"They found a depression in the ground here as well. You can see the warming tent. They'll start digging in an hour. Your face looks grey, Stella. Time to quit?"

"No. Let's find out what's in the two plastic bags the workers collected in the outbuilding. I need a look inside for myself, too."

"Okay," he replies, although his eyes reflect confusion. "Come with me."

As they approach the pathologist's vehicle, Aiden produces his ID and introduces Stella as a consultant in the investigation. "May we see the pieces of potential evidence retrieved by one of the staff from the garden shed?"

"Not pleasant, folks." He reaches into a dishpan for the bags. "We found what appears to be the remains of a cat, along with a collar and an empty cat food tin. There's a sack of some sort, made of twine. The latter is empty and frayed in places." He holds the items in the air by their closures. "The building is cleared now."

"May I go inside?" Her stomach knots. An image of Kiki, cuddled on the couch, floats before her. She shoves her hands, now chilled regardless of the warm afternoon temperature, into her pockets.

"If you want." He offers them both gloves and evidence bags. "If you notice something, don't touch it. Call one of us."

Stella pulls the gloves on and whispers as they trot toward the outbuilding, "Charlotte said she took food to a woman in a shed. Willy Saunders used a string bag. Both Connie Gee and Del Trembly described her purse," she pants. "She wanted a cat. Willy lived here, Aiden."

"Okay. Okay. Don't jump too fast. We'll give the place a once over. Two sets of eyes are better." He pats her arm. "We're gonna figure this mess out, Stella."

She trembles—perhaps the chill. Aiden turns on his flashlight and she takes tentative steps inside. The plywood floor of the shed sags when she stands in the middle. The edges are nailed but not the centre. The material appears reused—not unusual if one scrounges lumber for a garden shed. "This place isn't constructed well."

"Although the size of a single car garage, it's still a shed."

The walls aren't insulated. Even with the warmer weather, the damp and cold persist inside, with no light, no heat source, and no visible aids to comfort—like a blanket. She inhales but can't catch her breath. She pushes past Aiden toward the outside.

On their return to the car, she describes her emotions. "I sensed Willy Saunders in the shed. Maybe she's nearby."

"We inspected an empty outbuilding, Stella."

His response isn't meant to be condescending. She avoids further discussion for now.

****

Stella arrives home for supper, thankful when she finds Nick waiting at the door while she navigates the veranda stairs. "No hugs until I take a shower. Death has crawled over my skin today." She races toward their bedroom strips off her clothes, deposits them in the hamper, and dives under the hot water, which pulsates off her back and pounds her shoulders. She needs to cry, to wail, but no tears come. She wants her feelings to rush away from her and disappear down the drain. After ten minutes, she sags against the tile wall and her tension releases. She dresses in soft cotton pants and a bulky sweater. Suede moccasins cradle her feet. She makes her way downstairs, greeted by a bear hug, a Kiki snuggle, and a glass of white wine.

"Terrible?"

"I still don't know if I'm right, Nick. When I left the detachment, the latest report said two depressions were discovered on the Merlon property and another at Jane's. They also pulled the remains of a cat and a string bag from the garden shed at Jane's. Aiden will call me once they warm the sunken areas and dig."

Nick stands at the stove, stir-frying vegetables. "They've found three possible grave sites?"

"Three, yes, but I won't know more for a while. The outbuilding gave me the creeps, though."

"You didn't go inside?" His face pales.

"Couldn't help myself." She takes a sip of wine and meets his worried gaze. "Aiden entered with me. The space was empty since the dead cat and the string bag were removed by forensics earlier—no power, no water, no insulation. I can't imagine Willy lived or slept in such conditions so she could own a cat. And the floor seemed soft in the middle. Whoever built the unit used second-hand plywood and tacked the corners without securing the centre."

"Willy Saunders lived in a shed, in the back yard of a boarding house?"

She lifts her glass, and he adds more wine. "String bag and cat."

"Most people, when they build a garden shed, include at least one support joist underneath. They attach the plywood to this board and the frame, which prevents the springiness you felt and gives more strength when you store heavy items inside."

"You are a mine of information."

He shrugs. "Well, I know...."

"Forensics should remove the plywood." She jumps up from the table. "Hold supper for a minute. I'll call Aiden." She reaches for the phone on the wall while Nick studies her face. "No luck. He's left the station and I won't contact him at home. He said he'd touch base before the day's over. I hope he calls." She wanders toward the stove. "Your concoction smells fabulous."

****

Later—much later—the phone finally rings. In a hushed voice, he says, "I can't talk long. Rosemary's in the bathroom preparing for bed. They found three bodies—two at Merlon's and one at Jane's. The investigation will move fast now, with autopsies completed over the next couple of days. Maura Martin and Hector Greene were arrested earlier. We can interview them on Monday." He gasps while he talks. "Olive Urback has been directed to re-organize her staff and notify the board. All residents are being moved. I called because we located Luther, thanks to Vic Staples' lead. Halifax police will bring him to Shale Harbour. Are you able to come in tomorrow mid-morning and assist?"

"Sure. And I've an idea, too."

"Not much time, Stella."

With a clenched jaw, she continues. "Any chance they can lift the plywood floor in the garden shed where they located the cat's remains and the string bag?"

"What? Why? You don't expect they'll find a body buried under the shed?" His remark is more question than statement.

Her voice's hush matches his. "Willy's around, Aiden."

"The team will return for another sweep of the grounds. I'll order the process."

"Aiden. Where are you?"

Stella hears Rosemary in the background.

"Gotta run. Tomorrow at ten, right?"

The phone disconnects before she agrees.

She joins Nick in the living room. When the weather warms in the winter, the house develops a damp chill, and the best solution becomes a cozy fire. Her tea has cooled while she took Aiden's call in her office. Nick remains in his spot, glued to a *Perry Mason* rerun—one of his favourite shows.

He glances up when she returns, but she waits for a commercial before she explains. "Three bodies so far. Aiden wants me at the station in the morning for an interview with Luther. Maura and Hector were arrested. Autopsies will be performed and the team is scheduled to resume their search tomorrow." She watches him walk across the room and turn off the television.

"I asked if the searchers could remove the plywood in the shed and he said no problem. If we find Willy, the five missing people and extra cheques are accounted for. The difficulty comes when I break the news to Dad and Del."

"Let me help." He returns and sits beside her.

His hand warms her knee. "I expect a few changes at Harbour Manor. Aiden mentioned social workers reassessing the residents of Jane's and Merlon's. In my humble opinion, although I am not an assessor, they each qualify for nursing home care." She pauses. "Except for Jasper, and with the lowered rates, he might afford a move back. He helped me turn the corner on the case. Maybe I can make a plea to the board for an exception, given the circumstances."

"You amaze me."

Chapter 23

Sacred Trust

Sunday morning calm blankets Shale Harbour as Stella reaches the detachment at nine forty-five. At least Sergeant Moyer managed a day off. The constable on the front desk directs her to wait in the interview room as Detective North has been delayed. She asks, and they tell her Luther Greene will remain in a cell until the detective arrives.

Aiden must be embroiled in an issue with Rosemary—his current explanation for tardiness of any kind. She waits. She listens for the click of the door. She glances at the window, which gives a clear view of the hall. By ten-fifteen, she rallies her courage and returns to the front desk. Detective North is on his way.

He blusters into the conference room twenty minutes later, his dishevelled white hair the primary indicator of his stress. He hasn't been near his office because he tosses his coat on a chair. His complexion borders on crimson. He waves his hand and puffs for breath. "I'm sorry, Stella. I should have let you know but ran out of time. I've been awake most of the night with Rosie. I called Toni and Mary Jo, who refused any help unless I stationed a police officer nearby."

"Are you okay?"

"For now. Let's finish our interview with Luther before I leave again. I scrounged for an off-duty constable who needs extra money, and found one with a pregnant wife," he adds, as a means of explanation. "I'll struggle through the next three hours," he mutters, avoiding eye contact.

"And tomorrow? We'll re-interview Maura and Hector, correct?" She imagines their plans collapsing.

He nods while he digs for his notebook. "Let's manage today, for now. I'm sorry," he repeats.

A uniformed officer escorts Luther Greene into the room. With his head bowed, he sits with his hands folded in his lap. The heartthrob persona has melted away. Before her, she sees a young man, a father, both troubled and afraid. He understands. Before he says a word, he slides a crumbled piece of lined scribbler paper across the table toward Aiden. "I kept a list of the times I worked for Uncle Hector with the digger."

Aiden pushes the list in Stella's direction. She reads four dates—Luther's confirmation of his culpability. They represent the four bodies uncovered at the graveyard, at Merlon's, and at Jane's. "Are there more?"

Luther lifts his handsome face with the square jaw and dimpled chin. Tears run unabated along his cheeks. "No, Ma'am. I never wanted to do the jobs for Uncle Hector, but he said the people were dead and there was no family to pay for a funeral. He said he did the best he could by them. I know he was wrong."

"He paid you for your work?"

"Yup." Luther swipes at the wet streaks on his face. "He gave me money for my time and for the digger. I settled with Port Heavy Equipment Rental and Storage in cash, but I can remember the amounts."

"You knew what you did was wrong," Stella states, while she focuses her attention on the sheet of paper.

"I'm a single dad to my boy. My job don't pay much and Uncle Hector helps me sometimes. I couldn't say no. Uncle Hector put me in a bind."

"When Vic uncovered Ira Gold, you didn't tell us the truth. You impeded a police investigation, Luther," Aiden accuses.

"Right," he snivels.

"Explain why you ran away to Halifax." He's a nice enough young man, and Stella remains mystified at his behaviour after the discovery of the first body.

"I woulda come back. Needed thinkin' time. If I end up in jail, I won't see my little boy anymore. His mother will make it hard for me to see him." He blubbers in earnest.

"Understood," Aiden answers. "You're off to the cells for now, although I'll complete the paperwork for your release."

Luther's eyes light.

"Make no mistake. You'll be charged and your testimony required later, but I will emphasize your cooperation and current responsibilities as an attempt to keep you out of jail." He leans across the table. "The first item on your agenda, after we're finished here, is a visit with Otto King. Assure him you don't want to quit your job. Your child requires your support." The lecture ends.

Once Luther is escorted out, they make their way into Aiden's office, where he starts Luther's paperwork. "While I finish, will you find us coffee?"

She frowns. "I thought we were done. I'm off home."

"The front desk suggested I stand by for a forensics report from Jane's. I hoped you might keep me company while we wait for word from the search site." He stares at his desktop. "They were assigned the task of lifting the plywood in the shed."

"I'll pour coffee." She hurries.

When she returns, Aiden pushes a button on his phone and indicates she should sit.

"Tell me again what's happened. My consultant, Stella, has entered the room and you're on speaker."

"We removed the floor from the outbuilding at Jane's Retirement Home for Ladies. The earth appeared disturbed. We discovered the body of a woman, wrapped in a plastic sheet, and secured with wire. She was dressed in a man's topcoat. We believe her identity is Wilhelmina Saunders."

"And the evidence?"

"Her wallet was tucked into the inside pocket of the coat. We found her library card and a picture of herself and a man we expect was her husband, since he's wearing the same coat—we assume."

"Can you tell how she died?" Stella can't control the tremor in her voice. "How long has she been dead?"

"Hard with the plastic. I saw no overt signs of a struggle. An autopsy will tell the tale, but more than three months."

"Thanks for the call. I'll wait for the written report." Aiden replaces the receiver in the cradle and studies Stella's face. "Did you see a ghost?"

"I felt a ghost, for sure," she mumbles while she presses her index finger against the bridge of her nose. "Especially when we were in the shed."

"Go home, Stella. I expect a long day tomorrow. Interviews with Martin and Greene separately. They'll consume our morning. Afterward, I'll buy you lunch. Autopsy results on Tuesday followed by a joint interview."

"And Rosemary?"

"If her sisters can handle her with an off-duty constable on guard, I'm safe. If not, then I've exhausted the options. The good news is no one's called the office since I arrived."

****

Maura Martin, who has spent the last two nights in cells, arrives dressed in grey sweatpants and a hoodie. She wears sneakers on her feet. Either she expected the arrest, or she was at work in her home gym when she and Hector were brought into the local detachment Saturday evening. Stella watches from the hallway as the woman perches on the edge of a chair in the interview room. One of her boarding house staff must have informed her the forensics teams discovered the graves—Stella's sure. Maura has plastered a demented and vacant expression on her face.

The weather has turned. Their precious January thaw has ended with finality, as forecasters predict a blizzard for the weekend. Last night, she and Nick snuggled by the fire, with Kiki curled between them. She luxuriated in the comfort of her flannelette nightie and floor-length chenille bath robe, while poor Nick remained in corduroys and a flannel shirt until Kiki made her final zip outside. Stella was exhausted and remains tired beyond compare. Her work is complete except for the Martin and Greene interviews. Aiden's people will deal with JanlonNS staff, although she hopes to be included.

She nods when Aiden rounds the corner, pushing her thoughts of home aside.

"We can go in now." He opens the door for her. "Thank you, Constable. I'll call when we're finished."

They both seat themselves across from Maura, Stella slightly off-side.

Aiden studies his file folder and begins. "Ms. Martin, you are charged with pension fraud and improper interference with human remains—serious charges. Have you engaged a lawyer?"

"I don't need one, Detective. I am innocent. I am a good woman who cares for the sick and elderly. I am generous and kind to old folks with only their professional caregivers as support. I am an excellent employer. My staff are well-treated." She chews an already bloodied lip during her recitation.

"Maura, we'll know the identities of the people found on your properties before long. Besides Ira Gold, discovered in Mallory Gorman's grave, we suspect," she double-checks her notes, "Lloyd Gurney, Weldon Beck, and

Minnie Gardiner's identifications any moment." She leans toward the woman who stares at her hands, clasped in her lap. Stella notices the chewed nails—new behaviour. They were never bitten when she saw Maura at the nursing home. "Maura, look at me, please."

She lifts her face. The circles around her eyes are purple and blotched.

"Forensics found a person we are certain is Willy under the garden shed at Jane's. We've interviewed Luther. Although he assisted with the other four burials, he wasn't involved with Willy."

"I don't understand any of your accusations."

"Jack Lawson told us you gave her financial advice related to the disposal of her mother's body."

"I don't understand," she repeats, increased hysteria in her tone.

Aiden pushes. "Your husband claims you are responsible for the management of both boarding homes. He said you make the decisions, and he's involved in name alone."

Maura's face lifts. "Hector would never betray our trust—our sacred trust."

"What trust is that, Ms. Martin? The trust you put in him to dispose of dead residents, which enabled the business to collect their pensions after their deaths?"

"No more discussions without my husband here—and a lawyer."

After the constable returns and accompanies Maura out, Aiden turns toward Stella. The skin on his face droops. "I hope we learn more from Hector."

"He strikes me as the slimy type. I bet sacred trusts aren't a big concern."

****

Hector, dressed in a suit and tie, presents himself in the same manner as on the first occasion they met. "Good morning, Detective, Ms. Kirk. I must say, your accommodations require improvement." The contrived frown follows his upbeat remark and a swipe at two day's growth of beard.

"You've told my people you're anxious for an interview with us, and you don't want a lawyer." Aiden's abruptness illustrates he's lost patience with the couple.

"I'll request legal representation after I tell you our little tale, but I'm convinced advice won't be necessary. My wife and I are responsible citizens and employers."

"Go ahead."

Stella holds her breath.

"Dear Maura and I purchased and developed Merlon's Place for Gentlemen and Jane's Retirement Home for Ladies because we perceived a need. Through Maura's work, she saw many people who couldn't afford the exorbitant charges made by facilities run by the municipality. The legislation permits private homes with a capacity limit of three elders in residence, not related. We never house relations."

"You started your enterprises as altruistic ventures?" Stella remains doubtful.

"As a matter of fact, yes," he huffs. He turns his attention toward Aiden. "We are responsible," he repeats, with an elevated tone.

"Go on." Aiden glances at his watch.

"Look. The problem of options confronted us. When a resident with no means and no family dies while in our care," his eyes narrow, "who shall be considered accountable for the necessary events following their demise, like their funeral and the finalization of their affairs? After two such circumstances, where Maura and I bore the cost of a burial because no arrangements were made and no funds were forthcoming, we examined the idea that each person should provide directions."

"Direction is good, but what if there's no money?"

"I see you possess a modicum of understanding, Detective. Most residents of our two boarding homes—in fact, all of them—have no savings or prepaid funerals when they choose our facility. They grant permission for JanlonNS's use of any remaining funds for their final expenses."

"But the scheme became more fruitful when the cheques didn't stop."

"Yes. No one knows or cares what happens. We expensed their private burials and collected their cheques until we felt what they owed our company was recovered. The cheques are government money. We don't steal."

Aiden's face is flushed.

"Hector, your statement will say you and Maura buried people in the garden, labelled the process a private burial, and collected their cheques after they died to cover their expenses. Correct?" Stella sits stunned.

"Correct." He peers across the table toward her and nods with unexplained smugness.

"Mr. Greene, you pocketed Ira Gold's pension for two years."

"Oftentimes, government death notifications become lost in the paperwork. Management of a boarding home is a complicated business. Maura handles the money, and the daily operations. My job involved the private burials with the help of my nephew, Luther."

The use of past tense in the description of his role doesn't go unnoticed. "No harm done?" Stella's stomach heaves.

Hector expels a puff of air. "I am delighted you understand. If the truth be known, our problems began when we buried Ira. The appropriation of public property that might be disturbed later was a lapse in judgment." He sits erect, unapologetic.

"Call your lawyer to meet you here tomorrow morning. He may represent both you and your wife, or she can engage separate representation. My staff will help you sort out your decisions."

"I expect a withdrawal of the charges, Detective. Remember, we didn't kill anyone," he tut-tuts as he rises.

"Our charges stand, Sir. Come with me."

They adjourn to the café after Aiden returns to the interview room.

"I need a shower as much now as I did after our trips to both sites yesterday, Aiden." They're seated at Cocoa and Café with large mugs of hot coffee. Stella's stomach churns and twists after Tiffany describes salmon salad bunwiches and coleslaw. She opts for chicken noodle soup and a biscuit. "I'm pleased we can put off their joint interview until tomorrow."

****

Maura Martin and Hector Greene are scheduled for their interview after preliminary autopsy reports are received on Tuesday. Stella joins Aiden in his office, surprised when she discovers him surrounded by files, each with the name of a victim. She sees another stack on the credenza behind him, with the top folder labelled: "Jasper Nunn."

"I owe you an apology, Stella."

"Not unusual, but what's the reason today?" Her tease garners no reaction.

"The four additional bodies, two at Merlon's and two at Jane's, were identified. If we include Ira Gold, we can conclude they buried five people and kept the poor souls' pension money." He massages his temple while he closes his eyes. "Our case has overwhelmed even the most seasoned of the staff. Despite my preoccupations with Rosemary, you persevered." He meets

Stella's gaze. "I don't see how we could have progressed without you."

She sits, unnerved to hear Aiden pour out his emotions and compliment her in the process. He's conflicted and upset for personal reasons. The case has challenged them both. She opts to change the subject.

"Everyone died of natural causes?"

"Preliminary reports suggest each person died of natural causes, correct."

"Right. They found Willy's wallet in her pocket. Her pathetic string bag was full of holes." Her throat burns.

"There's a chance her cause of death was exposure, but they can't be sure."

Stella sits stunned into silence. After a moment, she gathers her thoughts. "And the files behind you?"

"Reports from the social worker assessments. Each is to move into Harbour Manor. They've rearranged rooms and can accommodate the seven, including Mr. Nunn. I expect considerable effort will be expended before the forensic accountants untangle their bank accounts, but the necessary people are involved. I assigned two detectives to search for any family of Willy Saunders, Lloyd Gurney, Weldon Beck, and Minny Gardiner. We've hit a dead end with Ira Gold. Notifications of death are now reported to the government. Hector and Maura are in the glue." He stands. "Here we go."

****

A joint interview with Maura Martin and Hector Greene took place in the presence of Brent Stephens, a cousin of Carter Stephens. Brent is soft-spoken. Stella sensed his discomfort throughout the meeting.

Maura maintained her denial in the beginning, despite her husband's admissions. Hector insisted they were good people and acted in the best interests of residents without family. He questioned who would bother attending the funeral of a man like Ira Gold? And no one wanted Guy Boucher in jail. "The old coot's demented," he said. He suggested they protected him from prison. Stella wondered how the "so-called" private burial service for Willy Saunders was respectful since her final resting place was under the floor of a shed. Answers were unsatisfactory.

Aiden went through each case with surgical precision. He asked the couple how every individual resident died and what happened afterward. Hector admitted he and Maura buried Willy. Luther couldn't lease the digger soon enough to be convenient, and they saw no other option with a body in the shed. They coerced staff at the homes into vulnerable positions by loaning money or providing housing. Maura mentioned how Charlotte, now a worker at Cliffs Guest Residence, worried her. She considered Charlotte too emotional for the job but remained upset when she quit. Charlotte became a risk to their livelihood.

"I am shocked at your treatment of us, Detective." Hector's exaggerated statement demonstrated high calibre buffoonery. "Most of the elderly are deemed unimportant by society. My wife and I gave them homes and supported them, with little in the way of compensation. We cared for people." He reached to pat Maura's hand, but she pulled away. "We are the caregivers. I cannot believe you intend moving forward with prosecution."

Stella and Aiden listened with less than genuine politeness.

By noon, she's bone-weary, and done with Hector and Maura. The charges of pension fraud and improper interference with human remains, five counts of each, stand. They are scheduled for transfer to Port Ephron. Brent Carter made subtle noises regarding their pleas. Aiden suggested the sale of their properties as an avenue to repay the government for the money collected in old age pensions after the victims died.

Once back in Aiden's office, they collapse and stare into space.

"Next on my list is a Harbour Manor visit, with explanations for Dad and Del."

"Will you wait in case there's more information uncovered? If you return at ten on Thursday, we can discuss my final report, since you completed most of the preliminary investigation alone. We need tomorrow for interviews with staff and a meeting with the Crown."

"Follow up with the JanlonNS employees?"

"Each is scheduled. No doubt charges will be laid in some cases."

"Am I needed?"

"No. There are members assigned. Thanks, anyway."

Sidelined again. She swallows her disappointment. "Okay. I'll call the nursing home and tell them to expect Nick and me Thursday for tea. Most of the JanlonNS residents should be moved and settled." She stands. "See you day after tomorrow."

Chapter 24

Anybody Dead?

After a quiet, although scrumptiously eventful early morning, Stella prepares to drive into Shale Harbour for a final review of the case. Her stay at home yesterday proved cathartic. They cooked, concocting two shepherd's pies—one for supper and one for the freezer—and she created one of their favourite desserts—a cranberry and apple crumble—with Nick's help. They make a great team, stronger every day.

Her mind explores the fates of the many players entangled in the boarding house cases. She hopes JanlonNS staff aren't held accountable for the behaviours of their employers. Yes, they were wrong when they assisted and wrong when they withheld information, but the lot of a minimum wage employee with no options often proves difficult.

With the memory of a delicious goodbye hug and the promise of more later, she makes the trip into town. The grey sky hangs heavy in anticipation of a blizzard predicted for the weekend. People will rush to complete errands and ready themselves for possible plugged roads, power outages, and treacherous conditions. Her sense of safety in the knowledge she'll be inside, warm, and loved comforts her.

The Shale Harbour RCMP detachment bustles with activity. Moyer motions her through. Aiden's behind his desk, ear glued to the telephone, with the now familiar file folders still heaped around him. She nods, enters, and sits.

"Thanks. Okay. The report will be delivered before day's end. A few details require review with my consultant. Yes, Stella Kirk played a pivotal role."

She watches his face and sees annoyance, anxiety, and impatience in rapid succession.

"I'm taking time off after today. I've assigned two detectives who can follow through with the Crown. Thanks." He drops the receiver in the cradle. "I'll soon be fired if I can't straighten out my personal life. Honest to God, Stella."

His outburst is unexpected. She hesitates before she reacts.

He continues. "Once I complete this paperwork, I'm on leave. I don't know for how long. Toni and Mary Jo arranged for Rosemary's hospital return, but readmission might take weeks."

"Oh, Aiden, I'm so sorry." She's lost for words.

"Right." He's gruff when he rebuffs her attempt at sympathy. "Let's focus."

"Once you document my details, we can discuss Essie Matkowski's status—and Rosemary." A conversation about medications is needed now.

He frowns, but nods and flips open his notes. "Will you review the interviews you completed in my absence?"

They spend an hour in discussions of the various lines of inquiry Stella followed on her own. She reminded Aiden of her telephone call from Caleb Hall, and how he told her Guy Boucher hit Ira Gold with an exercise weight when they lived at Merlon's. She mentioned Flora, at Jane's Retirement Home for Ladies, who revealed Monica Lawson's mysterious disappearance, Jack's involvement, and Minnie Gardiner's possible death. He did not need a review of Jasper Nunn's help; how he interviewed Horace at Merlon's Place for Gentlemen and learned the surnames of Lloyd Gurney and Weldon Beck. Horace confirmed Ira Gold's circumstances, too. She noted the assistance provided by Patsy, in the finance department at the manor, and Olive Urback's reluctance but cooperation, regardless. She detailed her sister's role. Trixie introduced her to Renée Tait from the post office. The interaction confirmed surnames, plus she met Mrs. McKechnie, Jack Lawson's next-door neighbour. She notes the need for confidentiality with the revelation of Renée's name.

"The bosses will think you do my work, Stella."

She silences her pride and answers with a simple, "Joint effort, Aiden. I sometimes think investigations involve more listening than the police are willing to do."

He plants his elbows on his desk, meets her gaze, and nods. "I can provide you with additional information now. The Crown tells me Maura Martin and Hector Greene want their day in court. Unbelievable. They still consider themselves caregivers for people with no family. In any event, Jack Lawson will be incarcerated. She'll testify, though, in exchange for a lighter sentence recommendation."

"And the boarding home staff?"

"They're out of jobs, which remains the biggest punishment, although Harbour Manor or the other two boarding homes could hire them on eventually. They'll make statements and maybe receive probationary sentences because they helped their bosses and lied to the police. The same for Luther. Otto King says he'll keep him on. The Crown Attorney is convinced the case will play out as expected. And finally, the postal person won't be involved."

"Guy Boucher worries me."

"No need. He and Caleb Hall are both absolved. The Crown sees no advantage in a move forward with charges due to Guy's mental capacity, and he's now in a controlled environment—at least as controlled as possible. Okay, what did you want to tell me?" His face muscles sag. His eyes hold little interest. She soldiers on.

"Two topics, Aiden." She struggles to maintain his attention. "One revolves around Essie Matkowski's potential return, and the other is your wife."

His eyebrows furrow for a moment. "Essie first. She's off for the foreseeable future." He lifts his right hand, palm toward her. "You're no longer on a continual contract, but I can engage you on a case-by-case basis, if you choose to help me. I appreciated your attention to detail this time. I couldn't focus and you managed the slack." The lines on his face soften.

Commitment isn't on her agenda right now. She remains silent. "Now, my next topic." Heaving a sigh and expecting the worst, she reveals details of the night of January the second, when Aiden and Rosemary joined her and Nick for dinner at the park. "You and your sisters-in-law need to be aware Rosemary has not taken her medication since before she was discharged home. Her so-called 'normal' behaviour is an act, enabled by habit reversal therapy she learned when in treatment."

"Did you contact her psychiatrist?" Aiden straightens in his chair. "Don't meddle, Stella." His face flushes a deep crimson.

"Rosemary spoke with me in private the night you were at my place for dinner." She maintains her composure. Important information will be lost if she reacts to his anger. "Your wife told me she stopped her pills. She said she learned control of her actions through a particular methodology. When she begins drifting toward the inappropriate, she acts in an alternate manner—habit reversal."

He leans back in his chair. The colour in his cheeks fades. "Why did she tell you? Although the absence of medications explains a great deal lately," he adds.

"Rosemary said she felt she should be fair with me. She emphasized how I represent the one person she might hurt. She wasn't, at the time, a danger to herself or anyone else—except for me."

"My wife threatened you and you never mentioned the incident? Why the hell not?"

"I didn't believe revealing her issues could help. She was cross with her sisters who meddle, as she reported, but she was scheduled for readmission to hospital the next day. I thought we were fine, but you kept her home, at which point I struggled. Nick and I discussed what happened the same night, though. I'm sorry. I should have told you sooner."

"Well," he puffs. "At least we now know she's taken no medication for almost a month." He pauses. "We watch her take her pills. I don't understand."

"A friend in the hospital taught her to pretend to swallow and make her mouth appear empty, even if checked. She's finding it difficult to maintain her act, I gather. She'll be readmitted, Aiden, which is good."

"Since you were the one threatened, I expect you're pleased, whereas my marriage remains on the rocks." Bitterness laces his tone.

Sergeant Moyer taps on the door. "Sir, I believe we have a potential altercation which involves stolen property. Will you attend the scene?"

"Anybody dead?"

"Not as far as I can tell, Sir."

"Can't someone else be assigned, Moyer? Report to finish." He waves a random file folder.

"No, Sir. The owner of the residence, a woman named," he glances at the scrap of paper in his fist, "Earlene Marigold, requested you."

Aiden nods. "Alright. Give me the address." He reaches for the slip from the sergeant's outstretched hand and turns to Stella. "Earlene Marigold is a friend of Mary Jo's. Earlene's an avid bridge player and Mary Jo spares when necessary."

"I've met her. The living arrangement of the fourplex she owns is unique.

I'll walk with you and explain."

"Ride along?"

She shrugs. "Sure. Scheduled for the manor at three, but I've the time."

On the drive to the address, Stella tells Aiden what she knows. Earlene's husband died. They were well off and owned a big house. She likes playing bridge and decided she wanted to live where everyone played the game. She designed a four-unit building and sold her home. Each apartment opens into an inside common area, accessible by each resident and equipped with a garden door and a deck. "The place is distinctive, from what I've been told."

"Who are the other renters? Or are they owners?"

"No. Earlene owns the property and rents to Velvet Carmichael, a retired teacher; and Tess Boone, an amateur writer who attended the Shale Harbour Writers Retreat—and she's Connie Gee's sister, by the way."

Aiden frowns.

"Connie Gee has ALS and provided me the list of local licensed and unlicensed boarding homes. She lives at the manor."

He nods in recollection. "And do you know the other person?"

"Her name is Deena Finch. She worked at the Groceteria. She hurt herself and they pensioned her off."

"Okay. We're here." He pulls into a generous parking lot in front of a single-story dwelling which presents as one bungalow until you see the sides, at which point the configuration becomes four bungalows pushed together. From the sky, the assemblage would resemble the letter G with a courtyard and garden doors into their common room.

They knock on the door of the suite which faces the street but elicit no response. A patrol car has arrived before them. They follow the sound of voices around the complex to the side. Despite the cold, the garden doors are ajar. They continue until they see four women in a heated discussion, while a police officer stands nearby.

"You hold the master key. If not you, who?"

"I never enter your apartment, unless invited, Velvet. The key is for emergencies. What if you fell and needed help?"

"Someone took my antique silver comb." Velvet pouts.

A frazzled constable attempts a modicum of order. "Okay, ladies. Detective North has arrived. He'll sort this mess out and we'll see who's been stealin' what." He saunters toward Aiden and Stella. "Let me introduce you."

"No need, Constable." He halts the uniformed police officer. "Good afternoon, everyone. I'm Detective Aiden North and please meet my consultant, Stella Kirk. Who owns the property?"

Earlene Marigold lifts her arm from the elbow and wiggles her fingers, still holding what Stella assumes is a master key attached to a long ribbon. She's short, petite, and fit. Stella believes her to be an avid swimmer in the summer. "I own the fourplex, Detective. Nice to meet you. Mary Jo often mentions you."

"And you are?" He gestures toward Velvet.

"I'm Velvet Carmichael. I rent what we call the spine of the G. My unit sits on the left side and faces the other street." She points behind her. Velvet's roundness doesn't detract from her most identifiable feature—her abundance of coal black and grey-streaked hair which froths and hangs past her waist. She caresses a few strands clutched in her hand while she talks.

"You're missing a comb?" Stella weighs in on the conversation.

"Correct, and this isn't the first time one of us has 'missed' a personal object from our apartments. Tell them, Tess."

"Hi, Stella. We met at the manor. Nice to meet you, Detective North. I'm Tess Boone. Soon after the writers retreat, my autographed copy of Elsbeth Strauss' latest book disappeared. I didn't call the police. Rather, I wrote Elsbeth a note and asked if she would be so kind as to send me another signed copy."

"Did she?"

"I haven't heard from her, sadly."

"Contact Yellow House. Brigitte has copies, Tess."

"Which unit do you occupy, Ms. Boone?" Aiden crosses his arms, emphasizing his impatience to return and finish his report.

"The right side. We call my apartment the thumb of the G. Deena's in the back—the top of the G, and, as you might expect, Earlene has the front unit—the biggest. Her place has three bedrooms."

"You must be Deena." Aiden extends his hand toward the fourth occupant.

"I've never complained, but items have been stolen from me, too. I never complain," she repeats. Deena's fashion sense overcompensates, in Stella's estimation. She's decked out in false eyelashes before noon.

They remain at Earlene's fourplex until eleven-thirty. Earlene insists her master key has not been used because they've never experienced an emergency. They all agree there have been no emergencies. In the end, statements are taken from each of them.

Deena doesn't object to their characterization of her as mildly disagreeable. She reports that she sees herself as a non-complainer, although considers her menopausal moods a permanent affliction.

Velvet, despite a contradictory appearance, sounds compulsive when referencing her personal possessions.

Earlene controls. As the owner, she prefers order and predictability, and isn't ashamed to emphasize those preferences.

Tess admits she spends most of her time in her own little world. She makes exceptions when she visits her sister, or plays bridge with the other three. She writes stories and self-identifies as an author. Stella senses the others might dispute her attestation if discussions were held in private.

The four of them play bridge a minimum of two afternoons and one evening per week, but more often in the winter when they're stuck inside. They reference their building as the "bridge-plex G."

Once in the car, Aiden rails on. The call proved unnecessary, although Earlene felt accused, and the constable wanted reinforcements. He dismisses their concerns like he dismissed the missing Willy Saunders. His patience has deserted him.

Stella keeps quiet. He has too much on his mind to listen to her criticisms. Once he drops her back at her Jeep, he races home. His report will obviously have to wait until after he sees his wife.

*****

With Nick by her side and behind the wheel, they drive to Harbour Manor. Olive said she would assemble those residents involved in the investigation.

"You were longer than I expected, Stella. Is Aiden okay?"

"The short answer's no. Toni and Mary Jo made an application for Rosemary's readmission." She watches him watch the road. "I told him about her threat and the habit reversal therapy she learned."

Nick turns toward her for a moment.

"He was mad." She acknowledges his unasked question. "I'm sure he would have said more, but a request came for his attendance at a scene, and he asked if I wanted to go."

"Nobody died, I gather."

She lifts her brows in mock horror. "How do you know?" Without giving him the opportunity for a smart retort, she continues. "The call involved the fourplex Earlene Marigold owns. I told him who lived in each unit." She says no more. No need for gossip, even with Nick. She doesn't work on theft investigations. "We were on site for thirty minutes. Earlene asked for Aiden because she knows Mary Jo. They'll sort the matter out, I'm sure."

They pull into the lot. Without Kiki in attendance, Nick holds her hand as they walk into the manor.

Olive Urback waits at the nurses' station. They see her glance at the clock and scan the entry as they make their way inside. "You're late." She bustles around the counter. "Everyone involved with your inquiries has been rolled or escorted into the lounge. Lulu and Stevie handed out snacks. Arlene will wander the halls and check on other residents while she keeps her husband company, which means I can stand by unless paged. Come on, now." She trots along the hallway, her mild annoyance illustrated by the swing of her hips.

"I'm surprised you're at work on a day shift, Olive. Did your daughter take time off to stay with Mr. Urback until the board finds a replacement for Maura?"

She takes a step back and turns. "After the fracas with Maura, the Board of Directors asked me to assume her duties. We found a spot here at the manor for my husband." She pauses. "Although we postponed the decision for far too long, his move here provided the best option for our family." She continues toward the lounge, avoiding further discussion.

The double doors to the common room are open. "Attention, everyone." Her voice possesses a new-found authority, and she sounds like she's announcing royalty. "Stella Kirk has arrived and will give us a report." She glances over her shoulder. "Lulu, please pour Nick and Stella each a cup of tea." Olive assumes a position near the door.

Although she can't reveal too much since Maura and Hector are pleading "not guilty," Stella's plan is to thank those who require her appreciation. She takes a big breath while she scans the assembled group. "Hi, folks. Most of you know me. I'm Stella Kirk and," she pats Nick's arm, "this is my partner, Nick Cochran."

"Can you talk louder?"

Stella can't determine who made the request but does her best. "Late last year, my father Norbert, and Del Trembly," she flutters a wave toward each of them, "expressed their concern for two residents they both thought had disappeared. One was Jasper Nunn—and we found you, didn't we?"

Jasper nods. He's seated beside Connie Gee, his hand resting on hers.

"The other person was Willy Saunders. My dad was worried. He said she always waved goodbye before she left for a walk." She pauses and gazes at rapt faces. "I must inform you Willy passed away almost six months ago. Willy moved into an unlicensed boarding home." She searches for Flora in the group. "Flora, raise your hand."

"Hi. Welcome to Harbour Manor. Flora lived at Jane's Retirement Home for Ladies and assisted with the investigation, as did most of the residents of both homes." She casts her eyes around the group. "I'm happy to see all of you here."

Flora leans sideways and cuddles Ethel. "Roxy went into a hospital, Stella. She ain't good."

"I'm sorry, Flora." She scans the group again. "There you are, Horace. I appreciated your help when you spoke with Jasper."

Swallowed by an overstuffed lounger, the old man salutes.

Jasper gives her a respectful nod.

"Caleb?"

He's seated beside Guy and waves.

"Your call was important." She sees the question in his eyes but doesn't react for the moment. "There's Patsy at the back of the room—your fearless financial person. Thank you, Patsy. You were fearless in more ways than I can tell. And Dewey over near Miriam. Both of you provided pivotal information. Connie, I learned so much from you." She turns and acknowledges Olive, poised in the doorway. "And you are all very blessed with Nurse Urback as your new head nurse."

Olive blushes and flits her fingers as if swatting a mosquito away.

"Are the homes gonna close?"

"Will they be sold?"

"Will Nurse Martin go to jail?"

"She should," Elmer mutters.

"Any questions about court cases and charges can't be answered today. What I can say," and she meets Caleb's fretful gaze, "is that no one who helped me need worry."

Caleb's nod is imperceptible, except to her.

"Thanks for your hard work, Stella." Del waves a flabby arm in her direction. "Willy's death makes me sad, but I'm happy you found Jasper and brought him back."

"I weren't lost," Jasper whispers while he pats Connie's hand. The trace of a smile touches Connie's lips.

They visit with Norbert for a few minutes before they make their way home. Her father was more distant today. Willy Saunders' death didn't elicit a reaction. He needed a prompt before he remembered Nick, and didn't recall her, even as Nick's wife.

****

"Long day." She's stretched on the couch with her stockinged feet on Nick's lap.

"You handled the meeting well. When I spoke with folks afterward, everyone understood what they heard, and the work you did."

Her response is pragmatic. "Although I provided little information, people always appreciate a thank-you. We can make another visit in a few days and take poor Kiki with us. She wasn't too happy we left her alone." Stella scratches the dog's ears.

"She pulled a book out of the bookcase and managed a wee read. Did you see the chewed corner on one of Greta Walmsley's books?"

"Yolanda Gordon?" She reaches for the dog. "Good choice, old girl." As usual, when the phone bleats, she jumps.

"I want an extension for here in the living room." She races into her office. "Shale Cliffs...."

"Hi, it's me," Trixie says. "I need your help."

"What for, Sis?" She knows the term of endearment annoys her sister.

"Can you or Nick drive the farm truck over to my storage unit tomorrow? If so, my move will take one trip with two trucks before the big storm arrives."

"Your new place is furnished, Trixie. What did you squirrel away in a locker?"

"As if my possessions are any of your business."

She sounds huffy, but Stella doesn't bite.

"Listen. I bought a set of bedroom furniture for Mia, but when Brigitte moved into Yellow House, she and Carter ran out and found the child a second-hand big-girl bed. I never mentioned what I'd done. Now, she can come stay with me in her own room at my place with her own furniture. Will you guys help or are you still on the dig for more old people?"

Stella replies to her sister's request first. "We'll be there." Stella's voice softens. "My role in the investigation is over, by the way."

"Great. At least this time, no one got murdered."

<<<<<<<<>>>>>>>>

About the Author

L. P. Suzanne Atkinson was born in New Brunswick, Canada and has lived in Alberta, Quebec, and Nova Scotia before settling on Prince Edward Island in 2022. She has degrees from Mount Allison, Acadia, and McGill universities. Suzanne spent her professional career in the fields of mental health and home care. She also owned and operated, with her husband, both an antique business and a construction business for more than twenty-five years.

Suzanne writes about the unavoidable consequences of relationships. She uses her life and work experiences to weave stories that cross many boundaries.

She and her husband, David Weintraub, now make the fabulous Summerside, Prince Edward Island, Canada their home.

Email – lpsa.books@eastlink.ca
Website – http://lpsabooks.wix.com/lpsabooks#
Face Book – L. P. Suzanne Atkinson – Author
Face Book – lpsabooks Private Stash

Titles:
Emily's Will Be Done (2012)
Ties That Bind (2014)
Station Secrets: Regarding Hayworth Book I (2015)
Hexagon Dilemma: Regarding Hayworth Book II (2016)
Segue House Connection: Regarding Hayworth Book III (2017)
Diner Revelations: Regarding Hayworth Book IV (2018)
No Visible Means: A Stella Kirk Mystery #1 (2019)
Didn't Stand a Chance: A Stella Kirk Mystery #2 (2020)
Sand In My Suitcase: A Stella Kirk Mystery #3 (2021)
Fictional Truth: A Stella Kirk Mystery #4 (2022)
Mallory Gorman Won't Be Buried Today: A Stella Kirk Mystery #5 (2023)

Watch for:

Fate Deals The Cards: A Stella Kirk Mystery #6

The sixth in a series of cozy mysteries, set in Shale Cliffs RV Park
Coming in the spring / summer of 2024

CPSIA information can be obtained
at www.ICGtesting.com
Printed in the USA
BVHW081440290123
657272BV00001B/6

9 781777 600549